THE
MOONLIGHT
MARKET

THE
MOONLIGHT MARKET

JOANNE HARRIS

To Chris Fowler
London misses you.

First published in Great Britain in 2024 by Gollancz
an imprint of The Orion Publishing Group Ltd
Carmelite House, 50 Victoria Embankment
London EC4Y 0DZ

An Hachette UK Company

1 3 5 7 9 10 8 6 4 2

A CIP catalogue record for this book is
available from the British Library.

ISBN (HB) 978 1 399 60474 1
ISBN (ETPB) 978 1 399 60475 8
ISBN (eBook) 978 1 399 60477 2
ISBN (Audio) 978 1 399 60478 9

Typeset at The Spartan Press Ltd,
Lymington, Hants

Printed and bound in Great Britain by Clays Ltd,
Elcograf S.p.A.

www.gollancz.co.uk

Prologue

Long ago and far away, the Moth King, known for his jealousy, uncertain temper and melancholy, courted the frivolous Butterfly Queen. They were very different. He was nocturnal; she loved the sun. He was sullen and taciturn; she was filled with merriment. Even so, they fell in love, and their wedding was held at sunset on the edge of a bramble wood, with all of their folk in attendance, and with dancing throughout the night and day.

But the qualities that had caused the Moth King to fall in love with the Butterfly Queen soon incurred his displeasure. She was flighty; she danced too much, laughed too often; drank nectar to the point of giddiness. He tried to reason with her, but the Butterfly Queen only laughed at him. Then, when laughter failed to melt the Moth King's stubborn heart, she retreated to the company of her friends and secretly hoped he would join her.

And so the Moth King brooded alone, while the Butterfly Queen spent her days with her friends in the treetops, rocking on a silver swing woven for her by the Spider Mage, who had always loved her, and whose webs reached as far as the Ninth World. The Spider Mage was loyal, and had never declared his love, knowing that the Butterfly Queen was born for higher, nobler things, but his heart ached when he saw her lord so cold towards his lady.

Time passed. The rift between the King and Queen grew deeper. While the Queen laughed and danced with her folk in the sunlight, the King would keep to his chambers. At night, he roamed the moonlit woods with his retinue of pale courtesans, while the Queen slept alone in her bed of spider silk beneath a quilt of woven thistledown, with crickets chirping at her side. Only the Spider Mage knew how unhappy this made the Queen; for during the day, she was always as bright and giddy as ever, sipping her nectar and rocking in her silver swing. And no one but he knew how little the King cared for those courtesans, or how he sometimes sighed to himself as he lay upon his silken couch under its canopy of leaves and listened for his lady's voice above him, in the trees.

More time passed. The King and Queen pined for each other in secret. But each was as proud as the other, and neither would yield or compromise. The King grew more taciturn than ever; the Queen grew more impulsive. The King disappeared from his chambers the moment the sun set over the hills; the Queen was always safe in her bed as the last rays kissed the treetops.

The Spider Mage grieved for them both. Looking into his web of dreams, he combed the Nine Worlds for a way to bring the Moth King and the Butterfly Queen together again in harmony. Finally, he found what he sought: a rare conjunction in the sky. In six months' time, so he observed, the Sun and Moon would intersect, so that night would fall at noon and all the stars awaken. Surely, thought the Spider Mage, this would be the time to bring the pair together. And so he wove his web of dreams, and by subtle means ensured that King and Queen were both at hand at the moment of the eclipse.

At last, the day came. The Sun in the sky yielded to the Moon's embrace, and in the midday twilight, the Moth King and the Butterfly Queen were reunited in love. Only for a short time – but enough that their child was conceived; a boy of both light and shadow, a prince of sun and starlight. The Moth King and the Butterfly Queen made ready to go their separate ways; but when the Prince was born, each tried to claim him for their own.

The Queen taught him to fly high, drink deeply and laugh at his enemies. The King taught him the secrets of the night-time forest: the way of the fox, the cry of the owl, the gleam of the moon on the water. Both taught him how to change Aspect: how to break from his human form into a cloud of butterflies; how to hide among the trees like a moth in the dappled shade.

The boy – living between their worlds – learnt his lessons faithfully. But his parents, who loved their infant son far more than they had ever loved each other, were jealous and greedy for his love. The King did his best to teach his son to despise his mother's frivolity, while the Queen did her best to teach him to mock his father's melancholy moods. Thus, the young Prince spent his infancy in a state of constant confusion. But the Spider Mage befriended him, and taught him the ways of his people, hoping all the while that the child might reconcile the King and Queen.

As he grew, the young Prince became very dear to the Spider Mage. He had his mother's charm and grace, without her volatile nature. He had his father's intellect, without his anger and sullenness. And he had a kind and loving heart, which longed for one thing only: for his parents to love each other, as he loved them both. The Spider Mage longed for this, too. But the situation seemed hopeless.

Finally, he went back to his web and combed it again for a solution. He searched all the Worlds of the Honeycomb, consulted every Oracle, sent his spider servants out to every point of the compass to look for a way of bringing together the Butterfly Queen and the Moth King. He spun his webs into every world, stretched his threads of spider silk into every place and time. Then he slept, exhausted, leaving his web of dreams untended, its filaments reaching out into every world in existence.

And while he slept, the young Prince crept into the Mage's chamber, and, seeing the gleaming spider threads leading into the many worlds, took hold of the nearest thread tightly in his small hand. The Spider Mage slept on, unaware, as the child pulled on the silken thread *shining in the moonlight. And when the Spider Mage awoke, he found his web in disarray and the young Prince nowhere to be found.*

The Moth King's rage was terrible. So too was the grief of the Butterfly Queen. The Mage soon guessed where the boy had gone – but the world into which he had disappeared was one of untold terrors.

'Not Dream,' said the Queen, her dark eyes wide.

The Moth King took her hand. It was day, but the crisis had roused him from his bed and he looked pale and drawn.

The Spider Mage shook his head. 'No, not Dream, Your Majesty. But to a world almost as dark. A world in which our people are weak, and magic works poorly, if at all.' His voice fell to a whisper, and he said to the Queen, with tears in his eyes: 'Your Majesty, somehow the young Prince has entered the World of the Sightless Folk.'

For a moment, the King and Queen looked at each other in horror. Both Courts – the Moths in their dark finery, the Butterflies in their merry madness – held their breath, and hoped that perhaps this crisis might lead to a reconciliation.

Then the Queen began to weep. 'This is your fault,' she told the King. 'You taught our son to love the night, and to hunger for secrets and mysteries!'

The King said: 'My fault? You taught the boy to disobey, and to defy my authority.'

The Queen went pale. 'How dare you blame me? When, for all you know, our son may already be in the hands of the Sightless Folk!'

'If he is,' said the Moth King, 'then your tears are unlikely to help him.'

The quarrel went on between the pair, becoming ever more bitter. Each blamed the other for the loss of the Prince. The Moth King grew colder in his rage; the Queen's anger more heated. Finally, she fled the Court, swearing an oath that no Butterfly would ever fall in love again. Instead, they would prey on love, she said, and feed on it like nectar, and drain the hearts of lovers without ever loving in return.

The Moth King, grieving, left his throne and hid himself in World Below, letting his kingdom fall to ruin.

And in their absence there came war between the Moths and the Butterflies, a conflict that will never cease until the day the lost Prince is found, and a Butterfly falls in love with a Moth once again.

Only the Spider Mage, crushed by guilt, believed the lost Prince could be found. Forgotten by almost everyone, despised by both warring factions, he watched the worlds through his web of dreams, hoping for an answer. But his web remained dark, and his wretchedness grew. One night, despairing, he spun a thread into the World of the Sightless Folk and crept through the door into that world, and let it close behind him.

Some say he remains there to this day, driven mad with guilt and grief, unable to return to his world, still searching for the lost Prince.

Some say that's only a fairy tale.

Part 1

Vanessa

I

In a city of magical things, of buses, and plastic, and concrete, and trains, there lived a young man called Tom Argent. This was in the old days of the great, lost cities of the Folk, cities with strange and beautiful names, filled with palaces and parks; tunnels that stretched for miles underground; markets, museums and gaming halls and gleaming towers of grasshopper glass.

This marvellous city was London. Tom's neighbourhood was King's Cross, though long ago it had once been known as Battlebridge. Tom had never asked himself why; as far as he knew, it was just a name. But names are secret, powerful things, not to be given lightly. And cities are curious places, where the skin between the worlds rubs thin, and sometimes things (and even kings) can cross from one side to the other.

Tom Argent worked in a little shop just off the Caledonian Road. The shop sold second-hand cameras and film; lenses, tripods, enlargers; books of glossy black-and-white photographs. All of these were magical things: boxes in which to trap memories; shutters that could stop Time; lenses that could turn light itself away from its directed course. But Tom was no believer in fairy tales and miracles. He could walk through a bluebell wood and not see a single fairy – not that there *were* any bluebell woods in London, but there were parks with ancient trees, and markets filled with spices and fruits from countries a thousand miles away, and people of all races and types, and cobbled alleys that echoed with ghosts, and ships that only appeared by night, and secret plague pits under the ground.

But Tom never saw these things. Instead, he saw litter, and traffic and smoke; and people on their mobile phones who suddenly stopped in the street when he was walking behind them; and angry cab drivers, and riotous drunks, and cyclists who never looked where they were going.

Tom Argent did not even see the magic at his fingertips. Instead, he saw the death of film, and the advent of the digital age, and the power of social media; and he worried about paying the rent, and about making art in a world in which artists are paid with exposure. He was no blinder than most, of course, but cities do that to people. They dull the senses; kill curiosity; make people look inwards instead of out. And the Folk are especially susceptible to this kind of numbness – which is why the Faërie scorned them, and called them the Sightless Folk.

The only time Tom Argent felt as if the world was truly *real* was when he could see it through a lens. Photography was his passion, and he spent most of his spare time around King's Cross, taking pictures of the streets. He saw the homeless people; the houseboats on Regent's Canal; the dogs; the vehicles; the railway trains; the station with its great glass roof and its faded, powdery, red-brick facades. Through the lens of Tom's camera, the everyday became magical; the commonplace, extraordinary. His camera brought forgotten things into sudden focus. Garish colours shifted to a crisp, nostalgic black-and-white, and Tom glimpsed the world as it really was, as if the camera's lens were an eye that saw beyond the everyday. And it was only then that he was ever truly happy.

He developed and printed his own work in his attic darkroom, which was the closest to magic he ever got – or, at least, as far as he knew. Sometimes he displayed his work, although he never sold it. He lived alone above the camera shop in a tiny, one-room attic flat with a view of the rooftops. His parents had died in a house fire during his first year at university, and he had no family, no friends – except for the kind of friends you greet without ever actually knowing their names. He had black hair, and thoughtful dark eyes, and a face that was pale from being too long indoors. He was twenty-nine years old, and he had never been in love.

His employer, the owner of the shop and of many others along the road, was called Mr Burnet. Tom had only met him once, the day he'd been given the job; after that, he'd only been in contact via email, and through intermediaries. Mr Burnet lived in a house on the far side of Regent's Canal, and was never seen without his long, dark overcoat, with only the flash of his grey-gold eyes visible under a broad-brimmed hat. Tom found him disturbing, although he didn't quite know why, and he was secretly rather glad he didn't see him more often. But Mr Burnet was by far the most generous employer Tom had ever had, never seeming to care how much money Tom made, or what (if anything) he had sold. The hours were short, the salary good, and the flat above the shop, though small, had a darkroom in which he could work. And Tom was doing what he loved most: working with cameras and photographs. It was the job of his dreams, and Mr Burnet never interfered.

On the morning this story begins, Tom had risen early and taken his camera and his bag in search of things to photograph. It was early April, when the light was at its sweetest, and on those sunny spring mornings, Tom sometimes felt the skin of the world ready to peel away at a touch, revealing beauty underneath – beauty, and sometimes horrors. A dandelion clock, growing between the cracks in the pavement. A girl, coming back from a night on the town, caught in an unguarded moment.

An old homeless man with a bundle of books, packing away his cardboard bed and muttering darkly to himself, unaware that the morning sun had given his head a corona of fire.

Tom reached for his camera. People usually realised quite quickly when they were being photographed. Sometimes they posed, which was bad – or, worse, became hostile, or ran away. But the old man was too preoccupied, and Tom, using a long lens, was able to rattle off a few shots before he became suspicious.

'What do you think you're doing?' said the man, as he finally noticed.

'I'm sorry. I hope you don't mind,' said Tom. 'It's just that … you have an interesting face. I'm a collector of interesting people.'

'Interesting,' said the homeless man. 'Yon Collector says we're *interesting*.' His voice was soft and hoarse, as if he didn't use it often. His accent was not that of London, or of anywhere else that Tom could identify. Behind his little round spectacles, his eyes were a clear and luminous grey, with a skein of gold running through them like a piece of *kintsugi*.

He grinned at Tom, who saw now that he was younger than he'd first assumed – not yet out of his fifties, with unruly white hair which gave him the look of a mad king.

'I'll tell you what's *interesting*, Collector. Breakfast.' He indicated a nearby café. 'That is, if you're minded to pay for the pieces of my soul you took without permission.'

Tom nodded. 'Of course,' he said. 'I'll get you something. A sandwich. All right?'

'And some tea, please. Two cups. Sweet. One for me, one for Charissa.'

Tom looked around, but as far as he could see the white-haired man was alone. He must be a little disturbed, thought Tom. The challenges for those who were homeless were rife.

He went into the café and came back with two paper cups of sweetened tea and a bacon sandwich. The man sat down on his parcel of books – neatly tied with coloured string – and ate the sandwich carefully, making sure not to drop any crumbs. Tom took a few more pictures of the man as he was eating. Now he reminded Tom of the feral cats that lived on his street; the way they took what food they could from the overturned rubbish bins, but delicately, like exiled queens forced to become cats at night and to fight for their food with the foxes.

'Don't mind Charissa,' said the man, finishing the sandwich and starting on his cup of tea. 'She don't much care for your regular food.' He paused to address the second cup, which he had balanced on a wall, and sat there with a cup in each hand, alternating mouthfuls.

Tom took a couple more pictures.

'Charissa sez she don't like that,' said the man. 'Cut it out, Collector.'

'Sorry,' said Tom, putting the camera back in his satchel.

'That's better,' said the man. 'You don't want to make them nervous. They get angry when they're nervous. They say it steals their soul away, although, of course, they never had any in the first place.'

Tom thought better of asking who the mysterious *they* might be. Instead, he said, 'What's your name?'

The homeless man looked wary. 'I'm not telling *you* that,' he said, as if Tom had suggested something too crazy to contemplate. 'We don't give our names to strangers. Give them away and anyone can use 'em, day or night. Names are for keeping to yourself, if you know what's good for you.'

Tom was taken aback. 'OK.'

The madman nodded. 'You weren't to know. Tell you what, Collector. There's daylight names and midnight names. Daylight names are safe enough. A spider brings good luck before midnight, but bad luck after. And you look to me like the kind of young man who needs good luck, and to keep out of dark rooms. You can have my *daylight* name. You can call me Spider.'

'Pleased to meet you, Spider,' said Tom. 'Hope you enjoyed your breakfast.'

'Thank you, Collector,' Spider said. 'And remember what I said about luck, and keeping out of dark rooms.'

And, at that, picking up his parcel of books, Spider began to walk purposefully down the road, a river of light at his ragged heels, his spindly shadow beside him.

2

On a normal day, Tom Argent would have developed his film after work. But this was not a normal day. This was the day that Tom Argent would finally, fatally, fall in love.

He had not intended to fall in love. He had intended to spend the afternoon quietly cataloguing his negatives, maybe drinking a cup of tea, and listening to the radio. On a normal day, he might have expected two or maybe three customers, most of them wanting to know if he would develop their old film, mend a broken camera or direct them to the nearest bookshop. On that day, however, the doorbell rang and in walked the most beautiful girl Tom Argent had ever seen.

Now, beauty is not a size or a shape, an outfit or a colour. Real beauty is something that *shines*. The rest is only glamour. This girl was both dark and luminous, like a copper beech in the sun. Luminous was her brown skin, and her eyes were every shade of leaf, from guinea gold to forest-floor black. She was wearing a yellow dress. Her hair was a crown of autumn fire. And yes, she was very beautiful. But her beauty was none of these things. And although by the time she had left, Tom could barely remember her clothes, or the shape of her face, or the colour of her eyes, or the exact shade of her skin, he knew he would always remember that shine. Tom Argent was changed for ever.

'Can I help you, miss?' he said as she came into the shop.

She smiled. 'I'd like to buy that print,' she said, indicating a photograph hanging in the window. 'I am assuming it's for sale?'

Tom had taken the photograph that winter. It had been snowing, which was rare in King's Cross, and, just for a day, the familiar streets had been new and clean again. A boy playing with his friends had thrown a snowball, and Tom had caught the moment, the light; the boy looking directly into the camera lens as the snowball began its trajectory; the brilliant swipe of powdery snow as it arced through the air towards him. The result had been a wonderful accident – the kind that only happens with film – and Tom was pleased with the result.

But he never sold his work. People had asked, but he had always refused. If he'd been able to find the right words, he might have told them that his work was more than just taking pictures. Every print was different. Even when they were taken from the same negative, each one had its character, its own individual markings. Each one was a piece of him, and the thought of it hanging in somebody's house, trapped under glass in the bathroom, perhaps, or providing a talking point in the hall, was almost intolerable. For a moment, he thought of Spider, and the way he'd referred to the photographs as stolen pieces of his soul.

He reached into the shop window and took out the print in its wooden frame. Then he showed it to the girl and said, 'I took that. Do you like it?'

'It's magical.'

Tom shifted from one foot to the other. 'It was just a lucky shot.'

The girl in the yellow dress smiled. 'Was it? You can see things others can't. If that isn't magic, then what is?'

'Well—' Tom began to explain exactly *how* he'd taken the shot; the lens he'd used; the shutter speed. Then he realised she had no idea what he was talking about, and stopped halfway through a sentence.

The girl gave her luminous smile again. 'Flutter-speed or glamorie-glass, lens of truth or coat of dreams: what does it matter how magic works?'

Her voice was slightly accented, though Tom could not place its origin. Her English, too, was slightly odd, slightly foreign, as if she'd learnt it from a very old primer. For a moment, he was reminded of Spider's off-kilter speech – but that was absurd. How could this girl and a homeless man have anything in common? He struggled to regain his composure, conscious that he was still staring.

'Well, I don't really *sell* my work,' he said. 'But if you like it – here. It's yours.' He handed her the picture.

The girl's smile became something so bright that Tom could scarcely look at it. Motes of dust in the dark air trembled and sang like golden bells.

'Wait. I'll wrap it for you,' said Tom, who by now was under the spell of something he'd never experienced before – something like drunkenness, or a dream in which he flew on magical wings and rescued maidens from dragons. 'Hang on. It might take a minute.'

He reached for a sheet of wrapping paper and some string, racking his brain for anything else that might keep the girl there a few moments longer. He wrapped the parcel with exquisite care; tied the string in a double bow; prayed for a sudden shower of rain that might force her to linger.

Outside, the sun was dazzling. The sky was perfectly cloudless.

The girl took the parcel and tucked it carefully under her arm. 'Thank you.'

Tom said: 'What's your da— Ah – what's your name?'

He was so dazed that he had almost said: *What's your daylight name?* The memory of Spider, combined with the girl's effect on him, had induced a kind of disconnection from ordinary language. In this new and luminous world, words like 'glamorie-glass' made sense, and daylight names were shields, designed to hold back the approach of night. The thought of this girl at night conjured up pictures of Van Gogh's *Starry Night*, and comets, and lightships, and the taste of her skin, torched to silver in the moonlight—

The girl looked amused. It occurred to him that she must be used to men being fools around her. 'I'm Vanessa.'

'*Vanessa.* Vanessa. I'm Tom,' he said. 'And where are you from, Vanessa?' It was an excuse to keep saying her name, which sounded to him like a cat's-paw of wind across the bright surface of a lake.

She smiled again. 'Oh, I'm from everywhere.'

'Near King's Cross?'

'Sometimes,' she said. 'Sometimes my friends and I come here. There's a champagne bar in St Pancras Station. Sometimes we meet for drinks in there.'

'Will you be there tonight?' asked Tom.

Vanessa shrugged. 'Perhaps,' she said. 'We don't make plans. But you might see us there.'

She left with the picture under her arm, in its brown-paper packaging. And Tom spent the rest of the afternoon saying her name and sighing, and trying to work out how a girl he'd never met before could have captured his heart as surely and as permanently as he had captured that snowball, forever now suspended in time like a fly in amber.

3

As soon as his day was done, Tom raced to St Pancras Station. He knew the champagne bar, but had never tried it, not being a connoisseur of champagne, or a lover of champagne prices. But Vanessa had said she might be there, and that was all the motivation he needed.

He waited two hours at a table and bought a glass of champagne that tasted like pulverised starlight (and which, of course, went straight to his head). Then, as he was starting to think Vanessa would never appear, he saw her, with a group of friends, standing at the bar.

The place had filled up since Tom had arrived. The tables and booths were all occupied, and there was a nasty gleam in the waiter's eye, as if to suggest that if he did not order again *very* soon, sharp words would be spoken. Tom, feeling reckless, now beckoned him and ordered a bottle (costing more than Tom had ever dreamed a single bottle of wine could cost) to be sent to the girl and her three friends. Then he left his seat and made his way, by now rather unsteadily, through the crowd towards them.

Tom was as unused to drinking champagne as he was to talking to women. His evenings were generally spent alone, watching television, listening to music or developing and printing his photographs. He felt very conspicuous in his jeans and T-shirt, surrounded as he currently was by people in evening clothes:

women in long dresses, their hair worked into complicated braids; men in bow ties and dinner jackets. Vanessa had changed her yellow dress for one of a vibrant butterfly-blue, and her curly dark hair had been braided into an elaborate coronet. Gold bracelets gleamed on her brown arms, reflecting tiny flecks of gold onto her skin. Surrounded by glass and chrome and lights, she was the most magical being Tom had ever seen.

He was not so sure about her friends. Two men and a woman, all striking, in brightly coloured clothing that looked both strange and sumptuous. Was one of the men her date? It seemed depressingly likely to Tom, but the champagne had made him reckless, and he pushed the unwelcome thought aside.

As he reached her, Vanessa was talking to a tall dark man with braided hair and a waistcoat of midnight-blue velvet. She looked happy; he looked bored. Tom felt a renewed surge of optimism.

'Vanessa,' he said.

She turned. 'It's you! *You* sent the champagne!'

He nodded, feeling absurdly cheered that she remembered him. Over her shoulder, Vanessa's friend glanced at Tom with a look of amusement that was not entirely kind. Tom liked him even less at close quarters than he had from afar. Handsome, tall and effortlessly elegant, he looked vaguely contemptuous, but mostly unthreatened – and unsurprised.

'Tom, meet Brimstone,' Vanessa said, speaking of the tall man. 'And this is Skipper, and this here is Pieris.'

Skipper was a woman – dark-skinned and shaven-headed, wearing a sheath of sequinned green. Pieris was slighter than Brimstone, cropped hair buzzed along one side, wearing a pink leather jacket over an orange T-shirt. He grinned like a flashgun and slung an arm companionably around Tom's neck.

'Stop it,' said Vanessa. 'He's mine.'

Pieris pulled a face at her. Tom could feel his head spinning. Had Vanessa really said *he's mine*? Or was he only dreaming?

'So, are you actors, or something?' said Tom. There was something of the stage, he thought, about the little foursome; a kind of self-conscious flamboyance, which was charming in Vanessa (*everything* was charming in Vanessa), but which, in the case of the others, now seemed quietly sinister.

The tall man, Brimstone, gave a smile. 'Yes, we sometimes *act*,' he said. His voice was low but carrying. Tom got the feeling he was being mocked, but was unsure of how to respond. Besides, what kind of names were they – Brimstone, Skipper, Pieris? Stage names? Foreign names?

Midnight names, he thought suddenly, and shivered without knowing why.

'Have you been in anything I might have seen?'

Brimstone smiled. 'I doubt it,' he said.

The others smiled too, as if at a joke at Tom's expense.

Vanessa gave Brimstone a stern look. 'Stop tormenting him, children,' she said. 'Tom's very sweet.'

'How do you know? Have you licked him?' Pieris gave Tom the kind of smile a child gives to an ice cream. Vanessa gave him a look of reproach, but behind it, Tom thought she was smiling.

Defiantly, he poured himself a glass of champagne and drank it all in one, and then immediately wished he hadn't, because the glass ceiling of St Pancras Station started to turn like a kaleidoscope, and he was suddenly in need of more air than he seemed to be breathing. He put out a hand to steady himself, found Pieris instead and flinched.

'Oops, I think we broke your friend.' Pieris' smile grew even wider. 'You should have brought a couple of spares. That way, we could all have one.'

Vanessa ignored him. 'Tom, are you all right?'

Tom said something about the heat.

Pieris grinned and said, 'That's fine. *Actors* like it sweaty.'

'Stop it, Pieris,' Skipper said in a voice that was calm but commanding. Then she looked at Vanessa and said, 'Better take it outside, no?'

Tom closed his eyes. The feeling of airlessness intensified, as did his sense of disconnection. Suddenly, none of this felt real; it felt like a dream, a fairy tale, smoke between his fingers. And then Vanessa was leading him through the kaleidoscope, away from the sounds of voices and the glare of lights, and the noise of railway trains and announcements, and into the magical London night.

London nights are never dark. Even at midnight, King's Cross was always ablaze with activity. Neon signs of all colours; taxis bringing people home; late-night passengers; rowdy drunks; and, later, the secret people: the homeless, the lost, sex workers, people in cheap cafés, people looking for places to sleep. At a certain time of night, all the bright colours disappeared, reverting once more to monochrome.

That was a time Tom Argent loved, not least for the chance it offered him to photograph the kinds of things the daylight people rarely saw. But that night, he'd left his camera at home. He felt lost without it. Shapes and colours seemed to blur all around him as he stood in front of King's Cross Station, feeling sick and miles from home, even though his little flat was less than ten minutes' walk away.

Vanessa saw his discomfort. 'Let's find you somewhere quiet,' she said. 'Come with me. You'll be all right.'

She took his hand and led him away, into the dark and the backstreets. Everywhere in London has them, and often where you'd least expect to find a quiet, deserted place. There are always quiet alleyways for those who know where to find them; places where the traffic sounds as remote as the sound of the sea.

Tom allowed Vanessa to lead him into one of these alleyways, feeling dazed and delirious but happy in her presence. He noticed that she still shone, even in the shadows; the flecks of gold on her dark skin dancing like tiny fireflies. And when she finally turned to him and kissed him softly on the mouth, he felt a surge of indescribable joy, and wished he could capture the moment; bottle and sip it, like nectar—

He suddenly felt unsteady again. The dazzling night spun him around like thread around a spindle. He reached for Vanessa and found himself clinging to her like a child.

'Come over here with me and sit down.' Gently, she guided him towards a bench by the side of a church. A row of flowering cherry trees seemed to float in the pale street light, and there was a scent of summertime, almost too heady for April. Tom had never noticed the bench – or the cherry trees, or the church – before, but he seemed to have lost track of time, along with his bearings. He sat on the bench and felt the world settle slowly back into place. Vanessa stayed on her feet, looking up at the night sky. 'The moon's so beautiful,' she said. 'But I always miss the stars.'

Tom would have liked to have said something about the stars. Or her beauty, like the night. Something about her eyes, perhaps, or how she seemed to shine – but somehow the words refused to take shape. The world was like a spinning wheel, turning common straw into gold.

Vanessa smiled and kissed him again, and once more Tom felt that sense of eerie disconnection, a feeling that somehow he might disappear into a shining vortex of stars—

Something near – a bird, a bat – made a sudden fluttering sound.

Vanessa flinched. 'Did you hear that?' she said.

'A pigeon?' said Tom.

She shook her head, and looked around, as if suddenly becoming aware of a potential danger. 'I have to get back to the others.'

'What, now?'

'I'm sorry, Tom.'

Once more came the sound of fluttering. Vanessa turned again, eyes wide. From out of the shadows came a shape, suspended in the hazy light.

It was only a moth, Tom saw; a plump and feathery light brown moth, caught in the arc of the street light. Some people were afraid of moths; but this one was so beautiful, with its curling antennae and dappled wings, that he was fascinated. It landed briefly on his arm, and Vanessa pulled away.

'It's only a moth,' he told her.

Now Tom saw that the moth had been joined by a handful of others. They fluttered in the street lamp's flare; they settled on the pavement. Soon, there were dozens – *hundreds* – of them; settling onto his arms and head, falling through the air like snow.

'What the *hell*?' said Tom.

But Vanessa was already starting to run, holding her blue dress with one hand, her snakeskin sandals tripping and tapping on the uneven cobbles. The pale moths whirled about her like confetti in a storm.

'Vanessa, wait!' Tom's dizziness had been replaced by a sense of alarm. He couldn't lose Vanessa now, not without knowing where she lived, or who she was, or even her full name. He stood up and started after her, holding up his arm to shield his face against the sudden blizzard of moths—

But the moths were gone, as suddenly and mysteriously as they had appeared. Not a single moth remained in the arc of the street lamp. It was as if they had never been there. He looked for

Vanessa and saw her, frozen to the spot a dozen feet away from him. She was facing a group of four people, who had stepped out from behind the angle of the church. Three women and one big man – almost a giant in stature – in leathers the colour of weathered stone. They wore mystic tattoos on their pale skin, with hair that was shaved or braided with beads, and soft, flat boots that made no sound against the stones of the alleyway.

One of the women stepped forward. 'Hello, Vanessa, darling,' she said.

'We've been looking for you,' said the man.

'And here you are at last,' said a third; a girl with a sharp, disquieting face studded with metal piercings.

Vanessa looked at Tom in appeal. Her face was naked with alarm, and for the first time, Tom saw her as imperfect, and loved her all the more for it.

'Please, Tom,' said Vanessa. '*Help me.*'

It was a call to action. Four attackers, one champion; and for a moment, Tom Argent felt like a hero in one of those books he'd read as a child, books which his father had deplored, in which knights rescue maidens against all odds, and magic is in everything.

He took a step towards the foe.

The woman who had first spoken, and who seemed to be the leader, looked him up and down with a kind of pity. Then she looked back at Vanessa.

'Really,' she said. 'Is that all you've got?'

Tom drew himself up to his full height (still she overtopped him). 'I don't know who you are,' he said, 'but if I were you, I'd leave us alone.'

The woman smiled. Her features were strong, with arched brows and high cheekbones. Tom might have been struck by her beauty, had his eyes not been on the knife in her hand: a small, dark, unshowy blade that looked as if it had been used often, and efficiently.

'You're in the wrong place, young man,' she said. 'Walk away, before you get hurt.'

Tom imagined the dark blade punching between his ribs. Then he imagined Vanessa's face if he failed to protect her.

With hands that trembled a little, he took out his mobile phone, set the camera app to video mode and held it out like a weapon.

'You think *that's* going to help you?' said the woman, looking amused. 'What do you think that will achieve?'

'I'm putting this online,' Tom said. 'Do anything to her, or to me, and your faces will be all over Twitter and YouTube. I can do it. I'm doing it *now*—' Behind him, he sensed Vanessa, backing slowly away from them. Once again, he waved his phone, wishing it looked more impressive.

The four strangers exchanged amused glances. 'Good luck with that,' said the woman who seemed to be the leader. 'Things like that don't work so well against the Midnight Folk.'

Midnight Folk? For a moment, Tom thought of Spider and his midnight names. But there was no time for questions. Behind him, he could hear the sound of Vanessa's feet as she started to run again, sending a spray of little stones skimming over the road in her wake. Two of the four started after her, running almost soundlessly in their flat and soft-soled boots. Spreading his arms, Tom stepped into their path.

'Atlas!' snapped the leader.

She and the giant leapt at Tom. The mobile phone flew out of his hand as the big man tackled him, slamming him into the wall of the church. The side of Tom's head struck the stone, and he felt the weight of the giant crushing his ribs against the cobbles as they fell. Then the pressure was released and he was left lying on the ground, dark flowers blooming behind his eyes, his vision pixelated with stars.

His last coherent thought was: *So, there are stars here after all—*

Then, for a while, there was nothing at all.

4

'*Collector. Hey! Collector! Wake up.*'

Tom awoke to find himself looking up into a face that he vaguely recognised. It was a girl's face, freckled and small, and with a corona of mousy hair, torched orange in the street light. One of the gang, he realised, and clumsily tried to sit up, provoking a sharp pain in his ribs. He gave a little whimper, suddenly sure that he'd been stabbed. But after investigation it seemed to be only the painful result of his fall – with luck, there was nothing broken.

The girl was standing over him. She looked to be only twenty or so; small and light and wiry. Bracelets of fine tattoos ran up and down her pale, thin arms. A gem – maybe a tourmaline – blinked at him from her eyebrow.

She looked at him dispassionately, then reached down to help him up. 'That was pretty stupid,' she said. 'Going up against Atlas.'

Tom pulled himself to his knees. The world was still spinning. Looking around, he could see no sign of the rest of the gang, or Vanessa.

'Where is she?'

'Vanessa? She got away. You're lucky. That's all I'm saying.'

Tom put a hand to his head. It hurt, but there was no blood. Using the wall as a support, he finally managed to stand upright.

'What do you want?' he asked the girl. 'I have no money. You broke my phone.'

That was true; he'd heard the sound as it hit the ground.

'You got in the way,' said the freckled girl. 'No one *wanted* to hurt you.'

'But what about Vanessa?' said Tom. 'What could she ever have done to you? She's—'

'Fragile. Helpless,' said the girl. 'That's what she'd like you to believe. Trust me, that bitch can look after herself. Thing is, she never has to.'

'I don't understand,' said Tom.

'It's complicated,' said the girl. 'I'm not even supposed to talk to you.' She looked around, then lowered her voice. 'I only came back to warn you,' she said. 'Because you were kind to a friend of mine.'

Tom was puzzled. 'A friend of yours?' He was fairly certain that any friends of this girl were unlikely to have come his way. 'And what do you mean, *warn* me? Warn me against what?'

The girl gave an impatient hiss. 'I mean, stay away from Vanessa,' she said. 'Her, and all of the Daylight Folk. They're dangerous to people like you.'

'And you're *not?*'

''Course we are. Just not in the same way *she* is.' She frowned. 'Now, can you get home?'

'I think so,' said Tom. 'But—'

'Then go home. Go home and forget all about her. She'll be fine without your help, and you'll be safer for it. Go *now*, before the others come back and decide to finish you, after all.'

Tom thought it sounded like good advice. But as for forgetting Vanessa, no. Vanessa's shine – her sunshine smile – was permanently imprinted on him. Might as well try to remove a face from a developing photograph.

29

The freckled girl seemed to sense his thoughts. 'Got to you, did she? Think you're in love? Give it a week and it'll wear off. I know you don't think that now, but you will. It's what her kind do to your kind.'

'Her kind?' Tom said. '*My* kind?'

The freckled girl smiled. Under the golden glare of the street light, it almost made her beautiful. 'Go home, Collector. Let it wear off. You've no idea how lucky you are. You've met the Daylight Folk and survived. Like I said, give it a week, and chances are you won't even remember her.'

5

Slowly, Tom Argent picked up his broken phone and made his way back to his little flat. His ribs hurt, and his head ached, but the dizziness had passed and he felt perfectly lucid again. That sense of being in a dream had gone. So had the illusion of warmth; he assumed the champagne was wearing off. Reaching home, he undressed, showered and tried to make sense of the night's events, which already seemed so very remote, like a half-remembered story. Drinking champagne with Vanessa's friends, who looked like something from Shakespeare; fighting the giant Atlas; the perfect kiss from the girl of his dreams—

Was this love? he asked himself. He had no point of comparison. But if love felt like drunkenness, and shooting stars, and flying on wings of starlight silk, then this *was* love – it *had* to be. Love straight out of a fairy tale – once glimpsed, never to be forgotten. The freckled girl had seemed so sure that he would forget Vanessa. How could she believe such a thing? And what did she mean by *Daylight Folk*?

It was late, but he couldn't sleep. His ribs still hurt and his head was filled with stars and unanswered questions. The undeveloped film with the pictures he'd taken of Spider that morning was waiting to be processed, and he'd always found his darkroom a quiet, peaceful place to unwind. Now, in the glow of the dim red light, he found himself relaxing at last; going through the ritual of bringing his pictures into the world. It was a ritual he loved, filled with possibilities; and as he hung the wet film to dry, he squinted at the tiny squares with eager curiosity. It felt like panning for gold. In every scoop of common grit, the chance of something magical.

But now, as he looked closer, he noticed something odd about his negatives. A double shadow on some of the shots that had nothing to do with the development process. An accident, he told himself. A thumbprint on the negative; a careless splash of chemicals. He waited for the film to dry, then put the roll of negatives under the enlarger.

Here were his pictures of Spider. A long shot, then a close-up, the man's white hair looking crow black in negative. And behind him, a doubled image, as if of someone standing there, a kind of angelic brightness. Of course it wasn't brightness, Tom knew. In print, it would look like a shadow. An ominous shadow, just out of shot, of someone at the edge of the frame.

Tom looked through the rest of his negatives. He could already see that they were good, and he felt a renewed excitement. He'd always felt that developing film was like a kind of alchemy. What had Vanessa called it? A glamorie-glass? He understood that. His camera noticed things he did not. Even now, looking closer at some of the frames, he could see details he hadn't seen when he was taking the photographs. A row of posters on a wall that he could have sworn had been faded to almost blank, now clearly legible and advertising something – a band, maybe – called the *Moonlight Market*.

But the thing that really caught his eye was in the pictures of Spider at breakfast. Someone *else* was there in the frame, someone who hadn't been there before. Sometimes they appeared as a shadow right at the edge of the photograph. Sometimes it was simply a hand, or a foot, or a knee extending into the frame. But in several images, the figure was there almost in its entirety:

not a doubled image, no, nor even an indistinct outline, but the very clear figure of a girl he was sure had not been there.

Tom printed out the negatives that featured the girl most clearly. There were almost a dozen of these. Some showed her standing directly behind Spider as he looked at the camera. Others showed her standing to one side, or turning away, or in motion. Two or three showed her clearly, looking straight at the camera. In one, she was actually in the foreground, seeming almost to mock him there with her presence, her *reality*.

Tom laid these images side by side and stared at the prints for a long time, trying to make sense of it, wondering if he'd gone mad. Here were his portraits of Spider, in the courtyard in front of King's Cross. Here was the man in his shabby old coat, eating his bacon sandwich. Here he was, with his bundle of books, leaning against the crumbling wall. And here he was, staring directly into the lens of the camera, his eyes full of piercing intelligence behind his little round spectacles.

But none of the prints showed anyone else, or anything unusual. The posters advertising the *Moonlight Market* were gone. There was no sign of the girl that he had seen in the negatives.

Once more, Tom placed the negatives on the enlarger. There she was: no figment of his imagination. In negative, her hair was bright; the spiral tattoos on her arms standing out like splashes of phosphorescence.

Now that he came to think of it, Tom could even remember her name. *Two cups. One for me, one for—*

Charissa.

Tom had assumed that Charissa was part of Spider's peculiar madness. But here she was beside him, *real*: caught in the moment, on celluloid. Here she was, cross-legged on the wall as Spider ate his sandwich; here she was, reading one of those mysterious posters; here she was, bending down to pick up one of the books from Spider's bundle. Here she was behind him now, head turned away from the camera; and here she was right in the lens, her eyes as bright as broken glass—

And now Tom understood what she'd meant when she told him he'd helped her friend. He understood what Spider had meant by *daylight names* and *midnight names*. Vanessa was one of the Daylight Folk, visible by light of day. And her would-be attackers – they must be the Midnight Folk, visible only at night-time; watching from the shadows; able to hide away in plain sight, but somehow visible on film. Tom knew this beyond a shadow of a doubt, and with the alarming knowledge came a thrill of both danger and delight. *Maybe my father was wrong,* he thought. *Maybe there* is *magic in the world.*

Because the girl in the photographs – the girl Spider called Charissa, who shone like the sun in his negatives, but who disappeared in print – was none other than the freckled girl who'd spoken to him in the alleyway.

6

Tom Argent had once loved fairy tales. When he was very young, he had loved to read about princes, and kings, and queens, and fairies, and goblins, and magic. He even liked to pretend that he was the son of a fairy queen, or a pirate king, who had been adopted by humans, and one day would claim his kingdom.

His parents had grown concerned at this. They had never hidden the fact that Tom was adopted, and they knew that all children like to pretend. But Tom's imagination was especially vivid. He loved his parents very much, but they were afraid that this daydreaming might lead him to reject them one day. And so, they had both gone out of their way to discourage his love of fairy tales.

Whenever they saw him with his books, they would tell him: 'Stories aren't real. Magic is just an illusion. Fairies don't exist, Tom. Only trust what you can *see*.'

Then, on his seventh birthday, they had given Tom a camera, and the books of fairy tales had vanished swiftly and silently overnight, to be replaced by magazines devoted to different types of lens, in which the young Tom Argent had found another kind of magic. But looking at these images of the mysterious girl, he felt as if he had returned to the world of those long-ago storybooks, and it felt both exciting and wonderful, and deeply, darkly dangerous.

Once again, Tom found himself going over the negatives. He

knew he hadn't seen Charissa when he'd taken them, but the eye of his camera – the eye that saw the world as it really *was*, and not as passers-by saw it – had managed to capture her on film. It must be some kind of camouflage, he thought, inspecting the image. The girl in the alley had been nondescript, her clothes the colour of mottled stone. But looking at her now, on film, Tom could see her beauty. It wasn't like Vanessa's *shine* – and yet, there was a resemblance. Perhaps it was something in the eyes; something fierce in the tilt of the head; the difference between a flower sold in a florist's shop and something growing out in the wild.

He remembered the amusement of the other woman in the alleyway as he'd tried to use his phone camera. *Things like that don't work so well against the Midnight Folk.*

What did that mean, anyway? Perhaps the phone would yield answers. He'd picked it up in the alleyway, hoping to repair the smashed screen. But the memory card might still be undamaged. Tom took out the card and transferred it into an older phone that he'd been intending to sell some day and had never got round to trading.

The video he'd taken was there. He called it up on the screen and watched. Turning up the sound, he found he could hear his own voice, tinny with fright: *I'm putting this online. Do anything to her, or to me, and your faces will be all over Twitter and YouTube.* Then a pause, and a dizzying blur as the phone was knocked out of his hand.

But of the Midnight Folk – Charissa, Atlas and the rest – there was nothing to be seen. Nor was any other voice discernible on the soundtrack. And to add another layer of mystery to the episode, Vanessa, who should have been in shot, was as absent as the rest of them. The alleyway was empty.

Vampires, thought Tom with a sudden start. Wasn't there some story about vampires not showing in photographs? Or was that just reflections? Charissa had been revealed on *film*, but not on the digital camera. Perhaps it was film that was special. Perhaps if he captured Vanessa on film, he might understand her secret?

Tom slept very little that night. Dreams chased around his head like moths, until he gave up on sleep at dawn, certain of just one thing. He needed to find Vanessa again. He needed to capture her image. He needed to bask in her *shine* again, to hear the sound of her laughter. But he had no idea of where she lived, where she worked or even her full name. All he knew was that she and her friends sometimes went to the champagne bar at St Pancras Station.

But *Spider* might know, he told himself. Spider, who saw Charissa even when no one else did. Spider, who had first told him about daylight names and midnight names. Surely, if anyone could help him find Vanessa again, if anyone could explain how she and Charissa's gang had failed to register on his phone camera, it would be Spider. So Tom got up, dressed quickly, picked up his camera bag and went back to King's Cross in search of answers.

7

The summery weather had shifted overnight to a thin spring rain. Once again, King's Cross was transformed; the sky a troubled shade of grey, the people drab and cheerless. Tom searched in all the places where Spider might have been sleeping. In front of the station; beside the canal; around the bins; in side streets. He searched the alleyways, the station; looked into all the cheap coffee shops. But try as he might, there was no sign of a white-haired man with a bundle of books, or of a freckled girl with tattoos and hair the shade of a moth's wing.

By nine o'clock, Tom was so tired that he went back to the flat. There, he had breakfast, showered, then slept until lunchtime, hoping that Mr Burnet would not choose that particular day to check on his business. He opened up in the afternoon, and spent till evening watching the street, half expecting Vanessa to call, half fearing Charissa might come in her place.

But no one called that day, or the next. Nor did Vanessa or her friends turn up at the champagne bar. For three days, Tom kept watch in King's Cross. But there was no sign of Vanessa, or Spider, or Charissa, or any of the Midnight Folk. And though he had no problem remembering the freckled girl in the alleyway, Vanessa's face had already grown strangely dim in his mind's eye, with only the memory of her *shine* to sustain his love.

He thought back to what Charissa had said. *Give it a week, and chances are you won't even remember you met her.*

He'd scorned the suggestion three days ago. But now Tom Argent was close to believing that he must have dreamed it all. He tried to hold onto the memory of Vanessa's smile; her *shine*; the sound of her voice; the scent of her skin; but the more he tried, the more the whole encounter seemed like some forgotten fairy tale. Except for those negatives, of course. Film never lies, he told himself, though memory can be mistaken.

Going over his film again, hoping for a clue, he paused at a shot of the wall against which Spider had eaten his sandwich. When Tom had taken the photographs, the wall had been bare London brick, with only the faded, ragged ghosts of ancient posters displayed there. But now, in the roll of negatives, a row of fresh posters announced the *Moonlight Market*. Another mystery, to which Tom had paid little attention in his search for Vanessa. Now he looked at the posters again, blowing up the image as far as his enlarger would go.

The print was slightly uneven, as if the type had been set by hand. In an intricate, cursive font, which would have been printed black on white, but which in negative seemed to float against a panel of darkness, it read:

Moonlight Market
Old London Bridge
Moonrise, Friday night
Forecast: mostly clear, scattered clouds
Enter at own risk

Tom reread the poster. He only knew of one London Bridge. Was there another? An earlier one? He supposed there might have been. The Thames had moved over the years, its banks shifting softly over the silt. There must have been bridges since Roman times; crossings; forgotten monuments. Maybe the

Moonlight Market was held on one of these earlier sites. He found both the weather forecast and the *Enter at own risk* line odd, but this was his only remaining clue to the Midnight Folk, and Vanessa.

Today was Thursday. The market was billed at moonrise the following day. There was no map, no address for the location. *Old London Bridge.* After looking up several guides to historic London, he discovered that although the old bridge itself was long gone, there were a few lasting remnants of the *original* London Bridge, one of which was built into the tower of St Magnus the Martyr's Church on Lower Thames Street.

Visiting the scene, he found a pedestrian entrance, once used to access the bridge before the river had shifted and made the passage redundant. Tom took the pedestrian entrance and searched the surrounding area, but found no sign of a market, or even a space where stalls might be set up the following night. It made no sense. The bridge was gone. There was no marketplace, or even a side street or cul-de-sac in which to set out stalls. And yet the posters were unambiguous. *Old London Bridge. Moonrise, Friday night.*

He thought back to those posters, invisible to the naked eye but perfectly clear in his negatives. Perhaps, if he took some pictures here, something might reveal itself. Images from a London long past; people who only appeared at night. His heart began to beat faster, even though the thought was absurd, and the memory of his father stood stern, reminding him that stories weren't real, but that the camera never lies.

For the next half hour, Tom Argent went from street to street, taking pictures. The drizzle of the past three days had stopped; the sky was clear again. He photographed the base of the old bridge; the archway to the pedestrian zone; the back of the church; the labyrinth of little streets leading to the river. He took pictures of old brick walls and of the sides of buildings; of cracked pavements and metal scrollwork. Finally, he went back home with six full rolls of film, and developed them all in his darkroom, and inspected them on the enlarger for signs of anything unusual.

What he found was astonishing. Every wall was plastered with posters and flyers. Some were like the ones he'd seen on the brick wall at King's Cross; others seemed to advertise specific market traders. Some were old and faded; some seemed much more recent. Some sounded quite ordinary – *Cocksfoot & Sable: Fine Ales and Cheeses*; *Clancy's Rustic Furnishings* – and some were more unusual. Tom frowned over *Yellow Belle's Night-Woven Yarns*, and felt his heart beat faster at *Spindle Ermine's Love Spells*. What kind of a market *was* this? He thought he understood *Bird-Cherry's Flowers and Fruits*, or *Straw Dot's Most Accurate Timepieces*, and even *Scarlet Tiger Sleeve Tattoos* – but what was he to make of *Pretty Pinion Wing Repairs* or *Mother Shipton, Laundress of Dreams*, or *Pale Eggar's Glamours and Charms*, or *Dusky Sallow's Evercoats*?

Once more, he scanned his negatives, searching for something more concrete. Then, there she was, caught in movement, her face turned away from the camera, but her luminous hair and spiral tattoos stark against the London stone. Spider's friend, Charissa, standing next to a stone arch, on which a faded sign read: MOONLIGHT MARKET – THIS WAY.

She must have followed him there, Tom thought. She must have been watching him while he searched for signs of the market. He considered this uneasily. Why had she followed him? What did she want? Could she be using him to lead her to Vanessa?

For a moment, Tom wondered if he should step away from the market altogether. But now he had found the entrance, he felt an even greater compulsion to investigate. Besides, if Charissa and her friends were visible at night, he thought, then surely he would be safe enough. And if there was the slightest chance that Vanessa would be there, then how could he risk losing her for a second time?

So, at sunset the following night, Tom Argent took his camera bag and set off once more for Old London Bridge – a place that existed now only in dreams – in search of whatever wares the Moonlight Market had to offer.

Part 2

The Moonlight Market

I

The Moth King and the Butterfly Queen grieved for the loss of their only son. The Moth King's grief was cold and grim; the Butterfly Queen's burned hot and bright. Both were unhappy, and longed for their son, and longed even more desperately for the love they once had shared.

But both were too proud to admit it, and so each went their separate way: the Queen into her world of air, the King down into darkness. Divided by grief, they slipped into the cracks between the worlds, sorrowing and incomplete, and were lost to their own world for ever.

Lost, in exile, they found their way to a city of stone and bridges and tunnels and underground vaults, built on a great, winding river. And there they held court; each to their own, alongside the people of that world, who, being sightless, could not see the events unfolding around them. The Butterfly Queen kept her word, and the Moth King his promise; that never again would a Butterfly ever fall in love with a Moth, but that both would feed on the hearts of their foes, and thrive on their quintessence.

And so, the King and Queen became rulers in that sightless world; he in the shadows, she in the light. And the many tribes of the Silken Folk – the Hesperiidae and the Lycaenidae, the Nymphalidae and the Papilionidae, the Frenatae and the Hedylidae – came to them in their thousands, with glamours and magic at their command, and swore them their allegiance.

And still they endure, after centuries of war, still grieving for their vanished son, too proud for reconciliation; taking their nectar wherever they can, within that city of ancient stones, and gleaming glass towers, and asphalt, and roads, and plastic, and concrete, and tunnels, and trains.

2

Moonrise was at ten thirty that night. Tom Argent waited beside the arch that marked the entrance to Old London Bridge, watching the sky as it darkened from blue, to rose, to sepia. The sky over London was never quite dark, just as the stars overhead never shone, eclipsed by the light of those man-made stars, but that night seemed different – darker, somehow – with the full moon rising over the Thames and streaking the water with silver. Looking around him, Tom realised that the street lights were still unlit.

There was no sign of a market, though – no stalls, no delivery vehicles – and Tom had almost given up hope when he saw something move from the tail of his eye. A figure, moving purposefully through the little archway. And now Tom could see a shape emerging from the shadows, the shape of a bridge that, seconds before, had been nothing but moonlight and air—

It must be an illusion, he thought. Sometimes things appear to us just because we want them to – or so his father had always said. But there was nothing wrong with his eyes, or with the lens of his camera, through which the arch of Old London Bridge appeared like the prow of a lighted ship pushing through the shadows.

With the moonrise, something was happening. Something that emerged from the night like a developing photograph. Two more figures joined the first. Then two more; then another two;

all of them passing through the arch onto the bridge, which seemed now to shine with a silvery light, like a flickering black-and-white movie projected against the buildings. Now Tom could hear voices, too – the cries of market traders – and see the shapes of market stalls rising against the bronze-dark sky.

This was no illusion, no dream. He could see the stone stanchions reflected in the silent Thames; hear the sound of footsteps resonating on solid wood. The bridge was a primitive design, and yet the absence of street lights conspired to make it seem perfectly in keeping with its surroundings, as if a hidden door had been opened on to an earlier time. And now he could see more people, moving purposefully through the arch and onto the wooden part of the bridge.

In the semi-darkness, Tom thought he saw faces – or were they masks? – that seemed to be covered in feathers or fur. And there was a summery scent of sun-ripened fruit; of night-blooming flowers; of new-baked bread; and frying mushrooms, and bilberry wine, and sandalwood, and cedar, and musk; and fresh-laundered sheets all wild from the wind. Now he could hear music, too; the sound of flutes and fiddles and distant voices raised in song; the soft, persistent rhythms of drums; the distant chirp of silver bells.

He took a step through the archway, and found himself on the cobbled path that led across the bridge. He could feel the weathered stone of the raised footpath beneath his tread. A woman driving a cart pulled by a team of small brown goats overtook him. Tom heard the driver's impatient cry – *Stand back, ye lobcock!* – as she drove her goats smartly through the narrow gate.

It sounded real. It *felt* real. Sounds, scents, sensations, lights: all of it was compelling. Tom started to walk up onto the bridge; below him, he could see the Thames, although he was sure the river had been much further away a moment before. Small boats with lanterns at their bows floated by beneath him. There were lanterns on the bridge, too; lanterns of every colour hanging from the balustrade, perched up on the stanchions, spilling multicoloured light across the stalls and tables.

Tom moved further along the bridge, pausing to photograph the boats passing over the river. People on foot overtook him, hurrying towards the market. The scents were overpowering: incense, and gingerbread; burnt sugar and spices. Around him, the throng of people grew, and he could hear the voices of individual traders hawking their mysterious wares:

Fat Boys! Sugared Fat Boys!

Faces! Get yer faces here! Yer genuine human faces!

Dreams freshly laundered! Dreams for tonight! Only three days each! Fresh dreams!

Tom continued towards the sounds and sights of the market, taking photographs along the way.

The cries of the vendors grew louder.

Charms, spells and glamours! Six days each! Garlands for your sweetheart!

Lutes and timbrels, viols and flutes! Steal away a lover's soul with songs from across the Nine Worlds! Yours for a fivemonth! Yours for a year! Guaranteed seduction!

Tom told himself he must have misheard. *Yours for a fivemonth? Six days each?* What kind of currency was this? But as he reached the first arch of the bridge, his attention was drawn by a woman in leathers who stepped in front of him, barring his way into the market.

'Your pass,' she said.

Tom stared at her. The woman was unusually tall, her hair braided with black and white feathers. A necklace made from

49

a crow's skull hung around her neck, and her eyes were a fierce and brilliant gold, and fixed disapprovingly on Tom.

'Your sigil?' she said.

'My what?' said Tom.

'Your sigil, my man. Your house. Your stripe. Your *tribe*,' prompted the woman impatiently, indicating a woven badge stitched onto the lapel of her leather waistcoat. It depicted a crow's head, flanked with a pair of crossed axes.

Tom gave her a helpless look. 'I don't have one,' he said. 'I'm sorry.'

The crow woman's face hardened. 'Then you shouldn't be here,' she said. 'How did you even find—' Suddenly, her gaze caught the camera hanging around Tom's neck. The sight of it seemed to give her pause, and she looked at Tom more closely. 'Oh, of course. Collector, it's *you*,' she said in a rather more friendly tone. 'I didn't recognise you at first. Come on in.' She waved him past. 'But mark this, and mark it well – anything you take from here must be paid for in full. Understand?'

Tom nodded, but already his attention was beginning to scatter like light through a prism. Before him, the Moonlight Market filled every available space on the bridge with stalls and stands and tables; displays of wares. There were fruits and flowers; spices and herbs; racks of musical instruments; kites that seemed to fly themselves. There were pedlars with packs on their backs, and cages filled with coloured birds; a tattooist working a wolf design onto the back of a kneeling man; and on the parapet of the bridge, there was a group of fire spinners, etching wheels of coloured light into the dark air around them.

Tom lifted his camera and took a quick series of shots – the birds; the fire spinners; a girl wearing a fox mask; a woman in a pair of wings that looked as if they might *almost* be real—

'What are you doing, Collector?' Tom turned and saw the

50

woman who had challenged him at the entrance. 'What did I just tell you?' she said. 'You can't have forgotten *already*.'

'How do you even know me?' said Tom.

The crow woman sounded impatient. 'You've been here many times,' she replied. 'Where's your friend?'

'Friend?' said Tom.

'The Spinnerman. He comes to buy books.'

Tom thought of Spider's parcel of books, tied with multi-coloured string, and the way Spider had called him *Collector*.

'*Spider?*'

'That's him,' said the crow woman.

Now Tom's head was spinning. 'But I barely know him,' he said. 'And I'm sure I've never been here before. How can you have seen us together?'

The crow woman shook her head, exasperated. 'I warned you about this before. *Everything* you take from here has to be paid for in full. Now put away your glamorie-glass before someone misses a piece of their soul. And for gods' sakes, keep a watch on the sky!'

Then she was gone before Tom could ask for further explanation. He glanced at the sky, where the rising moon looked enormous, ringed with silver. To his surprise, Tom realised that, from here, he could actually see the stars.

But the sounds and sights of the market were too enticing for him to remain distracted for long. He made his way along the bridge, wide-eyed, trying to look in all directions at once, hearing the calls of the stallholders, gazing at their astonishing wares. Here there were pastries, cooked on the spot, deep-fried and rolled in sugar; and there were displays of spices laid out on brightly coloured mats. There were fabrics of all kinds, and clothes of vibrant design, and tiny bottles of midnight glass with intricate silver stoppers. Behind a thin scarlet curtain, a woman was telling fortunes. Another tried to sell him a mask – except that the masks on her market stall winked and smiled at him as he passed. A man with no feet was making charms that looked like single grains of rice: Tom watched as, with a tiny brush, he inscribed the tiny grains with tiny, mysterious verses.

'Spells, curses,' said the man. 'Easy to swallow, easy to hide.' Tom glanced at the man, alarmed. The man gave a sly wink. 'Come on, son. What do you need? The woman of your dreams, perchance? Your enemies, dead and dishonoured? Yours for only a sixmonth. I promise you, it'll be worth it.'

'A sixmonth? What does that mean?' said Tom.

The man lifted an eyebrow. 'Don't tell me you've forgotten,' he replied. 'We traders deal in days, weeks, years. *That's* the Market's currency.'

'I don't understand,' said Tom. 'You mean – *time?*'

'*Memories*, Collector,' said the maker of rice-grain charms. 'Your *story*. Your quintessence. The memory of your first kiss. The tale of how your parents met. The twenty-four hours before you arrived. *That's* what we trade.'

Tom wondered if he was joking, but the man seemed serious. Memories? Days and weeks? *The twenty-four hours before you arrived?* Was this why the crow woman knew him? Could he really have been here before, and given away the memory? His head spun at the thought that, somehow, he could have been on this bridge before, seen these marvellous things before, and just *given* them away. And for what?

The woman of your dreams, perchance?

With a final glance at the charm seller, Tom Argent hurried on.

3

Walking over the moonlit bridge, Tom found himself drawn deeper and deeper into the world of the market. Here, it was crowded, noisy; buzzing with scents both familiar and strange. The sharp aroma of some herbal stuff seemed to dominate this part of the bridge; the scented smoke was strongest around a little stall named *Madcap*, from which a pipe-smoking vendor was selling brightly coloured pouches, marked at the price of *Three days a twist*. Next to him, a person of indeterminate gender was folding sheets of coloured paper into origami birds, which they released into the air with a papery flutter of wings.

In spite of the crow woman's warning, Tom snapped a few more pictures. A dancer on the side of the bridge, her wings spread wide against the night. A diminutive woman with a whole haberdasher's shop balanced on her head: tiny drawers full of bobbins and lace, and packs of slender needles, and pincushions, and safety pins, and multicoloured twists of silk. Next to her, cross-legged on the ground, an old woman in a drab overcoat was making garlands and buttonholes from baskets of strange-looking flowers that released an unfamiliar, intoxicating aroma. Her brown face lit up when she caught sight of Tom.

'Collector! What's it to be today? Another adventure? Your heart's desire? *I* know. True love!' And she picked up a white flower from one of her baskets and held it out to him with a smile. Its scent was complex, dark and sweet; the scent of a summer garden at night. Tom reached out automatically – then remembered the crow woman's warning.

'How much?'

The old woman laughed. 'You'd dare put a price on true love?' she said. 'Call it a twelvemonth. Cheap at the price.'

Tom inhaled the flower's perfume. *True love?* That was something else he'd heard could only exist in stories. And yet, over the past few days, so much of his experience had been of things his father had claimed were imaginary or impossible. Old London Bridge, forgotten for years but visible now by moonlight. Spider, the altered negatives, the market's unusual currency – and the way folk seemed to know him by name, as if he'd been here many times before—

The old woman laughed again. 'But can you afford it, Collector?' she said. 'There's no point in finding true love if you're going to forget her face. Tell me, do you remember her now? Or was she just another dream?'

At the words, Tom's heart gave a sudden leap. *Vanessa!* In all of the evening's excitement, he'd almost forgotten why he had come to the market in the first place. Vanessa, whose *shine* was imprinted in his memory, but whose face had mysteriously faded.

'I know her name's Vanessa,' he said. 'Tell me, have you seen her?'

The old woman's humour faded. '*That* bitch! She'll take more than a twelvemonth from you, and give you nothing in return. You won't see her or her kind here. The Daylight Folk have been banned from here since the Battle of Welkin Close.'

'Since the Battle of *what?*' said Tom.

'Never you mind,' the old woman replied. 'You'd do well to keep away from her. I'll give you *that* advice for free.' She reached into the pocket of her shapeless brown overcoat and drew out a tiny dried flower, shrivelled and colourless with age.

'Here. This might come in handy. Call it a gift, for old times' sake.' She held the flower out to Tom. A faint scent reached him, both musky and sweet, like the secret heart of a rose. He slipped it into his pocket.

'What is it?'

'A flower that blooms only once.' She smiled, Tom thought a little sadly. 'Of course. You don't remember,' she said. 'Never mind. It remembers *you*. Just take it for now, and keep it safe. And tell Spider he still owes me for the last time he was here.'

'Spider? You know him too?'

'Of course. He's a regular. Comes for the books, he does, every time, but still hasn't found what he's looking for.'

Tom thought of Spider's books, tied with their hank of coloured string, and wished he'd looked at them more carefully. 'What kind of books does he buy?'

The woman shrugged. 'His own, of course. Who else's books would he be looking for?'

Tom slipped the flower into his pocket and moved on, feeling slightly dazed. Books? What books did Spider want? And what had the woman meant by *his own*? He scanned the crowded display of stalls and tables in hope of an answer. Finally, he noticed an arrangement of books against the stone parapet, tied with the same kind of coloured string that he'd seen around Spider's books. Moving closer, he could see that the books were all very different, but of exquisite workmanship: some cloth-bound, in bright colours; some old and bound in leather, with intricate endpaper designs and cunningly inked edges. The titles were picked out in silver and gold, but were like no titles he'd ever seen. He read: *Magpie: 2 Years*; *Cinnabar, 6 Months*; *Willow: 3 Weeks*; *Hummingbird, 1 Week*. A hand-lettered sign above the collection read: WILLOWHERB'S BARTERED BOOKS. Below,

Tom could see a slender book, bound in sky-blue silk, entitled: *Vanessa, 13 Days*.

He felt his heart skip a beat.

'How much for this?' he asked the figure by the book stand, whom he took to be Willowherb. A figure; pale-skinned, long-legged, in a coat of shabby cloth emblazoned with embroidered stars.

Willowherb glanced at the book. 'That one's not for sale,' they said. 'I'm holding it for someone.'

'But I *know* her,' protested Tom.

Willowherb grinned, revealing small and very pointed teeth. 'Everyone knows Vanessa,' they said. 'Some even better than she knows herself. But her story's not for you. Now be on your way – unless you want to barter.'

Tom tried a desperate gambit. 'Are you holding the book for Spider?'

For a moment, Willowherb paused, their golden eyes gleaming like fireflies. 'As a matter of fact, I am,' they said, with a troubled glance at the sky. 'Have you seen him? I got to go.'

'He couldn't make it tonight,' Tom lied. 'But I can deliver it.' He put a hand on the vendor's arm and gave his most persuasive smile. 'You know me,' he said. 'You've seen me before. I'm Spider's friend. I'll take it to him.'

Willowherb looked at the sky again. 'You will?'

'I promise,' said Tom, recklessly.

For the third time, Willowherb glanced at the sky. They now seemed in a hurry to close whatever deal Tom had entered into. 'Swear on your name? Your *true* name?'

Tom nodded quickly, looking up, half expecting rain clouds, and saw the moon hanging overhead like a ripening nectarine. A little string of ragged cloud moved towards it from the west; just enough to hide the stars but not enough to threaten rain.

'Please, give me the books,' said Tom.

'All right,' said Willowherb at last, and reached for a short stack of books to which they added the sky-blue volume entitled *Vanessa, 13 Days*.

As Willowherb wrapped the books deftly in brown paper, Tom thought he glimpsed the titles: *Spider, 3 Days*; *Spider, 2 Months*, and on the faded spine of a book that looked older than the rest, *Spider, 10 Years: 1799–1809*.

Willowherb handed Tom the books, now neatly wrapped and bound with string. 'You give these to Spider as soon as you can,' they said, now packing their books into a battered suitcase. 'And keep your peepers on the sky. I don't much like the look of them clouds.'

Willowherb was not the only one who seemed concerned by the changing sky. Looking around, Tom realised that all over the bridge, the Moonlight Market was starting to close. He could see stallholders packing their things away into boxes and baskets and packs. Fire spinners doused their flames; pastry vendors packed their goods into wicker hampers; the flower seller hurried past, her baskets of petals strapped to the back of a small, energetic donkey. And it all seemed to happen so very fast, as if in response to an attack; the smiling faces turning grim, the cheery calls becoming urgent.

'What's happening? What's the rush?' said Tom to a woman hastily packing up a display of ceramics. The items – all pots of different sizes – seemed to be designed to nest inside each other like Russian dolls, so that all she had to carry was one very large and lidded pot, with which she was currently struggling. 'Here, let me help.' Tom lifted the pot – which was, unsurprisingly, heavy – and set it in place on the woman's head, atop a small embroidered pad that seemed designed for the purpose.

The woman gave him a grateful look. 'Thank you, Collector.

Well met, and make haste! I see clouds approaching.' Then she was gone, her enormous pot bobbing above the heads of the folk preparing to leave Old London Bridge.

Still carrying his parcel of books, Tom continued across the bridge, but by now the press of people was such that he could barely move forward. The welcoming sounds of the market had veered into something chaotic and strange. There was no music playing now; no cheerful Fat Boy vendors; only the hushed and fretful sound of many people under siege. Like refugees fleeing an earthquake, the traders had packed everything away: their stores, their bolts of cloth and baskets of fruit; their cages of birds and boxes of books and displays of singular objects. Several looked up at the sky, where Tom saw that the band of cloud had reached the very edge of the moon. The stars were no longer visible; below, the Thames was in darkness. For a moment, Tom thought he saw the river *through* a part of the bridge; but that was impossible, he thought. The bridge was made of stone and wood – and yet, for a second, it had been as ephemeral as moonlight.

There was cursing as something dropped through the gap in the bridge; a man selling musical instruments swore vividly as a long-necked guitar fell with a splash into the Thames. Tom gaped – *did I see that?* – then a hand fell on his shoulder and a familiar voice said: 'Time to be gone, Collector, while there's still moonlight to go by.'

Tom turned and found himself looking at a familiar face, framed by unruly mouse-coloured hair and constellated with freckles. His eyes opened wide.

'*Charissa?*'

4

'Oh, so you remember my name,' said Charissa, with sarcasm. 'Pity we don't have time to crack open the champagne.'

'What are you doing here?' Tom asked.

'Buying madcap.'

'Buying what?'

Charissa looked impatient. She was wearing a knitted hat and a long, full-skirted coat in many mottled shades of brown, with a lining that gleamed enticingly. Tom's eye was strangely drawn to it. For a moment, he stared, almost hypnotised, as it rippled and shimmered.

'Your coat,' he said. 'It *shines*—'

'No time,' said Charissa, grabbing his arm. 'You need to get off the bridge *right now*, before it disappears again.'

'Bridges don't just disappear,' remarked Tom, still staring.

'This one does,' said Charissa. With one hand still on his arm and the other on his camera strap, she started to pull him along. 'For gods' sakes, Collector, how can you keep forgetting *that*?'

Tom had finally decided that all this was a dream. It had to be, he told himself. There *was* no Old London Bridge, no Moonlight Market, no Midnight Folk. The girl in the strangely ephemeral coat was a figment of his fantasy; a remnant of those fairy tales he had so loved when he was a boy.

He looked at the moon, which had become a dim brass bauble in the sky. When he looked back, he saw that the bridge had become strangely insubstantial; a mist had crept up from the river to hide everything but the path ahead. And even so, Tom thought he could see the Thames through the spaces between the boards – spaces he hadn't noticed before—

'Where's Spider?' said Charissa.

Tom shook his head. 'He didn't come.'

'You mean you came up here alone? Please, tell me you didn't buy anything.'

'Why not?' Tom was starting to feel annoyed. It almost felt as if the girl thought he couldn't cope on his own.

'Why *not*?' She gave a staccato laugh. Her eyes fell on the parcel of books. 'Ye gods and little fishes,' she said. 'How much did *that* cost you?'

'Nothing,' said Tom. 'They're Spider's.'

She shrugged. 'That's something, I suppose. Where is he?'

'I was hoping you could tell *me*.'

Charissa gave him a scornful look. 'Who knows where a Spider goes? Over the rooftops, down the drains. Through the cracks between the worlds. Good luck in the morning, bad luck after midnight. Spider makes his own rules, and wise folk know to keep out of his way.'

'Oh.'

Now they were back by the archway that marked the old pedestrian path. The moon had gone, and so had the crowd that only minutes ago had thronged the Moonlight Market. Tom felt unexpectedly cold, as if the market had somehow belonged to a different season. Of the bridge, there was no sign. The river, too, which he had seen flowing beneath it, had gone. Of course it had, he told himself. The banks of the Thames had long since shifted.

'OK.' Charissa seemed to relax. 'Now, let's get you home, right? Give me the books.'

Tom shook his head. 'I can't. One of them belongs to Vanessa.'

Charissa made an impatient sound. 'If ever there was anything you *needed* to forget, it's Vanessa. Honestly, Collector, I don't know why he bothers with you. If it had been me, I would have washed my hands of you years ago.'

'Do you mean Spider?'

She shook her head. 'You need to forget about *him*, too. He's trouble, and trouble follows him.'

'But Spider's your friend,' protested Tom.

Once more, Charissa shook her head. 'Spider isn't anyone's friend. He's obsessed with making the impossible happen. Instead of simply accepting this world and building a life here for us all, he spends his time chasing butterflies, putting everyone at risk, and all for the sake of a dream that won't die, a dream of reconciliation.'

'I don't understand,' said Tom. 'You speak as if he knows me. And those people on the bridge—' He gestured vaguely into the air. 'They spoke as if they knew me too.'

'As well they might,' said Charissa. 'You've been to that market many times.'

'But I *haven't!*' exclaimed Tom. 'I'd *remember!*'

'Not if you traded the memory,' Charissa said with a twisted smile. 'The Moonlight Market deals in dreams, in spells, and charms, and glamours. The price for that is your life, your quin-tessence – your *nectar*. It's what Vanessa tried to take from you back in that alleyway by St Pancras. If we hadn't turned up when we did, she would have taken everything. Her kind always do. They're predators. Thieves. That's why they're not welcome at the Market.'

'So you're telling me,' said Tom slowly, 'that I've been to the Market before, but that I traded my memories?'

'Not quite,' said Charissa. She indicated his camera. 'Have you ever asked yourself why they call you *Collector*?'

'Because I take photographs, I suppose.'

'And what are *they*?' asked Charissa. 'Snapshots. Scraps of a life. Stolen moments. *Memories*.' She took the camera from Tom's hand and, with a single deft movement, pulled out the film to expose it. 'Every time, we warn you,' she said. 'Every time, since you were a boy and your father gave you the glamorie-glass.' She gave him a smile that was oddly, unexpectedly tender. 'Every time, you have sacrificed the memory of the Market, and every time, have tried to steal back some part of what you found there.' She handed the camera back to Tom, who was feeling strangely light-headed. 'Don't worry,' she added. 'The feeling will pass. The memory will fade. Now give me the books. I'll make sure Spider gets them.' She took the parcel from under his arm. 'You'll soon forget all this. You always do.' And then, most unexpectedly, she moved in closer and kissed him – a feather-light and fleeting kiss that felt like a moth's wing against his cheek. 'Stay safe, Tom Argent,' she said. 'Stay safe, and dream only sweet dreams.'

Then she spread the wings of her coat, revealing the shimmering lining. Except he saw it wasn't a coat. It was *wings* – huge, brown, beautiful wings, dappled in the street light. Not a bird's wings, but more like the wings of a moth, all silk and starlight spreading out against the smoky London sky. For a moment, she stood there, wings spread; shock-headed, wild-eyed, a thing from a dream.

Then, as Tom watched open-mouthed, she flew off, soundlessly, into the night.

Part 3

Spider

I

The exiled Spider Mage wandered the World of the Sightless Ones, searching for the lost Prince. He used every trick and cantrip he had; every charm and glamour. He spun his web between the worlds; observed the stars; cast arcane runes and searched the entrails of sacred beasts. But although he found signs of the lost Prince in every part of that cruel world, the boy remained elusive.

Years passed, and the Spider Mage passed through every land in that world. Everywhere, he seemed to find fragments and traces of the lost Prince – stories and legends, and sayings and songs – but still the boy eluded him. The Spider Mage collected these tales and spun them all into his web, which contained the memory of every place he had visited, every road he had travelled. He spun this collection of memories into the lining of his coat, so that they would never be lost, even when he was lost to himself. For all his travels in that world had taken their toll on his sanity. For years, he had wandered, friendless, alone, pursuing his obsession. For years, he had punished himself for the loss of the boy who was in his charge. And for years, he had pined for the Butterfly Queen, not knowing she too was in that world, holding court over her people.

Until one day he came to a place – a city of towers and underground roads, built on a great winding river – and saw her with her retinue, brighter in beauty than ever before, but feeding on the Sightless Folk and robbing them of their nectar. And the heart of the Spider Mage swelled with love and pity at the sight of her, and he knew he had to save her. And so he stayed in that city, and watched as the two tribes waged their war. And he determined to break the curse that the Butterfly Queen had brought upon herself and her people. Only through love could the curse be dispelled – the love of a Moth for a Butterfly; the love of a Butterfly for a Moth. But centuries had passed, and both sides were entrenched in their war. Still the Spider Mage persevered, and hoped for an opportunity to remake what was broken.

And so, time passed, until one year, at the time of the Moonlight Market, he saw a boy with a camera . . .

2

As he turned the corner, Tom felt a sense of déjà vu. It was a feeling he'd experienced often throughout his childhood; that sense that something *behind* the world had shifted for a moment, fleetingly exposing the truth, then slipping softly back into place.

As a boy, he had believed these were glimpses of a secret world. But his father had explained that it was only his subconscious mind retrieving unconscious stimuli, making connections with memories so old that he had forgotten them.

Tom supposed this must be true. And yet, every time it happened, he always felt the presence – gone almost before it registered – of some deeper truth, some deeper aspect of reality. It was ridiculous, he knew. But it kept returning. That feeling that there might be things hidden under the skin of the world; things unknown to science, explicable only by magic.

Tom checked his watch, then his camera, noting that it was past midnight and that his camera was out of film. Somehow he had managed to walk from Lower Thames Street back to King's Cross without even noticing. He supposed that his mind had been set on finding the woman of his dreams – but as he tried to remember her, he found that he had forgotten her name, just as her face and the sound of her voice had already slipped from his memory. He must be tired, he told himself. The stress of losing Vanessa – *Vanessa!* Of course! *That* was her name – must have taken its toll. What he really needed was rest, and a return to normality.

Just then, he noticed a man and a child on the station concourse. Both were dark-skinned and brightly dressed; the girl looked to be about nine years old, the man maybe thirty. They could have been anyone, he thought, travellers from anywhere. But there was something about them that caught his attention. The lateness of the hour, perhaps; or maybe their clothes set them apart – in a city in which most people wore varying shades of grey and blue, bright colours tended to catch the eye. As he approached, he saw they were watching him. And now, as he came closer, he noticed that the man was carrying under his arm a parcel tied with coloured string—

Books, thought Tom, with a certainty that seemed almost dreamlike. *Books, tied with coloured string, and containing – what? Bartered memories?* The thought was strangely persistent. And it seemed to come with a scent; a kind of drowsy, smoky scent, like dried flowers dreaming of summer.

'Hello! Wait! Excuse me!' he said.

The man turned once more to look at him. He was of around Tom's height, wearing a paisley shirt under his red velvet jacket. His eyes were a striking, luminous bronze behind his wire-rimmed glasses. The child at his side stared up at Tom with a candour that he found disconcerting.

'Excuse me. Where did you get those books?'

The man gave him a suspicious look. 'Traded for them.'

'At the market?' said Tom. A memory – or was it a dream? – blossomed sweetly in his mind. *A moonlit bridge. A dancer. A kiss. A woman selling flowers.*

'You know about the Market?' said the man, no less suspiciously.

Tom nodded. Somehow he knew, even though it still felt like

a dream. He put his hand in his pocket and felt dried petals, as light as lost love.

A flower, he thought. *A flower whose scent unlocks memories.* 'Those are Spider's books,' he said, knowing somehow that it was true. 'Where is he? Do you know him?'

The man shrugged. 'Never heard of him.'

'Those are his books. I know they are.'

Once again, the man shrugged.

'I'm trying to find him,' insisted Tom. 'Are you sure you don't know him?' Then, inspiration struck. 'Spider's just his *daylight* name,' he said. 'His *midnight* name is something else.'

Both the man and the child went very still and Tom felt his heart beat faster.

'You know where he is, don't you?' he said. 'Please. I'm his friend. I'm on his side. How else would I know about daylight names? How else would I know about the Moonlight Market?'

The man and the girl exchanged glances. Then the child looked up at Tom. 'We'll take you,' she said. 'He isn't far.'

'Are you with Vanessa?' said Tom.

He wasn't sure why he'd asked that, but there was something about them that reminded him of Vanessa's friends. Something vaguely theatrical; a shout of colour against the grime. A *shine*, which was more than the warmth of their skin or the luminous quality of their eyes. Just as Charissa and her friend had seemed to be creatures of the night, these people were the opposite. Light seemed to radiate from them somehow, reflecting against the sooty stones.

The little girl smiled. 'I'm Swallowtail. This is Argus. We're friends of Vanessa's. We'll take you to her.'

And, catching Tom's hand in hers, she and Argus led him through the silent streets of King's Cross, towards his doom and his heart's desire.

3

The child had been right; it wasn't far. She and Argus led Tom around the side of St Pancras Station to what looked like a fairy-tale castle. Turrets and arches of rosy brick; Gothic windows; roof tiles that resembled gargoyles and lions and dragons and gryphons and elephants. It was all the more bizarre to Tom as he'd never really *seen* it before, in spite of walking past it every day for the last five years. But this city was full of hidden things. Rooftop gardens; concealed parks; aerial pools suspended in glass. One of his favourite haunts as a boy had been the Natural History Museum, not just for its collections, but for the astonishing diversity of the stone creatures worked into its facade like ammonites in rock. There was something magical in the way those creatures clung to the stone; a magic that even his father could allow himself to enjoy. St Pancras reminded him of that, and not for the first time that evening, Tom Argent felt as if the world he knew had conceded a layer of reality, revealing something luminous underneath.

Swallowtail and Argus escorted Tom through a small arched entrance. There was a lift with no floor numbers, just a keypad. Argus entered a four-digit code, and they were taken up to a penthouse overlooking the city.

'This is where Vanessa lives,' said Swallowtail, ringing the bell. Tom took a deep breath and summoned his most eager smile—

But when the door opened, the first thing he saw was the

dark, unsmiling face of Vanessa's friend Brimstone. He was wearing a green feather waistcoat over a black T-shirt and jeans, but there was nothing frivolous or playful about his expression. His eyes narrowed angrily when he saw Tom.

'What have you brought *him* here for?' he said.

'He was asking after Spider,' said Argus, adjusting his glasses. 'And the scent of the Market's all over him like madcap on a mushroom.'

Brimstone opened the door wider, and Tom found himself escorted inside. It was a large and luxurious apartment, covered in rugs and wall hangings. Soft cushions on the floor. Stained glass in the windows. The whole, a bright kaleidoscope of mirrors and candles and colourful lamps.

Vanessa was sitting reading a book, dressed in scarlet velvet. Skipper, dark and elegant, was standing by the window. Pieris, the dandy, was on the sill, in a floor-length coat of purple silk over a moon-blue waistcoat. Bottles of champagne stood on the low table between them; empty bottles gleamed on the floor. The whole scene looked like something from an Arthurian tale, in which dark ladies watched the world through mysterious mirrors, and pale knights were their prey.

'Vanessa,' he said.

Vanessa looked up. She'd changed her hair since Tom had seen her last. Now it was bright gold, and very short, framing her dark face like the petals of a sunflower. He liked it less than her natural style, but that *shine* of hers – that magical shine – overrode the details. She looked at Tom for a moment, then looked away without smiling.

'Vanessa, it's your little friend,' said Pieris in mocking reproach. He stood up, displaying boots with six-inch scarlet heels, and came to stand too close to Tom, extending a hand to touch his hair.

71

'Pieris, no,' Vanessa said.

Pieris pulled a comic face. 'You ordered home delivery, and now you don't want to share?'

'You shouldn't have brought him here,' Vanessa said to Swallowtail. 'Why couldn't you have left him alone?'

'He mentioned Spider,' said Swallowtail, who no longer looked like a child at all. '*And* he knows the Market. He recognised the books. He's got to be the Collector.'

Collector. The name rang a distant bell. Hadn't Spider called him that? And hadn't Charissa used it, too? It seemed to him now that she had, and with the memory came the scent of flowers grown by moonlight, and fried Fat Boys, and madcap—

Tom put his hand on his camera. He knew that it was empty of film, just as his mind was empty of memories, and he wondered how he could have forgotten a whole evening, including, it seemed, a market...

'Give that to me,' said Vanessa to Tom, her eyes narrow and unreadable.

He passed her the camera. She looked at it, then passed it to Brimstone, who looked at it even longer. His eyes were a violet, velvety brown, crazed with coloured reflections. Tom saw intelligence there, and understanding, and a troubling kind of weariness.

'You were at the Market tonight. What did you buy?'

Tom shook his head. 'I don't remember a market. All I remember is seeing the posters in my negatives.'

Books. A bridge. The scent of smoke and roses. A dancer in the moonlight. A kiss...

Brimstone tossed the camera aside. 'There's nothing here. It's already gone. Skipper! Find out what he knows.'

Tom did not see what happened then. Her movements were too fast for him. One moment he was standing there, watching Vanessa; the next he was face down on the floor, one arm locked behind his shoulder blades, Skipper's knee in the small of his back. The thick pile of the carpet muffled his cry.

'Shut up and pay attention,' said Skipper, straddling him. Her elegant hands were incredibly strong. 'You're going to tell me all you know about Spider, and the Midnight Folk, and how you remember the Market.'

'But I *don't* remember,' cried Tom. 'I don't remember anything!'

Brimstone came to lean over them, his long braids almost touching Tom's face. 'But you can see things others don't. You can see the Midnight Folk. You know how to collect them. How long has this been going on?'

'I don't know what you're talking about!' Tom's arm was close to breaking. 'There was a girl. Charissa. I saw her in my negatives. I didn't see her before that. Let go of my arm! *Please!*'

The pressure on his arm relaxed by the tiniest fraction.

'Charissa?' said Brimstone.

Tom nodded. 'I was taking pictures of Spider. I thought he was crazy, he was talking to someone who wasn't there. Then I looked at my film, and saw her there beside him.'

'And the Market?'

'I saw the posters,' explained Tom.

'So. You *were* there,' said Brimstone.

'*No!* I mean, I don't know. I don't remember anything. Except...' *A sky-blue hardback book with Vanessa's name on the cover. A woman selling flowers. The fire spinners on the bridge. A girl with eyes like flame.*

'He's useless,' said Skipper, her knee in Tom's back. 'Whatever he knows, he's already traded it, or it's been taken from him.' She pressed a little more firmly into his lower back. 'What did you buy, Collector? Charms? Glamours? *Stories?*'

Tom tried to lift his face away from the dusty carpet. 'I don't know what you're talking about. Please, let me get up.'

Skipper gave an impatient hiss. 'Why are we wasting our time with him?' she snapped at Brimstone. 'He's one of Spider's projects, that's clear. He knows the Market. Knows the Moths. Knows Charissa. Knows *you*. Who knows how long he's been using him?' She dug an elbow into Tom's neck. 'Don't move. It'll soon be over.'

'Over? What do you mean?' said Tom, in a voice that was little more than a squeak.

Pieris gave his predatory grin and said, in a low voice: '*Nectar.*'

Tom felt a chill of fear move through his body like a purge. It made him feel almost euphoric, almost as if some part of him refused to see the danger that was approaching.

Pieris smiled, showing his teeth. Once more, Tom thought of vampires – but weren't vampires nocturnal? Surely a group of people who called themselves the Daylight Folk couldn't be actual *vampires*—

'Please, let me go,' he said. 'I don't know what this is about. I just wanted to see Vanessa again.' He squinted at her imploringly. 'Tell them, Vanessa. I'm not a spy. I'm not working with anyone. I love you. I've loved you ever since you walked into the camera shop. All I wanted was to see you again.'

Pieris yawned extravagantly. 'You should have stayed in your tame little world. Now you're in ours, and this is the *wild*.' He knelt down, so that his face and Tom's were only inches apart. Tom could smell him: a combination of iris, rose and something feral, like tomcat or fox. He struggled, but could not break Skipper's grasp.

Pieris moved still closer. Tom felt the other man's breath on his cheek.

'You smell delicious,' he growled. 'What *is* that? Madcap? Asphodel?'

Vanessa spoke up. 'Pieris, you can't.'

The dandy gave his flashgun smile. 'Who's going to stop me? Last time I checked, you were partial to a sip of nectar yourself. What? Are you on the wagon now?'

'Pieris, I *owe* him.'

'Owe him *what*?'

Brimstone raised an eyebrow. 'Do tell.'

'The Midnight Folk cornered me in an alleyway,' she said. 'Tom stalled them while I got away. Brimstone, I *asked* him to help me. He would have given his life for mine.'

Tom saw a flicker of something pass across Brimstone's angular face.

'You asked for his help?' he said at last.

Vanessa nodded. 'You know the rules.'

For a moment, the tall man was still. Then he said, 'Skipper. Let the man go.'

Skipper immediately released her grip. Tom lay on the colourful carpet, rubbing his arm and trying to breathe. Brimstone raised him to his feet. His eyes were bright with anger, but his voice was calm as ever.

'It seems I owe you a debt,' he said.

'I don't understand—' Tom started to say, but Vanessa interrupted him.

'*I* owe you,' she said. '*He* owes you. Now listen, and pay attention.'

Brimstone nodded. 'Yes, Tom, do. The debt will be honoured, and paid – in full, in whatever currency you choose.' His words seemed suddenly formal, and Tom had the strange impression that he and the others were almost afraid. The colours of the bright little room seemed to grow dim.

Everyone watched Tom in silence. The air was suddenly thick as tar.

'So. What's your price?' said Brimstone at last.

'I don't understand,' repeated Tom.

'It's really very straightforward,' said Brimstone. 'I'm asking you to name your price. What do you want in payment for the debt the Daylight Folk owe you?'

'I don't want *money*,' Tom said, more confused than ever.

'So what *do* you want, Collector?' There was impatience in his voice, and, beneath it, Tom seemed to recognise something like apprehension.

'Nothing,' replied Tom. 'That's not why I came. I thought…
I was looking for Spider. Argus said you knew where he was.'

There was a moment's silence. Everyone looked at Brimstone.

'Is *that* what you want?' he said at last.

'I don't know what you mean,' said Tom. 'Is Spider here, or isn't he?'

Brimstone seemed to be thinking hard. 'Are you sure?' he said at last. 'I'm offering you *whatever you choose*—' There was a weight to the tall man's words, as if Tom was supposed to hear some kind of unspoken message. But whatever it was, Tom Argent either didn't understand, or was too stubborn to change his mind.

He nodded.

Brimstone gave a sigh. 'All right,' he said. 'But that pays our debt. Cross my path again – *either* of you – and there'll be no mercy. Do you understand?'

Tom didn't understand, but he nodded again.

Brimstone gestured to Skipper, who left the room, returning within a few moments with the man Tom knew as Spider. His hands were bound with plastic ties, and his face bore marks of violence. One of the lenses of his wire-rimmed glasses was cracked, but behind them, his eyes were very bright as they alighted on Tom.

'Collector?' he said. 'Are you with *them* now?'

'Be grateful,' said Brimstone. 'I owed him a debt.'

For a moment, Spider stared at Tom. '*Me?*' he said incredulously. 'He asked for *me?*'

'A deal's a deal.'

Spider looked at Brimstone and said, 'What about my evercoat?'

'Your what?' For a moment, Tom thought he had heard him say *evercoat* for *overcoat*.

Skipper smiled and cut the plastic ties from Spider's wrists. 'Never mind your coat, Spinnerman,' she said in her silky voice. 'Be grateful that you still have your life – and what remains of your sanity.' Then she turned to Tom and said: 'Take him. He belongs to you now. May he bring you better luck than he has brought the rest of us.'

And with that, Skipper opened the penthouse door and escorted them outside.

Tom had only a moment to look back at Vanessa. She had not moved from her place during the whole of the strange little scene, but now she stood up, and seemed to reach after him as he moved away. Her luminous eyes were bright with tears, and Tom felt his heart was close to breaking. What was wrong? What power did Brimstone have over her, and what was the bargain he had struck?

'When can I see you again?' he said.

Skipper shrugged. 'You had your chance.'

'What does that mean, I had my chance?' Tom said, still addressing Vanessa.

But it was Brimstone who answered. 'What it means is *never*,' he said. 'You'll never see Vanessa again. Not even in your dreams. Now go home, count your blessings, and don't let the sun rise on your good luck.'

With these words, he closed the apartment door. The click it made as it closed was soft, but mercilessly final.

4

Tom turned to Spider. 'What just happened? Why were you tied up? Why was Vanessa crying?'

Spider grabbed him by the arm and started to drag him towards the lift. Tom struggled, but Spider was stronger than he looked. The homeless man from King's Cross had changed almost beyond recognition. Gone was the bulky overcoat, and without it he moved with surprising grace. His clothes – torn jeans and a faded shirt – were spattered with what looked like blood; and there were traces of blood on his face, in his hair and his four-day beard. He looked in a bad way – one eye was blackened, his lip was cut – but, even so, he seemed vigorous, and overjoyed to be free.

'You can't be here, Collector,' he said. 'The amnesty won't hold for ever. You heard what he said. I have to get under cover before the sun rises. If not, it's goodnight, sweet prince.'

Tom stared at him. 'I don't understand. What amnesty? What were you doing there anyway?'

'The Daylight Folk always honour a debt. Though why you chose *me* as your prize...' He grinned. 'Not that I'm complaining, of course. But you could have had anything. Power. Gold. Your heart's desire. Brimstone's life, if you'd asked for it. No wonder he looked jumpy.'

Tom kept staring as the lift bore them down to the ground

floor. There was so much here to digest that he hardly knew where to start.

'Who are they?' he said at last. 'And what do you mean by the Daylight Folk?'

'Keep walking,' Spider instructed. 'We need to get to safety by dawn. Maybe if you're lucky, then there'll be time for a story.'

They were back in the empty streets of King's Cross, but Tom felt as if part of him had stayed behind in the penthouse, in that kaleidoscopic world of dangerous colours and crazy lights. For a moment, he looked up at the sky, hoping maybe to see the stars, but the night sky had faded to dishwater grey, and the only lights he could see were those that shone out over King's Cross.

'Who are those people?' persisted Tom. 'And why is Vanessa with them?' Already, he felt her absence like an ache inside him, the memory of her *shine* so great that it eclipsed her features.

Spider gave a weary sigh. 'Listen to me, Collector. You need to put her out of your mind. Vanessa doesn't care about you. All she wants is nectar.'

'What do you mean, *nectar*?' said Tom.

'Nectar's what they feed on. The energy they need to survive. Didn't you ever ask yourself why so many London people wear black? Why they're so rude and cross-tempered? Why they never look you in the eye, even when you're talking to them? It's because they've been *tapped*, that's why. Tapped without even knowing it. Leached of their quintessence, their joy. All to feed *their* glamours.'

You're the one who's tapped, Tom thought. *You're crazy as a clockwork mouse.* But Spider didn't sound crazy to him. A week ago, perhaps he had – but not now. Scruffy, bruised and running on adrenaline, he nevertheless seemed intensely alert; *awake* in a way few people were. And wasn't there something else, Tom thought, something close to Vanessa's *shine*; a strange, ephemeral quality?

Spider gave Tom a humorous look. His grey-gold eyes were gleaming. 'Think I'm touched by the moon, eh? You might be forgiven for thinking as much.' He was starting to slow down a little; Tom saw that he was limping. 'But we need to find somewhere safe. They watch. They've got eyes everywhere.'

Tom looked up automatically. 'Cameras?'

Spider nodded. 'Argus-eyes. There's one on every rooftop. In your computer, on your mobile phone – you got a phone?'

'Not anymore.'

'Good,' said Spider. 'Then they can't track you that way. But that's only one of their tricks. And the Midnight Folk will be on the move. This is their time. We have to move fast. They won't stop hunting us, you know. Me, because they think I know how to find something they've been looking for. *You* – well. That's another tale.'

Tom wondered if he was going to regret befriending Spider. The man was clearly paranoid, for all his charisma. What if he was dangerous? What if he became violent? He'd already saved him from Brimstone's gang. He didn't owe him anything. Perhaps it would be easier to let him go his way and try to forget what had happened—

But *forgetting* things was the problem, wasn't it? The thought was sudden and striking. Tom had been forgetting things ever since Spider had entered his life. Forgetting things, and seeing things that other people didn't. The way he'd forgotten Vanessa's face. The way he'd captured Charissa on film. The Moonlight Market, the memory of which seemed to have been snipped from his mind. His camera, empty now of film. How Brimstone had said *You can see the Midnight Folk* – as if they were meant to go unseen…

As a child, Tom had felt the presence of something hiding *behind* the world. He'd called it *magic* because he had no other word for it, and his parents had persuaded him that it was nothing but fantasy. But Tom Argent had never really stopped believing. There *was* magic in the world, magic hiding in plain sight; a magic that sometimes showed itself in photographic negatives – or sometimes on a forgotten bridge that only appears by moonlight—

Once more, Tom felt that troubling sense of déjà vu. It came with the sound of voices; the memory of a woman's smile; the drowsy scent of flowers that bloom only once in a lifetime—

Tom felt a sudden flash of some emotion he hadn't felt since childhood. There *was* magic in the world. Spider was the proof of it. Spider was the key to the truth about his stolen memories, and to Vanessa, whoever – *what*ever – she was. Spider was a mystery. A fairy tale. An *adventure*.

He turned to him. 'My place isn't far. You look as if you could use a rest.'

'Thank you, Collector.' Spider smiled. 'They tapped me for my memories. Not that there's much sweetness left. Only the dregs and the doldrums. But I've been running on empty for days, and a rest sounds pretty good right now.'

Tom thought of Pieris, his hungry smile. 'But *why?*' he said. 'What do they want?'

'What they *always* want. A way back to the Kingdom. Or maybe just to punish me. I don't really remember. I traded so much of myself, you know, for madcap and the quiet it brings. It was all so long ago. And we pay such a high price for memories.'

He really *must* be crazy, Tom thought. *A way back to the Kingdom?* It sounded like a fairy tale. Yet his heart was beating as fast as the wings of a moth at a candle flame. 'But I thought the Midnight Folk were the dangerous ones,' he said. 'That night when they ambushed Vanessa—'

Spider gave a weary shrug. 'Daylight Folk, Midnight Folk. They all want the same thing. Different sides of the same bloody coin.'

'But I thought Charissa was your friend.'

'It's complicated,' said Spider. 'Let me rest, and give me something to eat, and I'll try to explain.'

By then, they were approaching the shop. Tom let himself in through the back door and showed Spider into the little flat. A bedroom, a bathroom, a living room with a tiny kitchen. Tom found a first-aid kit and a spare set of clothes, then sent Spider to shower and change while he prepared a hasty meal of bacon, beans and noodles.

Five minutes later, Spider was back, wearing a pair of Tom's jeans and a plain grey T-shirt. Now, in his wire-framed glasses, with his wet hair combed back from his face, he looked less like a mad king and more like an English professor who had fallen down some stairs.

Tom brought the food to the table. He had never seen anyone so hungry. He watched in fascination as his guest ate two bowls of the noodles, a small loaf of bread, then drank a full carton of milk.

At last, he seemed to have finished. 'Thanks.'

'You look a little better,' said Tom.

Spider nodded. 'You saved my life. Now let me return the favour.' He looked across the table at Tom. 'Forget about what happened tonight. Forget about the Daylight Folk. Most of all, forget about *her*. Forget about Vanessa. I know you think you can't do that. I know it feels like you love her. But she can't love you in return. All she can do is beguile you, and ruin you, and consume you.' He stood up. 'This pays my debt. Goodbye, Collector. Have a good life. And stay away from dark rooms.'

'Hang on. You can't go now,' said Tom.

'You heard what Brimstone said. The longer I stay, the more likely you are to get hurt on my account. A spider brings good luck before midnight, but bad luck after. Everybody knows that.'

Tom looked at his watch, and was surprised to see that between preparing the meal and eating, and talk, more time had passed than he'd thought. It was close to two o'clock, and in the streets below the flat, everything was quiet.

'But you said you'd tell me *everything*. You can't just disappear. I want to know what happened back there. About nectar. The Market. Vanessa—'

'Trust me, Collector. You *don't* want to know. You'll be safer – and a lot happier – if you forget all about it. Some secrets are meant to stay secret. And some stories aren't worth the candle.'

He looked so earnest right then that Tom almost believed him, and might even have let him go – if he hadn't been in love. But love makes wise men into fools, and Tom Argent was only half wise to begin with. The rest of him was as foolish as any love-struck, bedazzled young man, and so he ignored the warning.

'You said I saved your life.'

'So?'

'So that means *you* owe me a debt. Just as Brimstone owed one to me. And that means I want answers.'

For a moment, Spider stayed silent. Then he sighed. 'I see how it is. She got to you. She showed you that smile, and it was as if the sun had never shone before. Am I right? And then when she kissed you, you felt the whole earth shake and spin, as if the dice were rolling. That's what she does. I've felt it too. And I know what happens.'

Tom shook his head. 'You don't understand.'

'Oh, I understand all right. But she isn't yours. She never can be. She belongs to someone else, long ago and far away. She could never love someone like you, although she can make you *feel* like she does. She can make you feel as if you're the King of Fiddler's Green, for just as long as it takes to steal the nectar from between your lips.' He gave a harsh and humourless laugh. 'This is her *modus*. That's what she is. She's a predator, like all Daylight Folk. She'll tease you with her glamours, she'll draw you into her orbit, and then – *poof!* Don't fool yourself. To her, you're just a flower growing by the side of the road. A source of nectar – here today, faded and dead tomorrow. Or worse – she could decide to claim you, and make of you a thing like herself, cold and dead and hungry inside, feeding on something you'll never feel. That would be worse. That would be like a living damnation.'

But Tom was still thinking about Vanessa. Her beauty, her warmth, her words, her *shine*. The thought that he might not see her again made him feel slightly dizzy with fear. What was it Spider had said? *Power. Gold. Your heart's desire. Even Brimstone's life, if you'd asked.* And Skipper had told him: *You had your chance.*

Tom felt suddenly cold. *Your chance.* 'What did you mean back there, when you said that I could have had anything?'

Spider pulled a face. 'I meant, you could have had *anything*. Brimstone *said* he owed you a debt, didn't he? He asked you to name your price.'

Tom said: 'But this is ridiculous. You're making it sound like a fairy tale, where some kid gets three wishes.'

Spider seemed genuinely amused. 'Now that *would* be ridiculous. Whoever heard of *three* wishes? Brimstone hasn't acknowledged a debt in a hundred years. *Three* wishes?' He shook his head, still grinning.

Tom took a deep breath. Somehow, he told himself, he had been caught up in an alternate reality, where strange men offered him wishes; where people fed on human energy; where madmen thought he was crazy; where invisible girls appeared mysteriously in photographic negatives. Too many things to believe, he thought. Too many things to dismiss outright.

'But fairy stories aren't real,' said Tom.

Spider shrugged. 'What does *real* mean? Is love real? Or magic, or hope, or joy, or the quest for enlightenment? Are any of those things less real just because they're woven in words? Only you people would question the existence of what you can't see. Fairy stories matter. They're how we understand what's true.'

'So, tell me a story,' Tom said, going into his tiny kitchen and taking two beers from the fridge. He opened them, handed one to Spider, and kept the second one for himself. 'Beer,' indicated Tom. 'To help you talk, and to help me believe. Now sit down. You're staying here. You're going to tell me everything.'

Spider looked at the bottle. 'We're going to need a lot more beer,' he said. Then he sat down in a chair and began.

'*There is a story the bees used to tell, which makes it hard to disbelieve.*'

Part 4

Chrysalis

I

There once was a girl of the Moth Folk, dark-winged, strong, and fearless. Her eyes were like the starlit sky; her footfall soft as shadow. And although she was lovely, love had no place in her heart, for hers was the tribe of the Moth King, who had waged a war on love, for ever and ever.

But love, like all forbidden things, was fascinating to her. Every night of the clear full moon, she would go to the Moonlight Market and watch the traders sell their wares: printed books of every kind; pomegranates from the south; wines from the islands; gems from the north; flowers that bloomed only once in their lives. But she only had eyes for the sellers of charms and glamours. Here, there were spells for a broken heart, or to spin dead leaves into gold, or to rekindle a memory, or to summon the western wind. Most of all, there were love spells: tiny bottles of coloured glass with stoppers worked in silver filled with potions made from the heart of a rose, or the tail fin of a mermaid. Here were glamours to melt a lover's heart: candles of every colour; tokens of remembrance; silk-bound books of poetry.

But among all the love-knots and bonbons and pressed flowers and handkerchiefs, the Moth girl never truly saw the nature of her enemy, for it seemed to her that Love was weak, and simpering, and faithless. She told herself she was too strong to fall for its blandishments. Until one day, at the Market, she saw a boy with a glamorie-glass in his hand, standing by a display of books, and stories, and legends, and memories.

Beside the stall was a bright-eyed man, bundled into a heavy drab-coloured overcoat. In the moonlight, the lining shone with skeins of spider silk. The boy approached, the glass in his hand, looking like someone in a dream.

'Is this real? Am I dreaming?' he said.

The man in the heavy overcoat shrugged. 'Dream is a river that leads to all worlds. Which one are you looking for?'

The boy gave a smile of peculiar sweetness. It lit up his face like a glamour, and made his rather ordinary features suddenly look exotic and strange. The Moth girl drew closer, hoping to hear his answer, drawn to his smile in spite of herself.

The boy replied: 'My father says magic doesn't exist. He says to believe only what I can see. But here, there are things that no one sees. And I thought that if I showed him—'

'Then he would have to believe you?' The collector of books gave a hard, bright grin. 'Don't think I don't see you with your glass. Don't think I don't know what you're taking.'

The boy flushed. His gaze went to the glamorie-glass in his hand. 'You mean my camera? I only took a few photographs.'

Once more, the collector of books gave his grin. It was the look of a man who has seen and forgotten more than most men ever know. 'Maybe so,' he said. 'But here, everything must be paid for. Every cantrip. Every fragment of soul. Even a blackened soul such as mine costs more than you would be willing to pay.' He moved in closer to the boy, looking suddenly dangerous.

The boy looked uneasy. 'I'm sorry. I—'

The collector of books showed his teeth. They were very white, very sharp. 'I'm a collector of sorts myself,' he said, putting an arm around the boy's shoulders. 'I collect stories. Memories. Lives.' He indicated his stand of books. 'Every book here is a life,' he explained, 'or a piece thereof. Between these pages lie lost loves, sleeping kings, forgotten queens. Here too lies a vanished prince, stripped of his memories by a charm, lost to himself by the very love of the folk who claimed to have found him.'

'*I don't understand,' said the boy.*

'*I know,' said the seller of books with a smile. 'Time after time, you come back here, trying to bring back wonders.' And at this he picked up a book from his stand, a thick green book emblazoned with a name across the cover in gold.*

'*That's my name,' said the boy, perplexed.*

'*Go on, read it,' said the man. 'You'll forget it again, anyway.'*

The boy's eyes widened as he turned the pages of the green book. 'But if this is true,' he said at last, 'then everything I thought I knew about my life, my parents, is a lie!'

'*Yes,' said the man, his grey eyes agleam.*

'*But how could I have forgotten all this?'*

The girl of the Moth Folk stepped forward. 'Because our wares must be paid for,' she said. 'Whatever you take from the Market is paid for with memory. This man is stealing your life, piece by piece, in exchange for something he knows you will forget as soon as the moon sets.'

The young man turned to look at her. His eyes were very dark, she saw, and filled with tiny, dancing lights. He was not unpleasant to look at, she thought; and was a little surprised at herself for thinking something so trivial.

'*Not stealing,' said the collector of books. 'Believe it or not, I mean the boy nothing but love and happiness.'*

That word again. The girl wondered why it made her feel so lonely. She came a little closer.

The boy continued to look at her, his eyes reflecting pinpoints of fire. 'What's your name?' he asked.

Far away, across the Thames, a church tower clock struck midnight.

2

It was as if Tom Argent had fallen into some alternate world. Gone was King's Cross, gone London, even England itself was gone. In this world, magic was commonplace; nothing was quite what it seemed. Kings and queens fought bitterly for kingdoms built on stardust. And the homeless man he knew as Spider was a powerful mage in search of a lost prince who, the stories said, would bring together two tribes who had been at war with each other for centuries.

'But that's a fairy tale,' he said.

Spider finished his bottle of beer. 'I never called them *fairies*,' he said. 'That's what *your* people call them. And the Silken Folk are nothing like those creatures you call fairies. The Silken Folk are old, and proud, and wild, and dark, and dangerous. They have existed since long before the first of your people. You call them *fairies* because you don't have any other name for them. In your stories, you tame them, and make them small and delicate, because if you saw what they *really* were, it would send you all insane.'

Tom sighed. This was crazy, he thought. He was talking with a madman about impossible things, and for what? Because he'd had a scare? Because of a girl in a picture?

'I know that look,' said Spider. 'You are starting to rationalise. That's what their glamours do to you. In a week, you'll have forgotten us all.'

'Not Vanessa. I won't forget her.'

'You think?' Spider leaned closer and smiled. 'So tell me, Collector. You saw her just now. How old is she? What length is her hair? What colour? What shape are her eyes?'

Tom frowned. For a moment, he almost saw Vanessa in his mind's eye. But as soon as he tried to answer Spider's questions, she was gone, eclipsed once more by that *shine*.

'I ... I don't remember,' he said.

'Of course you don't,' Spider said. 'The Silken Folk have glamours to protect themselves from people like you. They haven't been living in your world for as long as they have without learning something about camouflage. And, of course, your people don't know how to look. They don't even see what's in front of them, right under their noses.'

Tom shook his head. 'It's impossible.'

'As impossible as taking a photograph of a girl who wasn't there? Or going to a market and then forgetting all about it?'

'I could have overlooked her,' said Tom. 'It's easily done, when you're trying to concentrate on something else. As for the market—' *The sound of the night. The gleam of the moon on the water. A kiss from a girl you met in a dream. A fleeting scent of woodsmoke.* 'I haven't been sleeping,' he said at last. 'I've been under a lot of stress.'

Spider laughed. 'Good try,' he said. 'But you don't believe that. Daylight Folk like to hide in plain sight. But Midnight Folk are good at camouflage. You didn't see Charissa that day because she didn't *want* to be seen. As for Vanessa – she let you see exactly what you wanted to see, just for as long as it suited her. For as long as it took her to pull you into her orbit.'

Tom took another bottle of beer. He didn't want any more, but his head was swimming, and suddenly being drunk seemed like the best of two bad alternatives. He thought back to his childhood, his father saying, 'Trust only what you can see.' But his camera *had* seen Charissa, even when she was invisible. And why could he still remember her face, when Vanessa's features eluded him?

He put his hand in his pocket. Once more, he felt papery petals there, and caught that distant, wistful scent. *A flower that blooms only once*, he thought. *That woman at the Market.*

The memory was luminous, sharp and bright as Kodachrome. How could such a memory have faded out of existence so fast, and be summoned back into being by the touch of a faded flower?

Spider gave him a sharp look. 'Did you say something?' he asked.

Tom shook his head.

'I thought I heard something,' Spider said. 'Or maybe—' He stiffened. 'You didn't bring anything back, did you? From the Moonlight Market?'

Tom shrugged and shook his head. 'Like what?'

'Like anything,' Spider said. 'A bead. A button. A bauble.' He paused. 'Perhaps even a *flower*?'

Once more, Tom shook his head. Some instinct warned him not to speak of the flower seller's gift, or her instruction to keep it safe. 'You're wrong about Vanessa,' he said. 'She cares about me. I know she does. Why else would she have saved my life?'

Spider shrugged. 'I know how it feels. But that's what she is. A butterfly, passing from one of your kind to another, sipping nectar as she goes. She may look like a girl to you, but underneath she's a predator, incapable of feeling love. That's what happened to her kind when the son of the Butterfly Queen and the Moth King disappeared between the worlds.'

Tom was feeling rather dazed. He sat in silence, drinking his beer, and then at last he looked up and said: 'I don't believe in fairy tales. But I *do* believe in love. And I'm going to find Vanessa, wherever she is, whatever disguise she's using.'

'Doesn't matter what you believe,' said Spider. 'You're a part of the story now. Brimstone warned you. *I* warned you.'

'But this isn't a story!' said Tom, who was starting to feel as if he were speaking a different language.

'There's truth to be found in stories,' Spider went on. 'Sometimes, strange as it may seem, it's the only truth that matters. Stories help us separate what's real from what's ephemeral. You know that, Collector.'

'Why do you keep calling me that?' said Tom, exasperated.

'Because you collect them,' he replied. 'You catch them with your camera. You capture them on rolls of film, where their glamours cannot pass. Thus you can see them as they are, and not as they choose to be seen by you. You have power over them. *That's* why you're the Collector.'

'I'd rather you called me Tom,' said Tom.

'That's your *daylight* name,' said a voice from behind them. 'Your midnight name is different. The name you gave to a girl on a bridge, in a dream, all those years ago. *That's* the name you'd rather hear. Isn't it – *Prince Argent*?'

3

Tom turned round so quickly that he almost spilled his bottle of beer. Charissa was in the doorway, an unremarkable figure in a long, mottled coat, her ragged hair pulled back from a face that was constellated with freckles. Once again, Tom Argent was struck by the way every freckle, every tattoo, seemed perfectly *familiar*, illuminated in his mind like a childhood memory. How was it that he remembered *her* so well, and not Vanessa? And *what* had she just called him?

'How did you get in here?' said Tom. 'What—?'

'Midnight Folk can get in anywhere,' said Charissa, sitting down. She was a good head shorter than Tom, and a good deal lighter, and yet she seemed to project an air of indefinable danger. One arm was bare, the sleeve torn off, and her delicate spiral tattoos appeared to chase each other like birds.

'Why did you call me Prince Argent?' asked Tom.

Spider gave Charissa a look. 'Because she likes to make trouble,' he said. 'Ignore her. She's nobody, anyway.'

Charissa's eyes narrowed. 'That's rich, coming from you,' she remarked. 'Didn't I tell you to leave him alone?'

'Charissa, he came looking for *me*.'

'So what? He isn't ready,' she said. 'He hasn't even got his wings.'

'Hang on,' said Tom. 'Did you say *wings*?'

'Excuse me,' said Charissa. 'All this may seem very exciting to *you*, but to me it's just another job, like hundreds I've handled before. So, please, let me get on with it, and *maybe* I'll keep you alive.'

Tom was taken aback by her tone. So much so that it silenced him for over a minute. By then, she and Spider were engaged in an acrimonious debate, in which Spider tried to explain what had happened in the penthouse, Charissa warned of the displeasure of someone she called Cinnabar, and Spider lamented the loss of his *evercoat*, which he seemed to find more important than any item of clothing should be.

'Er, excuse me,' repeated Tom. 'Did you say *wings*?'

Charissa raised an eyebrow, in which an emerald stud sparkled. 'What did I just say?' she said.

'No, but *wings*?' repeated Tom.

'Never mind that,' said Spider. 'What about my evercoat?'

'What's so important about a coat?' asked Tom.

Charissa ignored him. 'Maybe I could help retrieve it for you. For a suitable price, of course.'

'Name it,' said Spider grimly.

Charissa smiled. Tom noticed that her teeth were pointed, like a cat's.

'*Wings!*' said Tom. He flapped his arms. It should have felt like a joke, but instead he found himself feeling something like disappointment when nothing much happened, except that he finally knocked over his beer.

Spider assumed a patient expression. 'Tom, you don't *have* any wings.'

'Thank goodness for that,' Tom started to say. 'I thought the world was going mad.'

Spider went on. 'You've a long way to go before wings are even an option. And until I get my evercoat back, I can't spin a line to the Kingdom. So let's concentrate on that, shall we?' he said, addressing Charissa. 'Unimportant business can wait. I *must* have my evercoat before dawn.'

Tom wasn't entirely pleased at being dismissed as *unimportant business*. But he was relieved that talk had been diverted to something more practical. Just *why* Spider was so attached to a musty old overcoat was a mystery to him, but in a world of mysteries, this seemed the least alarming. Lost princes and warring tribes were too close to those tales he'd loved as a boy, and which his parents had warned him against, saying: *Tom, you have to understand the difference between reality and dream. This is the real world. Those other worlds – in storybooks – they're just fairy tales.*

And yet, in spite of their protests, the thought of other worlds had always enchanted him. Places where magic wasn't just a fantasy. Maybe that was why he had fallen in love with photography, the magic that made images from nothing but light and chemicals.

For a moment, Tom struggled between a pair of opposing realities. He had never taken drugs, but he was sure that if he did it would feel exactly like this. Was he really expected to believe that he was part of a fairy tale? Had Charissa called him *Prince Argent*? Had he really been to a market that only appeared by moonlight? And at the heart of the mystery, Vanessa, always Vanessa, like a gleaming monolith in a clearing in the woods.

He turned to Charissa. 'This coat,' he said. 'Vanessa's people have it, right?'

She nodded.

'So, why don't we just ask for it back? I mean, it's only an old coat.'

'It is not only an old coat,' Spider said. 'It's *my* old coat, with *my* old things hidden away inside. And if Brimstone has any sense – which he has – he'll be keeping a close watch on that coat to make sure nothing happens before dawn.'

'What's going to happen?' said Tom. 'It's a *coat*!'

Charissa ignored him. 'Where do you think they're keeping it?'

Spider shrugged. 'Not in the penthouse, for sure,' he said. 'Too risky. Too many prying eyes. Brimstone wouldn't want to risk Pieris or Vanessa getting their hands on it. Not that they could loosen its tongue, not if they were to tear it to shreds. But that wouldn't stop them trying. Skipper, though...' His grey-gold eyes gleamed. 'Maybe there's potential there. She's no friend of the Kingdom. Perhaps we could do some kind of deal.'

Tom had heard little of the exchange, except for the mention of Vanessa. Even her name seemed to raise the little hairs on the back of his neck. Even her name made his heart race, although the shape of her face was unclear in his failing memory. But Vanessa's *glamour* remained, like the memory of a beautiful dream. A sudden idea occurred to him. If he had a photograph, then maybe he could capture the dream, like a butterfly under glass, so that he would never forget—

'Let me come with you,' he said.

'Out of the question,' Charissa said. 'You can stay with Spider. I'll deal with this. I can get there and back before dawn breaks. If Skipper has the evercoat, or knows where it is, I can turn her. She wants to stay. I know she does. She's lost hope in the Kingdom.'

'What does that mean? What Kingdom?' asked Tom.

She looked at him. 'Will you trust me?' she said.

Tom started to protest. But Charissa's expression was so fierce that he thought better of it. How could someone be so small, he thought, and yet so supremely confident? How could she look so dangerous, so very sure and powerful?

He nodded. 'Yes. I trust you,' he said.

She gave a sudden, luminous grin. 'Typical chrysalis,' she said. 'Pretty as peaches. Thick as mince.'

Then she turned and made for the door, looking almost insubstantial in the shadows. Tom watched as she vanished down the steps. And looking down on to the street, he saw her hesitate, and then, finding the street deserted, spread out the skirts of the garment that he'd assumed was a long brown coat...

Except that it wasn't a coat. It was *wings* – wings the colour of cobweb, and dappled sunlight on water, and rain...

I've seen this before, said a voice in his mind. It came with a fleeting memory – a voice in the moonlight, the touch of a hand, a scent of smoke and roses. *I've seen this before*, thought Tom once again, as Charissa flew into the night.

His hand crept into his pocket, where something – *a dead leaf? No, a flower* – seemed to be caught in the lining. With the thought came a memory: of a moon like a Christmas bauble; a kiss as light as a moth's wing; a long-necked guitar that fell from a bridge into the moonlit water.

I must have dreamed that, Tom thought, and yet it didn't feel like a dream. And it came with the sound of voices of vendors selling flowers and fruit, and the scent of marchpane and gingerbread, burnt sugar, and smoke, and spices.

The Market!

He picked out the piece of debris that was stuck in his pocket lining. It looked like a flower of some kind; old and almost transparent with age. And yet its aroma reached him from afar, and with it the voice of the old woman selling flowers on the bridge: *You'd dare put a price on true love?*

That happened, thought Tom. *I remember this. I've remembered this before. And forgotten it again. But this time? This time is different. Why?*

He lifted the flower to his face. Its scent was sweet and potent, like jasmine under the full moon. And with it came the dream of a girl, with wheels of fire in her eyes—

That happened, he told himself again. *It happened, and it wasn't a dream.*

And now came the rest of those memories. The crow woman; the seller of charms; the sickening way a part of the bridge had slipped into non-existence as a scrawl of cloud had covered the moon. And Charissa—

Charissa's ephemeral coat. Her eyes, pinned with reflected fire. The jewel in her eyebrow. Her freckles, like sun-dappled shadow…

Once more, he looked at the flower, small and shrivelled in his palm. It looked so unimposing, and yet it felt charged with significance. He remembered the words of the vendor now: *A flower that blooms only once. Of course. You don't remember. Never mind. It remembers you.*

Now he remembered Old London Bridge, and the sounds of the Moonlight Market, and the people in their animal masks, and the fire spinners against the sky. And he knew with a sudden certainty that he had seen this all before, many times, since his childhood, but that he'd traded the memories. Traded them for the hope of bringing back proof of what he'd seen – proof, to convince his father.

Except that his father was dead now. Dead, though his legacy of disbelief and scepticism endured. *Why* had he tried so hard to persuade Tom to abandon stories? Why had words like *adventure* and *magic* been so completely forbidden? A complex sensation welled up in Tom – of hope, and shame, and furtive joy. *My father is dead,* he thought. *I'm free. Free to believe whatever I want. What if all those things were true? The magic? The dreams? The stories? And what if I could be a part of them, like the hero of a fairy tale who turns out to be a prince in disguise?*

4

Tom awaited Charissa's return with a nervous impatience. Spider had fallen asleep on the couch, and as time passed and no one came, he positioned himself by the window and, reloaded camera in hand, began to watch for any sign of activity.

The troubling cascade of memories that had assailed him earlier had died back to a kind of drone, like the sound of the sea in the ear of a shell; but they showed no sign of diminishing. The Moonlight Market had been real. Tom could remember all of it: the flower seller; Willowherb's books; the fire spinners; the tattooist; the crow guard at the entrance – and yet, Vanessa eluded him. *Why?* Why was Charissa's face so clear, while that of his true love stayed hidden? Could it be something to do with the fact that he'd taken her photograph?

Trust only what you can see, Tom, his father had always told him. Now, even the things he *could* see were as wild as his imagination. But his camera had never lied. His camera had shown him the truth. Maybe it would do so again. Heart beating wildly, he pointed the camera at the street, the telephoto lens in place. If Vanessa, or the Daylight Folk, were to make an appearance, he would capture them on film and fix them in his memory. This time, he would not forget. Was he not the *Collector*?

With this in mind, Tom waited, watching through the window. Through the eye of his camera, the silent street was very clear. His mind, too, seemed clearer. He'd always found that through the lens, reality seemed less chaotic, less filled with random elements. There was a kind of harmony to the world of photography, and a beauty that revealed itself – sweetly, unexpectedly – in even the darkest of places. That beauty was what moved him, he thought. People are so unaware of the beauty that shines within them. The tilt of a stranger's chin; the spray of freckles on their face. The eyes that shine like mica from within a nest of wrinkles. A mother with a sleeping child. The bright burst of laughter from a girl talking to a friend on the phone. They didn't see it, but Tom did. Tom did, and he collected it.

There is a kind of separation between the people who walk the streets before midnight and those who walk them afterwards. Before midnight, there would have been couples coming out of restaurants; families back from the theatre; maybe a few late-night joggers with running shoes and backpacks. After midnight, he saw people coming back from clubs, some lingering to piss in the street under the arch of the doorway. The doorway of the camera shop was a frequent target for these late-night revellers, something that enraged Tom's employer, the otherwise calm Mr Burnet. Then came the homeless with bundles of bedding, looking for places to sleep for the night.

But, by now, they had all come and gone. Now the streets were mostly still, but for the shadows, the rats, the occasional cat and one urban fox, resplendent in the yellow glow of the street lamps. But now Tom knew that the shadows were filled with possibility. Who knew what might be revealed – what wings, what peering faces, half glimpsed from the tail of his eye, but safely trapped on celluloid?

Dawn was approaching. Spider slept on. By now, Tom had shot three rolls of film, and the streets had begun to awaken. Soon would come the morning crowd: the early joggers, the dog walkers, delivery trucks, collectors of bottles and garbage. Soon, the homeless would be awake, shivering and stiff from the cold, packing their things into plastic bags; folding their tents and blankets away before the police came to move them on.

In his darkroom, Tom developed the films, then waited for the rolls to dry, and spread them onto the enlarger and went through them slowly, frame by frame, looking for what went unseen.

Here was a girl with only one shoe, lurching drunkenly homewards. Here was a man in a battered top hat, pushing a shopping trolley. Here were two young people with a broken umbrella, sitting in a doorway beneath a single grubby blanket. So far, Tom saw nothing unexpected. But when he came to the end of the final roll, to the place where the very last image had been sliced across the middle, he saw, right there, right at the break, in a shot of what had been an empty street, the figure of a crouching child perched on the top of a nearby roof.

Tom's heart began to pound. With fingers that trembled a little, he cut the negative and slid it onto the enlarger. The more he looked, the more certain he was that the child on the rooftop was Swallowtail. There was something about her posture, something wild and predatory. He found that he could almost believe she was only *disguised* as a child, to feed on human energies.

Once more, Tom picked up his camera and went to the window. This time, he worked almost blindly, taking shots of the empty street; the darkened buildings; the rooftops. Then he ran back to his darkroom.

It was his last roll of black-and-white film. Fifteen minutes' developing time. This time, Tom did not wait for the developed film to dry, but put it directly onto the enlarger with hands that were unsteady with impatience.

And there they were. The Daylight Folk, looking out from every frame. Faces pale in negative; perching on the rooftops, standing on the parapets. Invisible to the naked eye but revealed to him on film. Brimstone, Pieris, Swallowtail; dark eyes looking into his, velvet wings against the sky—

It was daybreak.

5

Tom's cry awakened Spider. His response was quick; he took no more than a moment to glance, first at the negatives, and then out of the window, closing the blinds and furtively peering out between the slats. A small brown butterfly – or moth, Tom couldn't tell the difference – flew out from between the curtains, fluttering into the daylight. Another joined it, settling for a moment on Spider's arm.

'Come on,' said Spider. 'We have to go.' His face was pale, the bruises now standing out all the more starkly. 'A spider's bad luck after midnight, and even worse after daybreak. I told you, Collector. We have to get going, and quickly.'

'But – I don't understand,' said Tom. 'We had a truce. Didn't we?'

Spider went to the door of the flat and quickly glanced through the spyhole. 'Charissa said she'd be back before dawn. She must have failed to turn Skipper. That means Skipper knows our plans. Thus ends our truce. We need to go.'

'What about Charissa?' said Tom.

'Charissa can look after herself. For the moment...' Spider dug into his pockets. 'If only I had my evercoat!'

'Too late for that, Spinner, my dear,' came a voice like crushed silk. 'Hand over the chrysalis.'

It was Skipper. Tom turned to see her standing by the window, her dark face still, her eyes intense. Her wings were patterned in orange and brown, half spread like the colourful lining of her coat. Except that it wasn't a coat at all; and the matching waistcoat underneath seemed a part of her miraculous skin. At her side stood Pieris, smiling like a switchblade.

'How did you even get in?' said Tom. 'That window doesn't open.'

'No time for that,' hissed Spider, and he grabbed Tom's hand and pulled him backwards into the darkroom, closing the door behind them and blocking it with his shoulder.

Outside, Skipper's cool voice said: 'There's no point trying to hide from us. We know you can't get out that way. Give up the chrysalis, Spinnerman. It's over.'

'Shows what you know,' muttered Spider, and from somewhere about his person, he produced what looked to Tom like one of those little sewing kits you sometimes get in hotel bathrooms: a piece of card with a safety pin holding three short lengths of thread – one black, one white, one scarlet. 'Lifelines,' Spider told Tom. 'Good job I had them on me.' He took hold of Tom's hand again and, with his teeth, pulled out the black thread. 'No time to prepare,' he said. 'No time to check the details. Just stay with me, and keep hold of my hand.' With that, he took the piece of thread and pulled it sharply towards him—

Tom had only a moment to grab hold of his camera. There was no thought behind the gesture; simply an instinct to cling to something that had never let him down. For a second, he felt dizzy, as if the atmosphere in the room had changed, or the floor had shifted suddenly beneath his feet. Perhaps it had; his vision blurred, there was a bright flare of light, and then the pair of them were in darkness.

Under his feet, Tom could now feel some kind of yielding gravel. The air felt damp, with a musty scent of engine oil and stone dust. And it was *cold*: the temperature had dropped by ten degrees or more. Tom tried to make out where he was, but the dark was absolute. Not even the tiniest smear of light. For a moment, Tom was sure he'd gone blind.

Then came a sound like a match being struck, and a light appeared. Not firelight, but something that fluttered like a neon tube nearing the end of its functional life. Spider was holding the scarlet thread between his hands, now glowing like a filament of reddish light from a half-dead bulb. Something skittered away from the light.

Rats, thought Tom. *In my darkroom?* But this wasn't his darkroom. The temperature, the dusty smell, the rats – this was somewhere else. Momentarily, he thought of the story of the children and the Pied Piper: of how the man in the coloured coat had lured them all under the mountain. And although he was afraid, the part of him that loved stories seemed to open up like a rose.

'Where are we?' Tom asked.

'Safe. For now.'

In the red glow between Spider's hands, Tom could see that they were in a tunnel. Narrow enough to make him feel slightly claustrophobic, it was built from some kind of brick, deeply stained with damp and soot, and with a cinder floor that gleamed like scattered crystals underfoot. At intervals, he could see vents, and there was a slight draught coming from the nearest one, which suggested a link to the outside.

'What's that?' he said, of the piece of thread still gleaming between Spider's hands.

'Stitch light,' replied Spider. 'Didn't have much. But it should last us long enough to find our way to safety. Of course, if I'd had my evercoat, we wouldn't have had to come here at all.'

'Where's *here*, exactly?' asked Tom, ignoring the mention of the evercoat, which seemed to him an entirely separate delusion.

Spider shrugged. 'Dead space,' he said. 'There are tunnels under King's Cross that haven't been used in a hundred years. Tunnels that served a purpose that has long since been forgotten, except of course by the Silken Folk, and the few of your people who found their way in. There's passages here that lead all the way down to London Beyond and the Court of Queen Orfeia, and further still, to the Night Train, and the many stations it serves. Now follow me, and don't look back. There may be worse things than rats down here.'

6

Tom had no idea how long he followed Spider through the tunnels below King's Cross. Time seemed to have no meaning here, and it might have been hours or minutes. Spider's stitch light was the same dim red colour as the light in the darkroom. Tom found this strangely comforting and, with the familiar feel of his camera around his neck, could almost believe that this was real, and not a very persistent dream.

'How did we get here?' he said at last, when Spider paused at the junction between two brick-lined tunnels. 'I mean, one minute we're in my flat, and the next we're down here. How did you do that?'

Spider shrugged. 'I'm a spinner,' he said. 'Spinning thread is what I do. Brimstone's crew took most of my stuff, but I always have a thread up my sleeve. I happened to have a piece on me that leads into World Below. And if I had my evercoat, with all its lining and pockets intact—' He shrugged. 'No chance of that,' he went on. 'They thought they were thorough last time. They took all my glamours, my trinkets, my maps. They thought they could use them against me. But there were things they *didn't* find. My threads and needles. My knots. My web.'

'Your web?' repeated Tom, vaguely wondering if this could be a reference to some electronic device. 'You mean, like the internet?'

Spider shook his head. 'Not quite. Yet there *are* lines that link the worlds, and webs that connect them together. Even worlds that some believe to have been lost for ever.'

'Like...' Tom found his voice faltering over the words. 'Like – the World of the Butterfly Queen and the Moth King?'

'*Just* like that world,' Spider replied, and suddenly all Tom's resistance began to unravel like a piece of knitting. Within this story, it made perfect sense – the Silken Folk: Vanessa, Charissa, the Butterflies, Spider, whom some folk called Spinner, who had literally *pulled* them out of the world on a thread – and, of course, his rolls of negatives, that showed him the truth behind the disguise, the faces behind the glamours they wore—

'Oh, my God,' he said. 'This stuff, it's all real, isn't it? There really *are* Daylight and Midnight Folk. And *you're* the Spider Mage—'

'Gods,' said Spider. 'You're a slow one, even for a chrysalis. Your parents must have really done a number on your childish imagination. What did they tell you? Not to believe in fairy stories and old wives' tales? Did they tell you monsters aren't real? That people who see things are crazy? That you'd go crazy, too, if you tried to look beyond your world?'

'Er, more or less,' said Tom Argent.

'Where are your parents now?'

'They died.'

'I know,' said Spider irritably. 'They died in a fire. You were twenty-one. And you were adopted when you were small, and your one attempt to get in touch with your birth mother ended when the agency said she didn't want any contact with you.'

'How could you possibly know that?' said Tom.

Spider gave him a tight grin. 'Tom, I know all about you. I've been watching you for years. Do you think you're the first chrysalis that's ever come my way?'

'People keep calling me that,' said Tom. 'What do you mean, *chrysalis?*'

Spider grinned. 'Let me tell you a tale.'

And so Tom Argent listened once more as he followed the Spider Mage through the tunnels of Battlebridge, squinting at the shadows cast in the flickering stitch light and hearing, far above his head, the occasional thunder of trains.

Part 5

—

Dead Space

I

By an accidental conjunction of stars, the young son of the Moth King and the Butterfly Queen had been lost in the World of the Sightless Ones. It was a dark and cruel world, even then – and it has grown so much darker.

It was a world in which nothing made sense; where kings and queens had no power of their own, but left their kingdoms to be ruled by madmen, clowns and profiteers. It was a world in which magic was just a word to be found in stories: a world in which dreamers were scorned and mocked, and where those who sought out beauty and truth were mercilessly hounded.

In this world, the old and infirm were left to beg for food on the streets, and strangers asking for shelter were driven back into the sea. In this world, children went hungry; those without work were treated like criminals; poor people were made to pay for the greed of the wealthy. In this world, the blind man was denied his stick; the lame man robbed of his crutches. And though there was beauty in the woods and wonder in the oceans, the Folk of this world – the Sightless Folk – did all they could to destroy it wherever it could still be found.

The young Prince arrived in this world, lost and very frightened. The thread he had followed was broken, and he had no means of spinning another. His friend, the Spider Mage, was too far away to hear his cries, and this world of cruelty and noise was too much for him. Even the air was unbreathable. And so he crept into World Below, and wept to himself in the darkness. As he wept, his grief was so great that he broke into a cloud of butterflies and moths, each one a fragment of himself, that scattered into the darkness of the tunnels beneath the city. Some of them found their way to the light. Others stayed in the darkness. Some slept. And they became two separate groups – one living underground, one in the light, both yearning for the world they had left, and for the chance to be whole again.

Time passed. The Butterflies and Moths, like those of the World of the Sightless Folk, adapted to suit their surroundings. They learnt to take on the Aspects of those who moved among them, and to take what nectar they could find. The Butterflies hid themselves in plain sight, growing ever more prosperous and beautiful in the sunlight. Living among the homeless and poor, the Moths remained nocturnal, keeping to the dark alleyways and the tunnels under the city.

Meanwhile, the exiled Spider Mage still searched for the Prince. Through his magic, he tried to locate all the missing fragments, hoping that in one of them the lost child might be found again. But in the World of the Sightless Ones, real magic works but poorly. The Mage's powers were almost gone, and his web, which had once spanned the worlds, had shrunk to little more than rags.

And yet he clung to the hope that somehow the lost Prince could be found; his Aspect made whole, his inheritance restored. Using his web of dreams, he found fragments of the Prince that had been forgotten and overlooked, cocooned in the darkness of London Beyond. And he placed each one of these cocoons with a human family, good folk oblivious to their origin, unmindful of their destiny. Thus were these royal hatchlings kept far away from the two warring tribes until it was time for their coming of age, and for the plan that the Spider Mage had formed to be put into action.

The Butterfly Queen had vowed that none of her folk would ever fall in love with a Butterfly again. The Moth King had sworn the same oath, and for centuries war had raged between the Butterflies and the Moths. But the Mage still believed that if a Moth could learn to love a Butterfly, and be loved by them in return, then the curse would fail, and the Prince be made whole, and the warring tribes be reconciled for ever.

But it was not as easy as that. In the World of the Sightless Folk, the Butterflies, thriving in the light, had come to enjoy the freedoms that this rich new life had brought them. And as time passed, they came to care less and less for the world they had left, and instead considered how to stay in their new home for ever. So that even as the Moths continued to dream of a way back to their home world, the Butterflies sought out the hatchlings, to kill them before they could develop to full maturity. For they knew that if that ever came to pass, were one of them to find true love with one of the enemy, then the ancient curse would be broken. The divided tribes would be made whole. And the Prince would lead them back to their world, and put an end to the long, long war . . .

2

Tom listened in silence as he followed Spider's stitch light through the tunnels of London. There were many more arches here, some bracketed with daylight. That must mean they were approaching the surface, thought Tom. How long had they been down there? He had no idea. His feet hurt; he was hungry; but his head was filled with stars. So much had happened since the day when he had first met Spider. That was only a week ago, but since then, his life had been overturned. Moonlight markets, lost princes, bridges that slip in and out of Time. And now, this. This waking dream, that somehow wasn't a dream at all.

'So – you're saying I'm one of you?' he began. 'One of these – what do you call them – hatchlings?'

Spider shrugged. 'There's only one of me,' he said. 'Thank all the gods.'

'But – a *cocoon*,' insisted Tom. 'A chrysalis? A potential prince? So that's what Charissa meant when she called me Prince Argent! But how can that be? I can't be a prince. I was born in *Guildford*!' His tone was flippant, but a sense of profound excitement had begun to take hold of him. 'I mean, I always knew I was different,' he said. 'I always sensed there was *something* special about me—'

'Oh, that,' said Spider dismissively. 'That's just human entitlement. It's nothing special, I'm afraid. All the Sightless Folk have that.'

'Oh,' said Tom, crestfallen.

'But it does put you in danger.' Spider snapped his fingers and the stitch light went out, leaving them in a semi-darkness to which Tom's eyes soon became accustomed. 'A full-grown prince might possibly – *possibly* – win their loyalty. But you're still just a hatchling. You haven't shown your colours yet. So pay attention and do what I say. We're about to enter the territory of the Midnight Folk.'

'But I thought the Midnight Folk were friends.'

'Not *friends*, exactly,' said Spider. 'Our interests coincide, that's all. They used to dream of going home, of finding the lost Prince, of restoring the Kingdom. But they don't want peace. What they want is to rule alone, without interference. The Spider Mage had always meant for the two tribes to come together, but all either side wants is to win this war. It wouldn't be the first time the Midnight Folk have neutralised a chrysalis that they deemed to be compromised. And as for the Daylight Folk – well. They're predators. They had to discharge the debt they owed, but you heard what Brimstone said. Next time they see you, you're toast.'

'*Toast*,' said Tom Argent longingly, realising how long it had been since he'd had anything to eat. 'What I'd give for a piece of toast, with smashed avocado and chilli and lime. Or hot buttered crumpets, with strawberry jam ...'

'Shh,' said Spider, testing the air. In the distant daylight, his face looked sharp and very sane. Tom wondered how he could ever have thought the man crazy, or simple, or slow. Come to think of it, he wondered how he could ever have thought Spider a man at all.

'What is it?' said Tom.

Spider said nothing, but Tom saw that the tunnel diverged ahead of them. Two arches faced them: one was faintly illumin-ated, the other remained in darkness. A distant scent seemed to come from afar, like spices on a summer breeze. It was so different to the damp, musty smell of the tunnels that Tom was drawn, involuntarily, to the illuminated arch and that warm and spicy scent. Coming closer, he saw that the brickwork here was lavish, with carvings of animals and birds and magical creatures, like those of the Natural History Museum he had so loved as a boy. And now came a distant fluttering sound, like pieces of paper on the wind, fretting the air and making the tiny hairs on Tom's neck stand on end.

'What is it?'

'Shh,' said Spider.

Shhh. The tunnels echoed his whisper.

The fluttering sound grew louder. Tom felt his hackles rise. Something – some kind of debris – flew from the darkened tunnel, like clothes moths from a wardrobe.

'Stay close,' Spider said. 'Just stay with me and do what I say. Whatever you do, whatever you see, don't r—'

Once more came that sound from the tunnel mouth, like wings against a lampshade. And out of the darkness came the Moths, in their midnight colours: golden-eyed and cluster-clawed and terrible—

'Run,' finished Spider.

Tom ran.

3

The tunnel on the left was dark; the one on the right gave out a dim glow. Ignoring Spider's call, Tom fled instinctively towards the light, through the right-hand arch with its many designs, and into a tunnel that led him over a barrage of broken bricks and a rivulet of water. The light looked like daylight – at least at first – but as Tom ran down the passageway, it seemed to flicker like neon overhead, then dance before him like a will-o'-the-wisp. Behind him came the sounds of pursuit, fragmented by the brickwork, but Tom raced ahead without thinking, taking turns at random – he thought – but following those flickering lights.

After a time, Tom realised the tunnel around him looked different. Gone were the patches of damp on the walls and the whitish trails on the brickwork. Instead, there was vegetation: ferns were growing from the bricks, brambles from the gravel path. Here the carvings on the brick were growing increasingly intricate: bears and bees and dragonflies, lizards, wolves and antelope. There was a new scent, too, like summertime; like sunshine on fresh foliage. The sounds of pursuit behind him had ceased. Now he could hear birdsong through a gap in the ceiling, and see the dapple of sunlight through leaves.

Feeling dazed, he pushed onwards, emerging into an open space, where the path plunged alongside a hawthorn hedge into a sea of bluebells. The scent of the flowers was dizzying, and Tom was suddenly aware that he'd gone much too long without sleep. To simply lie down among the bluebells now seemed to him the sanest thought he'd had in the past twenty-four hours. They would be soft, he knew, like a woven rug in every shade of blue, and their fragrance would be like a coverlet made with the discarded feathers of the bluebird of happiness. And were they *singing*? He thought they were – a song he seemed to recognise:

> O'er grassy bank True Thomas lay,
> Rockabay, rockabay
> And he beheld a lady gay,
> Rockabay, rockabay
> She was the Witch Queen of the Fae,
> Rockabay, rockabay
> From o'er the sea to Norroway,
> Rockabay, rockabay—

Tom could think of nothing more wonderful than to obey the call of the bluebells. But just as he was about to lie down, his hand crept into his pocket, where the flower seller's gift still lay hidden, its petals disintegrating at his touch, but its scent still potent enough to combat the song. Tom shook his head to clear it, and, remembering why he had fled, stood up and moved down the grassy path towards what looked like a little stream, leaving the bluebells behind him.

Where on earth was this, anyway? He remembered Spider mentioning dead spaces, and London Beyond, and some kind of court, but this was neither a dead space, nor any version of London he knew. For a start, it was *summer* here: a summer effervescent with life. Bees hummed in the hawthorn hedge; neon-green dragonflies skimmed the little stream ahead, which was spanned by a stone bridge, Tom could see its perfect arch reflected in the water. There were carvings here, too, of creatures he did not recognise. And on the other side stood a girl – no, not a girl, a *woman* – of such astonishing beauty and *shine* that for a moment even Vanessa was eclipsed in memory.

Behind her stood two figures, wearing masks of terrifying aspect: one was eyeless, the other had eight eyes, like a spider. Looking at the eyeless one, Tom realised that its eyes were in the tips of its long fingers, which beckoned to him gracefully.

'True Thomas,' said the woman. 'At last.'

'Do you know me?' Tom said. He was starting to get used to being recognised by people he didn't know.

'Of course I do.' The woman smiled. Tom saw that she was wearing a green velvet coat, with tiny bells sewn into the hem and lining. The bells made a silvery sound as she moved, a sound that was strangely distracting. 'Everyone here knows True Thomas,' she said, and the tiny bells whispered and shone. 'I am Queen Orfeia, and these are my servants, Cobweb and Peronelle.'

The two masked figures – but *were* they masks? – bowed and simpered behind her.

'Come. Join me, True Thomas,' the lady went on, and beckoned to him to cross the bridge. 'You'll be safe in my realm, I swear. You'll forget all your trouble, all your harm. Walk with me, and you will dine on the fruits of Atlantis and the flowers of Fiddler's Green, and drink the wines of Tír Na nÓg...'

Once more, Tom remembered how hungry he was. But, thinking of Vanessa, he paused and once again put his hand in his pocket. The withered flower was still there, and although repeated handling had worn it almost to nothing, its fragrance, like a dream, still lingered. *A flower that blooms only once*, he thought. *You'd dare put a price on true love?*

He shook his head. 'I have to go.'

'Go where?' said Queen Orfeia. 'There are only two roads

for you to take. One leads to our Kingdom. The other leads to certain death.'

'How can you know that?' Tom said.

She smiled. 'Death and I are old friends. There's Death in your future, True Thomas. I see him clear as I see you.'

In spite of the warmth of the bright summer day, Tom felt a shiver. The storybook phrase, *certain death* – like *true love* – did not seem clichéd or worn out here. There was something compelling about them, something that spoke of fairy tales passed through generations on the smoke of a thousand campfires, with nothing but words between them and the dark.

'You folk burn so bright,' said Queen Orfeia. 'So bright, and yet so brief a flame. Come with me, True Thomas, and that flame need never stop burning. Death has no power in my realm, and neither has Grief, nor Memory. In my realm, there is only Joy, and Sweetness, everlasting.'

Tom listened to her words, transfixed. A future without death? A world where sorrow had no purchase? He'd heard of such places, just as he'd heard of Atlantis and Tír Na nÓg, without believing them to be true. But now he felt as if he were on the edge of a marvellous discovery; a world in which monsters and mages were real, and fairy queens traded in memories.

Memories.

The thought was like a cold shower, breaking the spell. *I've been here before*, said Tom to himself. *At the Moonlight Market, where memories are currency. This is just another version of it. My memories for illusions. My future for a dream.* Putting a hand in his pocket, he remembered the Moonlight Market; the calls of the different vendors, the sounds of its seduction. *Enter at your own risk.* He'd read the warning signs, and yet he'd entered without a thought, giving away his memories for the price of a roll of negatives.

And now, here he was, by another bridge, about to do the same thing. To accept another bait and switch, a glamour to rob him of his memory. How many times had that happened? How many times had he lost his way? The thought of Vanessa – her *shine* – held him back. But the Queen's beauty spoke to him – a beauty born of something that transcended shape, or size, or age – commanding him to follow her, or die in pursuit of Vanessa.

'Well?' she said. 'Which is it to be? The rest of your life without her, or true love and certain death?'

Tom looked at her. The choice – *the rest of your life without her, or true love and certain death* – was mystic in its simplicity. Once more, he seemed to catch the scent of the withered flower in his pocket – a compound of jasmine and burning sage. An image, unexpected and startling in its clarity, suddenly flashed across his mind: a strange girl on a moonlit bridge, her bright eyes pinned with golden fire.

He answered in the flower seller's words: 'You'd dare put a price on true love?'

'There's always a price,' replied the Queen.

'I'd do anything,' said Tom, 'just to see her again.'

The Queen shrugged. At her side, Cobweb – or was it Peronelle? – waved their sea anemone fingers. 'A moth in love with a candle flame,' she said. 'Good luck, True Thomas. If you come this way again, remember – you have my favour. Use it, if ever you want to lose your way back to my Kingdom.' In a moment, she had turned and, in a jingle of bells, was gone.

Tom turned to go, and as he did, he noticed something on the ground. A single, tiny silver bell, no larger than a cherry stone, lay on the path by the little bridge. It must have come from her coat, Tom thought. He put it in his pocket, along with the faded flower. *A token, or a talisman? A keepsake, or a reproach?*

Then he followed the path through the glade of bluebells, and back through the tunnels of World Below, to the Midnight Folk, and dead space, and certain death – or true love, whichever came first. A moth, in pursuit of a candle.

Part 6

—

A Stitch in Time

I

And so the Moth girl and the boy continued to meet at the Market. Every time they met anew, the boy promised to remember her. But the Market was filled with wonders, and every time he attempted to capture some of them on film, he paid the price by forfeiting his memories.

The girl of the Moth Folk told herself it was probably for the best. The love of the Sightless Folk was a fleeting thing, their promises like fireflies. She told herself that it was good she had learnt this lesson early, and congratulated herself for her calm good sense in the face of the boy's inconstancy. And yet, she thought, there was still so much to learn from the situation. The boy would never remember her, but she would always remember him; *which meant she could tell him anything, knowing that her confidences would never be betrayed. And so the Moth girl told the boy the story of her people, and of her secret loneliness, and of her strange fascination with love. Together, they would explore the seductions of the Market: the entertainments, the acrobats, the fire spinners, the soothsayers. And every time, the boy would swear that he would never forget her; and every time, he forgot her as soon as he stepped off Old London Bridge.*

Meanwhile, the Spider Mage spun his web, watching the couple in secret. He had good reason to care for the boy, who had not yet shown his colours, but the Moth girl was a mystery. Could she perhaps be the one? Could she hold the future of their people in her hands? He watched as, over and over again, the couple met on Old London

Bridge, and the boy was stripped of his memories for the sake of his photographs. Many of these photographs were of the girl herself – but the film never survived the crossing between the worlds, and the boy returned with an empty heart, and no memory of why he felt so lost and lonely in the world.

And so, as he grew, seeking magic and love and always losing their substance, the young man began to believe in his heart that he would never know them. Instead, he turned to a magic that came from celluloid and chemicals. Photography became his love, his entry into the magical world, and, through it, he searched for what he had lost without knowing that it was barely a hand's breadth away.

Meanwhile, the Spider Mage observed the young man from afar. He had seen so many hatchlings come and go that he feared to hope – and yet, this one seemed different. Perhaps the Moonlight Market had left some trace in his mind; a memory, not of magic itself, but of what it made him feel. The girl, too, was intriguing; different to the rest of her tribe, seeking the forbidden in the face of all their teachings. However, he knew that until the boy reached his coming of age, he would be in danger: both from the Daylight Folk, who would seek to consume him before he showed his colours, and from the Midnight Folk, who feared his corruption by the enemy. And so the Spider Mage did what he could to keep the young man safe, and hoped that – this time – Love would find a way to reach him...

2

When Tom was still in his early twenties, he had become fascinated by the idea that living things had their own energy. He had discovered, almost by accident, that by using a long exposure, and photographing a flower with a 365nm LED light, passed through a filter to transmit only UV and infrared light, he could capture colours that could not be seen by the naked eye. The result was disturbing and beautiful, and had led in a roundabout way to Tom's current employment.

Mr Burnet had seen some examples of Tom's work in a gallery – his close-ups of flowers, gleaming darkly with secret light – and had offered him a job, including the use of his darkroom and unlimited supplies, on condition that Mr Burnet was kept aware of Tom's work, and given the opportunity to buy it, if he so desired.

Mr Burnet had bought a number of Tom's flower pictures, before Tom had tired of the process and moved on to other things. But now, as he entered the tunnel that led back into the lair of the Midnight Folk, he found that he could see blooms of luminescence, stark against the sooty stone, so like those LED images he had once found so exciting.

Why had he not seen them before? Tom had no idea how he could have missed them. But he was certain that the marks were somehow linked to the Midnight Folk, as if they had imprinted some of their dark energy against the walls. And now he could hear raised voices from along the passageway, and feel the charge in the air as he approached.

'Then where *is* it?' It was a woman's voice; scornful, coolly commanding. 'You say it was here, but it wouldn't be the first time you've reneged on a promise.'

'It isn't my fault he ran away. I *warned* you not to scare him off—'

The woman laughed. '*This* is your prince? A boy who runs the moment he sees something unexpected?'

Tom realised, with a sinking heart, that they were talking about him. *This is your prince.* He wondered if Spider believed that. And the woman was right, he thought. A *real* prince would not have run away. He felt in his pocket for his flower, but found instead the tiny bell that had fallen from the Queen's robe. It made a sound as he touched it; a tiny sound that nevertheless seemed to echo in his mind.

True love, sang the bell. *True love, and certain death.*

For a moment, Tom hesitated. His last encounter with the Midnight Folk had been less than encouraging. And yet... the Queen had called him *True Thomas*. She had given him her favour. She had promised him true love—

And certain death. Remember that.

In his pocket, the silver bell made its tiny chime. It spoke in the voice of every fairy tale, every story he longed to believe. *True Thomas*, sang the bell. *True Thomas, now stand and be true.*

In the shadows, Tom smiled to himself. *True love, and certain death.* It sounded like a fair exchange. If he could win Vanessa, he thought, then nothing the Midnight Folk could do would take away his happiness—

And with that, he stepped out from the darkness of the tunnel mouth to find himself in a kind of cave; the air was warm with sandalwood, and nutmeg, and allspice, and cardamom, and the Moths were all around him.

3

For a moment, Tom was breathless with the beauty of the Midnight Folk. In the semi-darkness, their wings shone with a faint luminescence and their skin gleamed with unearthly tattoos, like something seen under black light. Their hair was braided with feathers and rags, and all of them seemed to be covered with a powdery dust that twinkled and shone against their skin, setting the shadows darkly aflame. And all around them lay a pattern of those vivid tracks, as if the luminescence could be transferred to their surroundings by touch; each set of prints a different shade in troubled, alien colours.

Instinctively, he looked for Charissa's colours in the crowd. But she was nowhere to be seen. Instead, he was surrounded by the dangerous shine of the enemy. He saw them only in slices of light against the velvet darkness. The tip of a wing; the gleam of an eye; the mystic spiral of a tattoo that seemed to move across the skin. Then the shadows shifted, and the Moths were only people again, their wings hidden under long, shabby coats; their pale faces pinched with hardship. Tom recognised the two he'd seen with Charissa that night, the night they'd attacked Vanessa. The tall, strong-featured woman; the giant, Atlas; the rest of the gang, all now watching him warily. The woman was holding a long blade, its bright edge singing with sharpness.

'Stand down, Cinnabar,' Spider said. 'This is my friend, Tom Argent.'

The woman raised an eyebrow. She looked vaguely Icelandic to Tom, as did the giant at her side. Both were powerfully built, with pale faces, long hair and those spiral tattoos that a few moments ago had gleamed, but now showed black against their skin.

'Tom, meet Cinnabar,' Spider went on. 'And this is her brother, Atlas.'

'We've already met,' said Tom.

'Oh, that's good,' said Spider.

Atlas growled. 'Not really,' he said. 'He was with Vanessa.'

Tom's heart gave a tiny lurch at the thought of Vanessa. Here, in this place of shadows, the thought of her was brighter, more poignant than ever, though the details of her features were totally gone from his memory. In his pocket, he touched the flower that seemed to rekindle his memories, but it gave him nothing, save the scent of smoke and spices, and a glimpse of the freckles across Charissa's face and the gleam of her eyes in the firelight.

'You can't blame the boy. He was moonstruck.' Spider's voice was reproachful. 'Vanessa had him in her thrall. He was lucky to escape.'

Atlas gave a rich laugh. '*You* should know all about that, Spinnerman. What were you doing? You reek of them. I can smell their glamours on you. What did you give them in return for your life this time?'

Tom banished the useless memories. 'Nothing. I helped him escape,' he said.

'*You* helped him escape the Daylight Folk? How?' demanded Cinnabar.

'It was easy,' said Tom, trying not to sound too pleased with himself. 'Brimstone owed me a debt, so we just walked out together.'

Cinnabar's eyes widened. At her side, one of the other Midnight Folk gave a crow of laughter.

Cinnabar quelled him with a glance. 'Shut up, Diamondback.'

The person she had called Diamondback grinned. A slim, red-haired individual with a sharp and humorous face, he looked both clever and dangerous. 'Brimstone acknowledged a *debt*?' he said. 'How about that, girls and boys? And to a chrysalis, of all people. It just gets better and better.'

Cinnabar looked at Tom. 'Is that true?'

'True as Tribulation,' said Spider.

Diamondback laughed again. In the gloom of the tunnels, the sound was curiously disturbing. But Cinnabar looked reluctantly impressed. She turned to someone behind her and said: 'All right. Luna, tell me his story.'

The group of Midnight Folk parted to allow a young woman to step forward. Luna was tall, and slim, with long, pale, cobwebby hair and an oval face devoid of any expression. She alone had no tattoos, and her bare feet were totally silent on the darkly gleaming stone.

She stepped up to Tom and raised her hands to his face. Her fingers, too, were long and pale, the palms dusted with something that looked like chalk. Her eyes were blank and colourless, and Tom realised that Luna was blind.

'A common chrysalis,' she said, in a voice as colourless as the rest of her. 'Genus, Argent. Common as dirt. Already tainted by their glamours. Already in love with the Daylight Folk. No need to wait for him to show his colours. He's already compromised.'

'That's hardly fair,' said Spider. 'He's clean. She never tapped a drop of his life. Nor did any of the others. I'll set my warrant on it.'

'Doesn't matter,' Cinnabar said. 'This isn't what you promised us.'

'What do you mean? What promise?' said Tom. Turning to Spider, he saw the man shrug. 'You *meant* to bring me here?' he questioned. 'You meant us to come here all along?'

But Spider was talking to Cinnabar. 'We had a deal. The chrysalis for my evercoat.'

'That bloody coat again!' said Tom.

'Sorry,' said Spider. 'I'm fond of it.' Then, addressing Cinnabar: 'I brought you the chrysalis, just as you asked. It isn't my fault if he's been compromised. Who knows, you might still be able to get him to co-operate. He's not as stupid as he looks. He might end up being useful to you. Now, please – give me my evercoat.'

Cinnabar shrugged. 'The coat stays with us until you fulfil your promise to me.'

'No coat,' said Spider, 'no chrysalis.'

Tom was puzzled. 'But I thought you said *Charissa* was going to get your overcoat.'

Spider gave him a warning look. But it was too late. Cinnabar turned to face him, her dark eyes shining like a blade.

'Charissa?' she repeated. 'What do you mean?' At Spider's expression, she nodded. 'I see. You made a deal with her, too. You thought to cheat me of my prey. Playing your games again, Spinner? Just what did you promise her?'

'Er, what?' said Tom, who wasn't keen on being referred to as 'prey'.

'I had to do it,' Spider said. 'I owed the boy a favour.'

'And now he knows where to find us,' said Cinnabar in a quiet voice. 'He knows where to find us, thanks to you. Because *you* owed him a favour.'

Spider said nothing, but Tom thought he looked uneasy.

Diamondback gave an evil grin. 'Oh, my. This gets better and better.' He looked at Spider and bared his teeth. 'So *that's* why you tried to renege on our deal. Because of a debt to a chrysalis.'

He grinned at Tom. 'Good luck with that. Spinner isn't what you'd call trustworthy when it comes to paying his debts.'

Once more, Spider reached for a strand of thread from the little sewing kit pinned to the lapel of his waistcoat. 'You're right, of course,' he said quietly. 'I haven't lived as long as I have by granting favours, or paying debts. Ah, well—' He shrugged, and cast a sideways glance at Tom. 'No hard feelings, Tom,' he said. 'See you in another life.'

And then, once more, he pulled the piece of thread sharply towards him. A momentary flash of light, like something on the retina, then Spider was gone, leaving Tom alone with the Midnight Folk, under the arches of Battlebridge.

4

For a moment, Tom Argent looked around at the faces of the Midnight Folk, feeling more afraid and alone than he had ever felt before. Cinnabar stood watching him, her people standing guard behind her. Now Spider was gone, they looked even more dangerous, the knives in their hands gleaming balefully, their tattoos once more beginning to shine with subtle phosphorescence.

'Well, I guess I'd better go, then,' he said in a high and cheery voice that, even to his own ears, sounded less than convincing.

'*I guess I'd better go, then*,' repeated Diamondback mockingly. His intonation was so good that for a moment Tom thought he'd heard an echo.

Cinnabar smiled. He saw that her teeth had been drilled to take a row of diamond studs that shone like tiny LEDs. Once more, he remembered those flower pictures, taken through filtered reality. Those once-familiar daisies and ferns, roses and lilies and love-in-a-mist, had the same ominous beauty when stripped of the light we see.

'I'm afraid that isn't possible,' she said, with something like regret. 'You're already in love with Vanessa. That means you can't be of use to us. You could be a spy.'

'I'm not,' said Tom.

'But you *are* in love.'

He nodded.

'Sorry,' Cinnabar said.

Tom began to back away. Suddenly, the possibility of *certain death* sounded much less abstract than it had before. He tried for another angle. 'You keep calling me a *chrysalis*,' he said. 'So if I'm one of you, then—'

'You're not one of us,' said Cinnabar.

'But Spider said—'

'Spider talks too much,' said Atlas, his big face impassive. 'And that means now you *know* too much. It's a pity, but it's the way it is. Can't have you talking all over the place.'

'I won't,' said Tom, backing off a little further.

'No, you won't,' said Diamondback, with a grin that boded no good.

Atlas took a step forward. In spite of his enormous size, his movements were eerily quiet. 'It's really kinder this way,' he said. 'Better to end it all now, painlessly and easily, while you're still a chrysalis.'

'That's really not how I see it,' said Tom, taking another step backwards and finding a blank brick wall at his back.

'It's OK. It'll be over soon,' said Atlas, moving closer.

Tom looked wildly at Cinnabar. 'Please...'

Cinnabar shrugged. 'You had your chance. Brimstone owed you a favour,' she said. 'You could have ended this war there and then. You blew it. End of story.'

'But I didn't know!' said Tom.

'Too bad.'

Tom felt his strength begin to drain into the cold, damp wall at his back. There was nowhere left to go. He was surrounded by Midnight Folk. Atlas came a step closer, and now Tom could smell the scent of him, a compound of something like old books, patchouli and engine oil that he found both distracting and – strangely – pleasant.

Death smells of the seventies, thought Tom, and gave a cry of laughter.

'Soon be over,' said Atlas, with a patience that was almost kind.

'What about my last words?' said Tom.

'Be my guest,' said Atlas. Now his tattoos were ablaze with that uncanny witchlight. The others, too, were coming alive: Cinnabar's geometric sleeve; Diamondback's scatter of coloured stars. Luna's face was calm and sweet; a promise of true love, and certain death.

Tom felt his head begin to spin; his palms were damp and cold with sweat. *I'm going to die down here*, he thought, *without ever taking another picture*. The thought of his camera steadied him. Now he put his hands on it, feeling strangely disconnected. A tiny, desperate germ of a plan had begun to form itself in his mind.

'How could I have ended the war?' he asked. 'And how was I supposed to know that a favour from Brimstone could do that?'

'He's playing for time,' said Cinnabar.

'They call me the Collector,' said Tom desperately. 'I like to collect things. I want to know. What harm could it do?'

Cinnabar gave a long sigh. 'All right. Whatever. Brimstone is the leader of the Daylight Folk. What he says goes for them all. You could have ordered him to give himself up. To deliver himself to us. You could even have learnt his name, to bind him to you for ever.'

'But I know his name. It's Brimstone,' said Tom.

'That's only his *daylight* name. You could have asked for his true name: his *midnight* name. *A named thing is a tamed thing*, as my people used to say. You could have made him do anything. Anything you wanted.' She spoke very quietly, though Tom could hear the thread of anger in her voice.

141

'I didn't know. I'm sorry,' he said.

Diamondback laughed. 'Envious, Cin?'

Cinnabar's face hardened still more, a thing Tom would not have thought possible. 'Enough,' she said. 'Atlas, make it quick.'

And as Atlas lunged forward, Tom Argent raised his camera, levelled it at the Midnight Folk and fired the flashgun into the giant's face.

Boom!

He'd expected to cause a distraction. A moment of uncertainty, in which he might have had a chance to make a run for it. As it happened, there was a flash of light so intense that even Tom was temporarily blinded. For a moment, he was dazed, buffeted by shadows. A hand caught hold of his, and a very familiar voice hissed at him from the turbulence.

This pays my debt, Prince Argent, it said, and something was pressed into the palm of his hand. It felt like a little cardboard square with a skein of thread wrapped around it.

Use it wisely, Spider went on. *There isn't any more.* Then Tom felt a hard push in the small of his back and he fell into the darkness like a stone into a well, and for a time was lost to himself, lost between the cracks in the worlds.

Imagine a stone falling down a well.

Imagine a shimmer of bluebells.

Imagine the eyes of a girl, pinned with fire, on a bridge in London Before, her face reflecting something more than just the firelight.

Who are you? Tom asked himself. *Why is your face so clear in my mind? And why am I so drawn to you, when my heart is kept elsewhere?*

5

When his eyes adjusted again, Tom Argent was in daylight. The Midnight Folk, the tunnels, were gone. He was back above ground, on a street he did not recognise. The light was dim and wintry, and there was a heavy fog. This must be an old part of London, he thought: the street was cobbled, the buildings black with soot. Even the air smelt different, somehow: of woodsmoke, and sulphur, and horses...

A carriage went by, kicking up a mixture of mud and manure from the open gutter. Tom stepped back instinctively – and bumped into a young woman wearing a brown silk dress and a hat with what seemed to be a whole stuffed bird on it.

It's a film set, thought Tom. Ripper Street, *or* Penny Dreadful, *or yet another BBC adaptation of* Hard Times *or* Oliver Twist.

The woman made a sound of annoyance. 'Sir! Take care!' Her accent was slightly odd; more clipped than Tom was used to hearing.

'I'm sorry,' he said, standing back. 'I was looking for the way out.'

'Way out?' said the woman. 'The river? Whatever your troubles, that's no way for a Christian to think. Have you been drinking?' She fixed him with a suspicious eye.

'No. Of course not.' He looked at his watch. 'It's only half past ten.'

The woman looked unconvinced. 'Very well. But if you need help, turn to the Church, and not to the gin, or the river.'

Tom nodded, thinking how real she looked, how at ease in her surroundings. Another carriage trundled past, throwing up a flag of mud. It all looked very authentic, especially as there were no cameras, no lights, no staff to cordon off the street.

He said: 'What are you filming? I mean, it looks terrific.'

The woman looked puzzled. 'What do you mean?'

'Filming,' said Tom. 'What show is this?'

'You *are* drunk,' said the woman sternly. 'Here. Take one of these.' She reached into her reticule and brought out a yellow paper. Tom took it automatically, then, as the woman went on her way, glanced at it. He saw a woodcut of a hatless man holding a bottle, flanked with the title, in capitals: TEMPERANCE.

It was a tract.

Tom was feeling uneasy. Everything about this place – the narrow street, the unfamiliar smell of the air, the smog, the carriages, the gutter filled with mud and manure – but, most of all, the total absence of cameras, dollies or film personnel – troubled him deeply. He made for the end of the alleyway, which surely led into a main street. There would be cars, pedestrians; the clever illusion of isolation would be broken.

But when he reached the end of the alley, Tom could only stare in shock. It was Piccadilly Circus, but not as it had been the last time he had seen it. Gone were the screens, the Coca-Cola sign, the traffic. Instead, there were carriages of all kinds, and people in hats; and flower sellers, and pie merchants, and a man in a yellow driving coat drinking from the small fountain under the statue of Eros.

It may have been this detail that finally convinced Tom of the truth. The rest might possibly be achieved – with money and clever set-building, anything was possible. Even a fountain in a place where there had been no fountain before – but for people to *drink* from that fountain was surely taking authenticity a step too far.

He took a step back into the alley. It stank, but there was less there to take in; perhaps there was even less to fear. He turned away from the scene, deliberately looking at the ground. Even that was wrong, he thought. No London street – not even during the shooting of a film – had been so deep in filth for years. And it was *filth*, not studio mud: filth formed of excrement of various kinds, mortared with rags, stones and rubble, and pushed to the sides of the alleyway to allow for passage. A dead rat in an advanced stage of decomposition completed the picture.

Netflix, eat your heart out, thought Tom.

He was starting to feel quite faint. Too little sleep, too little to eat, too many surprises – it all conspired to fog his mind and to make him feel that all would be well if only he could just lie down and sleep. Too much had happened over the past twenty-four hours. Maybe he was getting sick. Maybe he was delirious. He stuck his hands in his pockets and felt the hard little beadlike shape of the bell he had found in World Below, and caught the sudden scent of a flower that blooms once in a lifetime. There was something else there, too. Something like a scrap of card.

This pays my debt, Prince Argent, said Spider's voice in his memory.

Tom pulled out the piece of card, around which was wound a skein of thread of a curious silvery colour. And now he re-membered how Spider had pressed it into his hand in the dark, whispering: *Use it wisely.*

Tom thought of the way in which Spider had transported him into the tunnels under King's Cross. Was this another lifeline? Could Tom use it as Spider had, to find his way back home?

He might have tried it there and then, if just at that moment he had not seen a woman passing the alleyway. He only saw her for a moment, but it was enough to banish all thoughts of escape from his mind. The woman was dressed in sky-blue silk, and was holding a parasol – presumably against the soot that fell like black snow from the rooftops. Her hair was a rich, dark shade of red, bound up in a generous bun, secured beneath a sky-blue hat. For a second, Tom didn't recognise her, and yet in that moment every part of him was awake. His heart began to race, his skin to tingle all over. Because he *knew* who the woman was, in spite of the fact that her colouring was different, and that seemingly they were both now part of a long-vanished London.

He might have forgotten her features, but in his heart there was no doubt. The woman was Vanessa.

Part 7

London Before

I

The war between the two tribes lasted many hundreds of years. Much
of the time, the conflict was one-to-one, in secret, or covered by the
glamours that kept them hidden from the Folk. Sometimes, events
in the world outside gave one side or the other a chance to launch a
direct attack on one of the enemy's strongholds, but most of the time,
the war was waged at night, in the alleys and parks and deserted
Tube stations of the city, where the Moths had their domain, and
where the Butterflies hunted the Folk and tapped them of their nectar.

The Moths were more particular regarding the source of their
nourishment. They took nectar from the Butterflies, and from those
tainted by their influence. They could keep a prisoner helpless in their
dungeons, feeding from them as they chose, safe from interference.
And thus they remained, their camouflage allowing them to walk
unseen among the Sightless Folk, while the Butterflies used their
colours to attract their unsuspecting prey.

Meanwhile, the Moth King stayed aloof, even from his own kind,
watching the world through his glamorie-glass, sullen and unreach-
able. But the Butterfly Queen ruled the daylight hours, surrounded
by her courtiers, sipping nectar wherever she went and shining like
a fallen star. Thus the Moths and the Butterflies endured, and built
their fiefdoms among the leavings of the Folk, and took their pleasures
where they could, and made their plans for the future. Some of the
Moths even found love – for it was hard enough to live in the dark,
without a little warmth in their lives – but never for a Butterfly.

The Butterflies were incapable of feeling warmth of any kind, and the Moths had lost too many friends to succumb to the enemy's glamours. Similarly, the Butterflies knew the Moths to be without mercy, and hoped to die in battle rather than be captured. Thus it was that when Brimstone, the leader of the Butterflies, was taken by the Moths in a raid, his people mourned his death, and hoped for his sake that it had been quick. In fact, he was a prisoner in the secret lair of the Moths. Kept in darkness, and weakened, his quintessence might sustain the enemy for months – even years – before he died. It was the fate all the Daylight Folk feared: a grim humiliation.

The captive was kept bound, alone, in one of the enemy's oubliettes, his situation overseen personally by a captain of the Midnight Folk. Cinnabar was her name, and she was strong, and brave, and true. She believed that her Folk would return one day to the kingdom they had lost. She believed in the triumph of virtue, and in the rightness of their cause. Most of all, she believed in love: the love that crosses oceans, builds worlds, even sometimes raises the dead. It was the hope of her secret heart that one day she might know such love; but none of her people knew this, for she kept her dreams close, and told no one.

Meanwhile, Brimstone waited alone in the dark, and made his plans. His cell was a stone-lined pit, accessible only if a rope or ladder were lowered towards him. The only light he saw was when his captors came to check on him. Then, and only sometimes, could he see the fugitive gleam of the sun, reflected from the passageway or in the glint of weapons.

He had not spoken a single word to his captors. He did not even acknowledge them as they came to jeer, or gape, or to tap his quintessence – which was the nectar of the Daylight Folk – into great glass jars that glowed with subtle phosphorescence. Not a word did Brimstone speak, not to beg for his release, nor to ask for mercy.

150

Instead, he stayed scornful and aloof, and as his shine dwindled, his energy died. But his substance seemed to elude them.

Cinnabar watched all of this, and felt a treacherous stirring in her heart. It was not warmth, or even pity, but rather a kind of reluctant respect. She found herself watching the prisoner rather more often than was required. Brimstone ignored her, and she was surprised to find how very much this annoyed her. She spoke to him coldly, but with meticulous politeness. He continued to ignore her. She found this infuriating. She offered him food and lodgings in accordance with his rank. Still he ignored her, preferring the squalor of his oubliette to the shame of addressing her. And so time passed, until one day she looked into the pit to see a tiny fleck of sunlight bounce against the seeping wall. The prisoner was using a discarded fragment of broken glass to reflect the light from the opening. He closed his hand almost instantly around the piece of glass, but Cinnabar saw how he kept it safe, as if it contained a vanished world, and looked at her for the first time, as if in silent entreaty.

She knew she should have taken the glass. Such things were not allowed in the cells. The Daylight Folk took their sustenance at least in part from sunlight. To allow even a scrap of it to enter might be dangerous. And yet that day, she left the trapdoor to the oubliette half open, as if by accident, so that her prisoner might see the light of the sun and be comforted.

She told herself she was simply ensuring the man's survival. His quintessence was running low, and he would be no use to her Folk if he were allowed to die. And at the next scheduled collection, instead of sending one of her guards, she took his quintessence in person, and gathered it into the glass jar, and found herself enchanted by his sullen luminescence.

After that, she came to tap the prisoner's nectar every time. Silence is confessional. His silence seemed to want something of her. Gradually, she started to speak of what was going on outside, in her life, and her thoughts, and her feelings. And he seemed to speak to her with his eyes, and in the way he watched her, and at last she realised that Love was not always a creature of light, but was sometimes a demon of darkness.

For many weeks and months after that, Cinnabar kept her secret. She was a warrior of the Midnight Folk, and she knew that this sickness would end her. And yet she found it impossible to keep away from Brimstone. In the dark of the oubliette, he seemed to speak to her without words, and when she was with him, she believed that a Moth could love a Butterfly, and be loved by one in return, and she was almost happy.

This could not go on, she told herself. This folly put all of her people at risk. Brimstone could not love her, she knew. He was simply awaiting his chance to exploit her weakness. She should have kept him in the dark, in silence, and allowed him to die. She knew this now, just as she knew that there was only one solution: she had to end his life, before this creeping sickness ended hers.

And so she went down to the oubliette one night, when the Midnight Folk were abroad. She went alone, and in secret, and closed the trapdoor behind her. In the dark, she could just make out the prisoner: he shone with a fugitive brightness, as if in response to her presence. Steeling herself, she reached to take his life, but sensed no resistance. Instead, there was the sweetness of nectar offered freely, of sentiments exchanged without words – of love with no conditions. She fell to her knees, and saw him standing above her like a prism; and she understood that, instead of taking his nectar, she had given him her own, and with it, the power to take her life, and thereby end the age-old war.

But Brimstone did not do these things. Instead, he knelt beside Cinnabar and whispered a single word into her ear. And then he turned and spread his wings and flew out into the moonlit night.

No one knows what Brimstone whispered to Cinnabar. Some say it was his true name. Some say it was a dreadful curse. Some say that, in that moment, the two of them exchanged souls, so that Cinnabar became Brimstone, and Brimstone, Cinnabar. Of course, these were only stories. They made no difference to the war. Because for some folk, making war is easier than making love. And anyway, Butterflies have no souls.

2

'Vanessa!' Tom barely had time to call her name before she vanished into the crowds of Piccadilly Circus. He thrust Spider's token back into his pocket and set off after the woman, this time paying scant attention to the crowds of strollers, vendors and horse-drawn vehicles of all kinds.

The sky-blue figure was easy to spot; most of the pedestrians were, like the Temperance woman, sensibly dressed in black or brown. Not so different to his own version of London, then, except for the long skirts, bowler hats and buttoned boots that seemed to predominate.

He was in jeans and a T-shirt, with his camera around his neck, which earned him a couple of strange looks, but Tom was far too preoccupied in catching up with Vanessa to care if he fitted in. He dodged behind a passing cab, half slipped in the road mud, almost hit the wheel of a high-sided carriage, to the shrill annoyance of a driver with an almost incomprehensible accent, and veered onto Piccadilly just in time to see the sky-blue dress and its matching parasol vanish into an alleyway. Tom put on a burst of speed, and saw Vanessa at the end of the street, about to turn the corner.

He called her name and she seemed to pause, although she did not turn around. But that pause was enough for Tom to catch up with the sky-blue dress, and to clutch at one silken sleeve—

She pulled away. 'How *dare* you, sir!'

For a moment, Tom was unsure if it really *was* Vanessa. She looked so different, bland and cold, and she faced him without recognition. And yet her curious *shine* was undimmed, calling him to follow her.

'It's me,' he said. 'From the camera shop?'

'I don't know you,' Vanessa replied. 'Kindly take your hand off my arm.'

'But it's *me*,' repeated Tom. 'I saved your life. Remember? Back in the alleyway?'

The woman in the sky-blue dress gave him a look of open disgust. 'I do believe you're drunk,' she said. 'Unhand me at once, and stop following me, or I shall call for a constable.'

At that, she turned away, keeping the hem of her sky-blue dress carefully clear of the kerb, and Tom had only time to say, *'But Vanessa—'* when a small, fierce hand caught hold of his arm, and he heard a familiar voice in his ear, hissing:

'Shut up, you idiot. What in the name of all that's dark do you think you're doing?'

It was Charissa, her usual garb hidden beneath a man's overcoat that looked several sizes too big for her.

Tom stared at her. 'What are you doing here? And where *is* here, exactly?'

She gave him a look of impatience. 'This is London *Before*,' she said. 'Thanks to your good friend, Spider. So help me, if he's sent me here to babysit a *chrysalis*...'

Tom wanted to say a number of things: first, that Spider wasn't his friend; second, that he didn't need help; and third, to ask why Vanessa seemed not to have recognised him. Instead, he said, 'London *Before*?'

'A stitch in Time. One of Spinner's lines. He must have sent us both here.'

'But why?'

'Maybe he thought he owed you something.'

'Well,' said Tom, thinking of the voice he had heard in the darkness. 'He *did* say he'd discharged his debt. But what about Vanessa? She didn't seem to know me at all.'

'That's because you haven't met yet, dummy,' said Charissa. 'The Vanessa you saw is Vanessa *Before*, from a hundred years before you were born.'

'Well, what about you?' said Tom. '*You* know me. Why aren't *you* Charissa *Before*?'

'Because I wasn't *there* before,' she replied. 'Tom, Vanessa's *old*. Older than you can imagine. She doesn't look it because she's lived in the light for hundreds of years, feeding on what nectar she can. Nectar, stolen from people like you. In the Kingdom, she had power. Here, all she has is glamours and tricks. But that's enough to blind the Folk. That's why we call you the Sightless Folk.'

'You make her sound like a vampire,' said Tom. 'But you're wrong. She saved me. And Brimstone must have known she had *some* kind of feelings towards me, otherwise he wouldn't have said that I could never see her again—'

Charissa laughed. 'You'll believe anything, won't you? Next you'll be telling me you're the one who can break the curse and unite us again.'

'But if I'm Prince Argent—'

'Princes are like bread rolls,' said Charissa. 'Stale before the day's over. And Spider should know better than to fill your head with stories.'

'I thought he was your friend,' said Tom.

Charissa shrugged. 'I don't have friends. I owed him a favour, that's all. Keeping you alive pays my debt. So let's get this done as soon as we can. Because, frankly, this century sucks, and I can't wait to get back home.'

'*Home*,' said Tom, sliding a hand into his pocket. Spider's token was still there, along with the bell and the flower. He could feel it: a square of card with a single skein of thread wrapped three times around it. *Use it wisely*, Spider had said. It must be a means of escape, Tom thought, like the one he had used in the darkroom. But he had no intention of using it. Meeting Vanessa the moment he'd arrived – that had to mean something, didn't it? Had he been given a second chance to make her fall in love with him? Was it even possible that he was here to *save* her?

He pushed Spider's token deeper into his pocket.

'You think there's a way to get back?' he asked.

'There's always a way,' said Charissa. 'Spider always has a way. But for now, if you're going to survive here, we need to get you somewhere safe. I know a place. Do you trust me?'

Tom thought about that. 'Er – not really.'

'Good,' said Charissa. 'You're learning. Now follow me – and *hurry*.'

3

Tom followed Charissa through the cobbled streets towards King's Cross. Or at least it *looked* like King's Cross, but not as he had ever seen it. Gone were the gracious walkways; the streets lined with cafés and restaurants. Gone were the restaurants, the parks, the little canals of Battlebridge. The roads were mostly cobbled, though a few were simply dirt tracks, and the whole area was crowded with people: passers-by and travellers, and ladies with silk parasols, and pie vendors and flower girls, and constables in tall hats, and street urchins, and pickpockets, and hackney carriage drivers, and hawkers and thieves.

He felt an overwhelming urge to confirm its reality. Lifting his camera, he had already taken several rapid shots before Charissa intervened.

'What are you doing?' she hissed at him. 'Do you *want* to attract attention?'

'I'm sorry,' said Tom. 'I wanted to be sure.'

'Put that away and follow me,' she said. 'The Daylight Folk may not recognise *you*, but they'll know a stitch in Time when they see one. And if they do, they'll follow the thread, and I'll be as dead as you'll soon be.'

Reluctantly, Tom put away his camera.

'You and your thrice-damned photographs,' said Charissa grimly. 'You'd think that after all this time, you might have remembered *somethi*—' She bit off the end of the word, looking fierce. 'Never mind. Just follow me. We're nearly there. And for gods' sakes, no more photographs!'

And so Tom followed Charissa through the streets of London Before, feeling at the same time fearful and euphoric. In spite of his brush with danger, he felt more alive than he'd ever been, as if until now he had spent his life asleep. His escape from the Midnight Folk, his encounter with Queen Orfeia, the stitch in Time to London Before – all of it might *sound* like a dream, but Tom no longer even felt the slightest doubt that this fairy tale was real. And if all this wasn't enough to confirm his present reality, there was that glimpse of Vanessa, which he meant to pursue once more as soon as his legs had ceased to feel as if they belonged to someone who wouldn't be born for over a century.

He became aware that Charissa had stopped in front of a row of brick buildings. 'Here we are,' she said. 'Welcome home.'

Tom saw that they were standing beside a building that looked vaguely familiar. The windows and door were different, and the brickwork was blackened with smoke and soot, yet Tom recognised his shop, and noticed a hand-painted sign that read:

IMAGO BURNET: PHOTOGRAPHER

Imago Burnet. Tom stared at the sign. It couldn't be a coincidence. Could this be his employer's grandfather – or his great-grandfather?

'Quickly,' said Charissa, pushing open the green-painted door. 'Don't just stand there gawping!'

A little bell rang at the back of the shop, and Tom followed the girl inside. The shop, already small, was crowded with equipment. The walls were covered with picture frames. A gas lamp stuttered overhead, giving the interior a drowned, undersea glow. There was a scent of pipe smoke, and books, and dust, and leather, and chemicals.

For a moment, Tom stared, fascinated, at the display of paraphernalia: the wreaths, the stands, the advertisements. And the photographs that crowded the walls; all of them of young people. Children, adolescents, girls with lilies in their hair; young men with soulful faces, all apparently asleep: some in bed, or lounging in chairs, surrounded by floral arrangements.

'What kind of photographer's *is* this?' he said.

Behind him came a familiar voice: 'The only kind that matters, Tom. The kind that stops Time.'

4

Tom turned towards the doorway which led to the back of the shop and saw a figure in a drab brown coat and a hat with a brim that covered his eyes. Not his Victorian ancestor, but the man himself: tall, pale, with eyes of a curious golden-grey, like gilding on the spine of a book that has been faded by the sun.

'Mr Burnet!'

The tall man smiled. 'Tom Argent. You're a long way from home, boy. Sit down and have a cup of tea.' There was a stove by the counter, on which a fat black kettle sat. Mr Burnet indicated a couple of leather armchairs and Tom sat, feeling slightly dazed.

Now he knew why Mr Burnet had always been nocturnal; why he'd never seen him without his overcoat and hat. 'You're one of them. The Midnight Folk. But how...?'

'Not quite,' said Mr Burnet, setting three cups on the counter-top. 'But yes, I am a part of the tale in which you have become entangled.'

'How can you remember me,' said Tom, 'if you belong to London *Before*?'

'Time,' said Mr Burnet, 'is a complicated thing. Part dream, part invention, built from the fragments of the past. We cling to it like lost children. We trust it, even when we should not. We look back, when we ought to look forward.' The kettle started to whistle, and Mr Burnet removed it from the fire, holding it with a padded glove. 'But, Tom, I *have* been here a very long time, and I've known *you* longer than you remember.'

'Vanessa didn't recognise me,' Tom said. 'She thought I was drunk.'

'Vanessa was never very wise,' said Mr Burnet, pouring hot water into the pot, then adding three spoonfuls of leaf tea. 'And one for the pot,' he continued and smiled, adding another spoonful. Turning to Charissa, he said, 'My dear, I rather thought *you* were supposed to stop young Tom from getting involved in all this.'

Charissa shrugged. 'Too late for that. Luna says he's compromised. Cinnabar thinks he's dangerous. He doesn't have his colours yet, and he's *crazy* in love with Vanessa. So.'

Mr Burnet gave a sigh. 'You're sure?'

'Sure as ships and starlight.'

Mr Burnet sighed again, and poured the tea. 'Then all we can do is protect him. Let him live out his life in this place. Keep him away from the Daylight Folk, and especially from Vanessa. That way, maybe—'

Tom put down his cup. 'Don't I get to decide for myself?'

'Decide what?'

'What to do with my life! Who to be with! Who to *love*—'

Charissa made an explosive sound.

Mr Burnet put a hand on her arm. 'With that approach,' he said, 'your life is likely to be brief.'

'You don't understand,' said Tom fiercely. 'All of this has to mean something. My memories. Spider. *Vanessa*—'

'Oh yes, it means something,' said Charissa tartly. 'It means you're an idiot with no attention span, always in pursuit of the nearest shiny thing.'

Tom shook his head. 'This is fate,' he said. 'What were the chances of me seeing Vanessa the minute I arrived in London

Before? Maybe I was *meant* to. Maybe Spider sent me here to give me another chance with her? And even if he didn't, I'd rather die than never see her again.'

Mr Burnet looked calmly at Tom. 'Your persistence is touching. But Vanessa, most of all of her folk, is wholly incapable of love. All she can do is shine for you, and draw you in, and consume you. Then, when she has drained you of every drop of nectar, she will move on to another man – or woman, she has no prejudice – until they, too, have been consumed.'

Tom shook his head. 'You don't know her.'

'Oh, please,' said Charissa fiercely. 'Tell me, *Prince Argent*, what do you think happened to all the others, eh? The other potentials, the other cocoons, the other young people who fell for her?' She made a furious gesture at the photographs on the walls. Hundreds of them, large and small; all young people. Young men reclining, eyes closed, on lounge chairs and on daybeds; young women, all dressed in white, sleeping among flowers.

Memorial photographs, Tom thought. A trend that had lost popularity as cameras grew cheaper. But in the Victorian era, they had been immensely popular. In many cases, these portraits of the dying – or recently dead – had been the only photographs of the subject in question. Artfully posed, frequently alongside their living siblings, draped in white, adorned with flowers, on stands, or under canopies, displayed like butterflies and moths under glass.

'You see,' said Mr Burnet with a smile, 'you're not the only collector here.'

'These were all like me?' Tom said. 'Potentials?'

'*Prey*,' said Mr Burnet. 'That's all they were to Vanessa.' He took a gentle sip of his tea. 'Tom, you have to understand that Vanessa and I have been playing this game for many, many centuries. But it is a game that cannot be won. And in the end, it will cost you your life.'

Tom shrugged. 'You can say what you like. I'm still going to look for her.'

Mr Burnet gave a long sigh. 'Very well,' he said. 'At least let me lend you some camouflage.'

And, putting down his teacup, he handed Tom his hat and overcoat. Without them, he looked different: taller, more alert somehow: his long grey hair pulled back from his face with a piece of black ribbon. The coat was warm and heavy, and smelt of cough sweets, tobacco and ambergris.

'You won't try to stop me?' Tom said, transferring his possessions to one of the coat's large pockets.

'No, Tom Argent. Go to her. Tell her you love her. Worship her. That will make her happy. And if she looks at you, even once, you'll be the luckiest man in the world – at least, until she looks away.' He smiled, but Tom thought his eyes were sad.

'Thank you,' said Tom. 'I owe you a debt.'

'We need not speak of debts,' said Mr Burnet. 'This world is a dark and cruel place in which those of us who still can see must try to enlighten the ones who cannot. Go then, now you have made your choice, but know I will not come after you.'

'I'm not expecting you to,' said Tom. 'In fact, I forbid you to even try.'

Then, opening the shop door to the sound of a distant bell, he stepped out into the sooty streets and alleyways of London Before.

Part 8

—

Wings

I

Under the eye of the Spider Mage, the Moth girl and the boy of the Folk met many times on Old London Bridge. Winter and summer, each time they met, the boy would fall in love with the girl anew; and every time they met, he would trade his memories for photographs. The folk of the Market laughed at him and called him the Collector, but the Moth girl did not laugh. Instead, every time, she told herself that she had had a lucky escape. The Sightless Ones were selfish, she thought, as well as being stupid. But Spider still believed in him. Spider thought he was different. And so she continued to keep watch over the young man as he grew, looking for the colours that would one day mark his allegiance. So far, like all hatchlings, he had none; but one day he would declare himself for one side or the other, and on that day she would have to either greet him as a Moth, or end him as an enemy . . .

2

Once more, Tom was struck by the stench and noise of this version of London. Smoke, soot, horse manure, open sewers, foul water; all were layered with the scents of sweat and grime and perfume from the passers-by. Flakes of grey soot fell from a grey sky, and the sounds of the city – the horse-drawn cabs and carts, the calls of vendors and hawkers, the deafening scream and clash of the trains – were so much louder than those to which he was accustomed that Tom felt overwhelmed by it all; and yet he was not discouraged. Spider had given him a second chance with Vanessa, and this time, he wasn't going to let anything get in his way.

He had no idea where he was going. But as St Pancras Station had been the home of the Daylight Folk, he headed in that direction. As he did, he became aware of a figure in a long drab coat, following him at a distance. They kept to the shadows and made no sound, and no one else seemed to notice them, but maybe Tom was becoming attuned to the ways of the Midnight Folk, because he knew immediately who it was. He made a turn into Gray's Inn Road, and saw the figure change direction to follow him.

He slowed his pace a little. The gap between them closed until the figure in the overcoat was almost at his heels. Then, turning abruptly, Tom shot out a hand and grasped a pale wrist, tattooed with a delicate spiral pattern.

'Why are you following me?' he said.

Charissa glared at him from beneath her shaggy fringe. 'I'm trying to save you from yourself,' she said. 'The Daylight Folk are as dangerous here as they ever were in your day. Show yourself, and your sanctuary is gone like a spider's web in the wind.'

Tom shook his head. 'Go back to your own time, Charissa. I don't need you to save me.'

'Believe me, I would if I could,' she said. 'But Spider neglected to throw me a line. I can only assume the idiot sent me here to help you. So I'm stuck here for as long as you are, and whatever stupid risks you run put *me* in equal danger.'

'I don't see why,' said Tom. 'This is about Vanessa and me. You have nothing to do with it.'

'Have you even been listening?' said Charissa fiercely. 'I knew you were stupid, but seriously. Listen, and try to understand. You'll never get near Vanessa again. As soon as you show your colours, the Daylight Folk will hunt you down and you'll end up on Burnet's wall with the rest of his collection. As for me... Call me selfish, but I happen to value my life; besides which, I'll never get back to *my* London if I let them take you.'

'Couldn't Mr Burnet send you back?'

She laughed. '*Him*! You heard him. An empty cocoon. All he cares about nowadays are his toys and his trophies.'

Tom gave a shrug. 'I'm sorry,' he said. 'But I didn't ask for any of this. I don't want to be part of your war. What matters to me is Vanessa. I don't expect you to understand, but from the first moment I saw her, I knew she was the only one. I stupidly gave her up. But if this gives me a second chance—'

'It won't,' said Charissa impatiently. 'You never had a chance at all. She only cares about one thing: winning the war.'

'You're wrong,' said Tom. 'She's not like the others.'

'You think?' Charissa made a sound that was both rude and

despairing. 'Of *course* she's not like the others. She's by far the *worst* of them. Besides, she could be anywhere. You'll never find her.'

'But I bet *you* could,' Tom said. 'With the right motivation.' He reached into his jeans pocket, where Spider's token lay against the flower and the silver bell. A tiny sound came from the bell – *True love, and certain death* – and the flower released a memory that was almost as quickly forgotten. He pulled out the card and the piece of thread and thrust it at Charissa. 'Look. I'm not asking you to believe. I don't even need your protection. But help me get close to her, just for five minutes. Help me make my case with her – and in exchange I'll give you *this*.'

For a moment, Charissa stared at the piece of card in the palm of his hand. 'A lifeline,' she said in a low voice.

'Spider gave it to me,' said Tom.

Charissa looked at the token in awe. 'And you'd give that up – the chance to go home, to pick up the threads of your life again – for five minutes' conversation with someone who won't even *remember* you?'

'I don't expect you to understand,' said Tom. 'Just get me into a room with her. Then you can go back to your own time, or anywhere else you want to be.'

Charissa looked at the token with a complex expression of longing and hope. Then she nodded. 'OK,' she said. 'I'll do it. But you're making a mistake, Tom. You think you've seen Vanessa, but all you've seen is her glamour. That's why you can't remember her face for longer than a couple of days.'

'I'll remember her *this* time,' Tom said. He touched his overcoat pocket, where his camera rested, loaded with film. 'Just find Vanessa. I'll do the rest.' He smiled at Charissa's scowling face. 'Have a little faith,' he said. 'I'm the Collector.'

3

They followed Gray's Inn Road to High Holborn. Tom frowned at the juxtaposition of familiar and unfamiliar landmarks: the narrow alleyways, the shops, the inns and public houses. Charissa guided him through the streets, keeping to the alleys and passageways, avoiding Ludgate Circus with its crowds of hawkers, beggars, newsboys and labourers, and heading through the maze of slums that sprawled across the city.

'It's best to keep to the backstreets,' she said. 'In daylight, I can't see their signatures.'

'Signatures?' repeated Tom.

'They're like … a kind of trail, I guess. All our people have them.'

Tom thought back to London Beyond, and the way the Midnight Folk had appeared to cast luminous tracks in the darkness. 'I think I've seen them,' he said. 'In the tunnels, with Spider.'

Charissa looked surprised. 'You did? Most chrysalises don't.'

'Maybe I'm starting to hatch,' said Tom. 'Maybe I'll start to grow wings next.'

Charissa gave him a sharp look. 'You shouldn't joke about things like that. Really, Tom, sometimes you behave as if you think all this is a fairy story.'

'Sorry. Learning curve,' Tom said, and lapsed into a subdued silence. Charissa walked surprisingly fast given her diminutive size, and Tom found himself struggling to keep up with her. 'Where are we going?'

'Fleet Street,' said Charissa. 'The Midnight Folk have always liked to be aware of what's happening. Newspapers, printers and photographers are our natural territory. And that's where we'll find the Daylight Folk. That's where they come in search of prey.'

Prey. Tom shook his head. Even after what he'd experienced, he still found it hard to believe. Vanessa and her folk, predators?

'You don't believe me,' Charissa said, seeing his expression. 'You will. You'll see them at work. Then maybe you'll understand.' She led him down an alleyway he found he almost recognised to a sooty public house, with a familiar sign that proclaimed it: YE OLDE CHESHIRE CHEESE.

'I think I know this place,' said Tom. 'It's one of—' He hesitated. In his version of London, the Cheshire Cheese was a quaintly refurbished pub, crammed with dubious memorabilia and mostly frequented by steampunk fans, Dickens enthusiasts, and tourists. But here, in London *Before*, the place was as much a part of the city as the sooty walls or the cobbled street. The mud and refuse underfoot; the stink of cheap tobacco and beer; the sound of many voices. And standing outside the half-open door was a figure he recognised, wearing a brown silk dress and a hat with a whole stuffed bird in it; it was the Temperance woman who'd been distributing tracts when he'd arrived, the one he'd been talking to when he first saw Vanessa— He put a hand on Charissa's arm. 'I know her,' he said in a low voice. 'She was there when I—'

'Shh,' said Charissa sharply, pulling him into a doorway. '*Look*.'

Tom stepped back – the doorway was deep and narrow, and in the enclosed space, he could smell Charissa's scent, a hybrid of wool and tobacco smoke and chypre and patchouli and spices. Her hair, escaping from beneath the brim of her old felt hat,

tickled his chin, not unpleasantly. He turned away, uncomfort-
able, keeping to the shadows.

'What are we looking for?' he said.

Then he saw someone else leave the taproom; someone who
shone like a Roman candle in the gloom of the alleyway. Striking
in his velvet coat, face shielded by the brim of his hat, he looked
up and down the narrow street, then, seeing it empty, sauntered
in his high-heeled shoes to join the Temperance woman, and
smiled.

'I have an addiction,' he said. 'I think perhaps you can help
me.'

It was Pieris.

4

'Don't move,' whispered Charissa. 'Where there's one, there are always more.'

'But it's Pieris,' Tom said. He knew what that meant. Pieris was a predator – the Temperance woman was inches away from succumbing to his charm. He took a step out of the doorway.

'Don't.' Tom felt Charissa's fingers tighten on the sleeve of his coat. 'He won't notice you if you don't move. Remember, this is Pieris *Before*. He doesn't know you. He won't suspect.'

'But I know that woman. She helped me,' said Tom. 'He's going to—'

'Tap her nectar. Of course. Don't you know what they are yet?'

Pieris was still speaking to the woman. Her reply was indistinct, but his voice was clear enough. 'Yes, I'd like a tract. Anything for a moment more of your delightful company.'

Casually, Pieris allowed his hand to touch the woman's arm. Her face, which was in shadow, now seemed only a pale blur against the sooty stone.

'But shouldn't we do something?' said Tom.

Charissa shook her head. 'Too late.'

The *shine* around Pieris intensified, and now Tom finally understood what Charissa had meant by *colours*. This was nothing like the dark and dangerous light of the Midnight Folk. Pieris' *shine* seemed to come from the very heart of him; to burn like banked embers beneath his skin; to radiate against the walls.

Tom could feel its reflected glow like the memory of Christmas: a spectacle of fairy lights, and church candles, and fireworks.

The Temperance woman steadied herself against the wall of the alleyway. Pieris moved closer, smiling. Tom was aware of something intangible passing between them, something that lingered in the air in a luminous moment of clarity—

'She's in no danger,' Charissa said. 'He won't tap *all* her nectar. There'd be too many questions if people kept turning up dead in the street. She'll just feel dizzy for a while, maybe even go to sleep. Then she'll wake up with a headache, and maybe a ringing in her ears, and after a few days she'll have forgotten all about it.'

'Really?' said Tom. 'Because when I was in their penthouse—'

'You're different,' Charissa said.

'Special?'

She shrugged. 'Special enough for that, yes. How do you think the others died? The other potentials? The Midnight Folk?'

'The Midnight Folk would have killed me, too,' said Tom, remembering Atlas and Cinnabar.

'Nectar is nectar,' Charissa said. 'Why should the rest of us go without?'

Tom thought back to the night of his only date with Vanessa. He hadn't had the chance to ask *why* she was so afraid of the Midnight Folk, but he remembered her look of terror when she saw the first moth by the street lamp, and of course, she'd *told* him he'd saved her life.

'But *you're* not like them, are you?' he said.

Charissa gave a bitter smile. 'Not like them? Of course we're not. We don't shine like they do. We don't have their glamours, their charm. We don't live in the sunlight. We have to make do with what nectar we can.'

'And that means—?'

'Taking theirs, yes. Oh, for gods' sakes!' she said irritably, seeing his expression. 'This is a war. Did you think we played for points?'

Meanwhile, back in the alleyway, Pieris was embracing his prey. The woman in the brown silk dress was leaning drunkenly against the wall. A luminescence like the Northern Lights seemed to ripple and bloom in the air, almost as if it were coming from the woman herself.

'Oh,' said Charissa.

'What?' said Tom.

Charissa shrugged, but did not reply. The cloud of luminescence grew as Pieris moved even closer. The leaflets fluttered to the ground. The hat with the stuffed bird slipped sideways.

'What *is* that?' insisted Tom.

The strange light had become more intense. Pinpoints of brightness danced in the air, stuttering like fireflies. The Temperance woman slid to the ground, and Pieris bent over her, shining.

Tom hissed at Charissa: 'Is that supposed to happen?'

Charissa shrugged. 'It's Pieris. That bastard plays by his own rules. And besides, those rules are just for the Folk. A chrysalis is anyone's for the taking.'

'A *chrysalis*? She's a *chrysalis*?'

'Another one for Burnet's wall. They got to her early. It could have been worse. She could have been one of Vanessa's.'

Tom felt his heart freeze as he observed the little seduction scene playing out in the alleyway. Now Pieris stretched out a gentle hand to touch the sleeping woman's face. The *shine* that Tom had always associated with the Daylight Folk was an almost unbearable glow. Tiny moths fluttered towards the light, like pieces of burning newspaper.

'That's her quintessence,' Charissa said. 'The force that keeps her life burning. Tap enough of her nectar, and—'

Tom stepped out of the doorway.

'Don't!' whispered Charissa.

Tom ignored her. Pulling away, he walked out onto the cobbles. In the carousel of lights, his shadow doubled, trebled.

Pieris looked up, eyes gleaming, and a curious expression came across his face. 'Hello,' he said. 'What have we here?'

Tom was aware of Charissa cursing softly from the shadows. On the ground, the Temperance woman gave a frightened little moan. The fragments of brightness in the air seemed to be moving towards her again. *Good.* For a moment, Tom had been afraid that Pieris had taken all her – what was it? Life force? Glamour? Energy? What was the scientific term for what these people called *nectar?*

'Step away from her, Pieris,' he said. 'I don't want to fight you.'

Where had that come from? Tom asked himself. The last thing he wanted was a fight, and yet he found himself prickling with a sudden nervous activity.

'You know who I am?' said Pieris.

'Yes, and I know *what* you are.'

'Is that so?' Now, Pieris reached out to touch Tom's arm with his fingers. Tom felt a sudden rush of something like electricity pass between them. A surge of multicoloured light blazed out into the alleyway. Tom was vaguely aware of Charissa calling his name, but he was unable to respond. The light was as heady as champagne; as clear as the purest oxygen. It lit him up like a birthday cake topped with a hundred candles. It flashed across his gleaming skin like a lit trail of gunpowder. It was the most exhilarating sensation Tom Argent had ever experienced, and he responded to it instinctively, like a flower to the sun...

Then the light slowly subsided. The sense of elation faded. A scatter of luminous particles burst into the smoky air, and Tom found himself staring down at something lying at his feet.

For a second, he wasn't sure what it was he was seeing. There was Pieris' velvet coat, the broad-brimmed hat, the high-heeled boots. But the man who had been wearing them was gone. Instead, there was a thing on the ground that looked nothing like a human being. It looked like something that had died many, many years ago; a mummy, a fossil—

A chrysalis.

The Temperance woman sat up. 'You killed him,' she said.

'No,' said Tom. 'I hardly even touched him.'

The Temperance woman shook her head as if in denial, not just of Tom, but of everything around her. Grasping for the fallen tracts as if they might hold the key to her salvation, she struggled to her feet, using the wall as a support. 'I *know* you,' she said, still looking at Tom. 'I know you. I saw you this morning. Did you make me drink something? Did you...'

And now, from the thing on the ground, there came a flicker of movement. Tom saw a tiny butterfly – white, with smudges of black on the wings – emerging from the chrysalis. Then came another. And two more. Soon, the air was filled with them, rising into a column of light—

The Temperance woman started to scream.

'No, please, don't. It's all right—' said Tom.

She screamed again; a good, loud scream that promised to bring anyone within earshot running. At least she was OK, thought Tom. That kind of noise could only come from a healthy set of lungs. He turned and saw Charissa, her eyes brimming with reflected lights. For a moment, a memory nudged his consciousness, a memory that somehow belonged to the Moonlight Market, and the scent of flowers that bloom only once in the course of a lifetime.

True love, and certain death.

You'd put a price on true love?

178

'We have to go,' Charissa said, in a voice that was pinched with urgency. 'We have to get you out of here. *Now.*'

She was right; the rising screams of the Temperance woman had brought a response from inside the public house. A door slammed open against the wall; a blurry face appeared, then another. The butterflies had almost gone, rising like burning paper into the smoky London air. Tom saw the last of them disappear, high above the rooftops.

He looked back at the Temperance woman. 'Miss, you're still in danger,' he said. 'You need to find Imago Burnet. He has a photography shop near King's Cross. Find him. He can help you. Trust him. He'll explain everything.'

Charissa tugged his sleeve. '*Now!*' The lights in her eyes were remarkable. Not just a metaphor, Tom thought; they must be reflecting something bright. And the walls, the walls of the alleyway – they too were touched with a brilliance that shot like searchlights into the sky…

Pieris was gone. His shine had been extinguished during their combat. And yet the light seemed brighter than ever, rebounding against the cobblestones like a magic lantern show. 'Where's all the light coming from?' said Tom, looking around to no avail.

'Never mind the light. Come *on!*' She tugged once more at the sleeve of his coat. 'We can't stay here any longer.'

Tom nodded and started to follow her, still staring over his shoulder at Pieris' discarded clothing. 'I tapped him, didn't I?' he said. 'I tapped him without even knowing it. But what were all those butterflies? Was that his…' He searched for the word. 'Was that what you meant by *quintessence?*'

Charissa looked grim. 'Never mind that,' she said. 'There'll be time for all that later. For now, we have to get under cover. Find ourselves somewhere safe to hide. And not just from the Daylight Folk. What you did there, in front of witnesses, is going to be all over London in a matter of hours. We'll have the police on our tail, as well as every damn Butterfly in the city, all hot as hell for the blood of our Folk. You've started a war, Tom, whether you meant to do it or not. Now follow me, for gods' sakes. Oh, and one more thing.'

'Yes?'

'Put those bloody wings away.'

5

'Wings?' he said. 'What do you mean, *wings?*'

Charissa was still dragging Tom away from the scene of carnage. Already, outside the public house, a crowd had begun to assemble. The Temperance woman had attracted quite an audience. All around them, reflected against the walls and cobbles of the alleyway, shone those eerie coloured lights, like those of a fairground carousel.

'It's me,' said Tom in disbelief. 'I'm creating the light, somehow. And what the hell's that?'

That was a shape, etched in colours against the dark; colours like those in his photographs; like the colours he'd glimpsed in the tunnels. They seemed to surround him somehow; to furl around him like shot silk. To open up around him like—

'*Wings?*' he said.

'Just put them away, for gods' sakes,' said Charissa. 'Anyone would think you'd never heard of flying before.'

Tom craned his neck, trying to see the wings, but all he could see was a kind of bright blur surrounding him. He tried to touch them – but felt nothing but the fabric of the borrowed coat he was wearing.

Charissa started to run, still dragging Tom behind her. 'We have to find somewhere safe,' she said. 'I know a place. Follow me.'

Tom ran, and realised that the colours around him had

faded. His 'wings' were ephemeral, he thought – or maybe they were only visible under certain kinds of light? In any case, as he emerged onto the main thoroughfare, the eerie shapes had disappeared and he and Charissa were once more part of the drab and featureless crowd.

'But does this mean I could fly?' he said, when Charissa slowed her pace.

'Oh, you *could*,' said Charissa. 'If you had a death wish, which, of course, you do.' She turned to check behind them, and seemed satisfied that they were not being followed. 'Talk about beginner's luck,' she said. 'So far, you've tapped a Butterfly, shown your wings in public and you still want me to set you up with *Vanessa*, of all people. There isn't a wall big enough to display all the near-death experiences you've had so far, and yet somehow you're still breathing.' She looked behind her again, and indicated a narrow passageway leading off from the main thoroughfare. 'Through there,' she said, and ducked under an arch, which was small enough to challenge even her diminutive height.

Tom followed her into a tunnel that led between the weathered facades, and opened in thirty feet or so on to a cobbled cul-de-sac. A cast-iron sign attached to the wall read: WELKIN CLOSE.

Charissa turned once more to Tom. 'I hoped this place would be here,' she said. 'I'd heard of it – it's legendary among the Midnight Folk – but it fell many years before my time. You should be reasonably safe here, at least until we decide what to do next.'

'What about Vanessa?' asked Tom.

'Oh, give it a rest,' said Charissa crossly. 'Until you can manage your colours, you're not safe to be around. We'll hide out for a few days here. It's protected by glamours, so we'll be safe, as long as you don't do anything stupid. And maybe, if it's safe—' She grinned. 'Maybe then, I'll teach you how to use your wings.'

Tom's face brightened. 'You'd do that? My wings?'

'I said maybe,' she said. 'As long as you promise you won't use them to fly off in search of Vanessa.'

'OK,' said Tom, whose mind had already been moving in that direction.

'OK,' said Charissa. 'But first, I need rest. I need to recharge. My glamours are almost exhausted just from trying to keep you safe.'

'Oh,' said Tom. 'I didn't know.' He realised now that Charissa was looking more than usually pale.

'You don't know very much,' she said. 'Come with me. Time for you to see what you've got yourself into.'

Part 9

——

Welkin Close

I

After Brimstone's release, there came an unspoken truce between the tribes. The Moths lay low in their stronghold in the heart of the city, and the Butterflies kept to their stone eyrie overlooking the rooftops.

For several decades, the war was limited to small skirmishes, with no great losses on either side. Some of the Midnight Folk welcomed this. Some even whispered of a possible reconciliation; a partnership with the Spider Mage to weave a way back to the Kingdom. But these were only whisperings. The Daylight Folk stayed united. One among them especially, an ambitious young soldier named Skipper, was alert for any sign of treachery. Although she was loyal to Brimstone, she feared he might have been compromised during his long imprisonment, and his refusal to speak of that time only increased her suspicions. To Skipper, the prospect of peace with the Moths was a betrayal of all she knew. Born outside the Kingdom, she only knew of their ancestral home through a handful of stories and legends. She believed their future lay with the Folk, and that only the complete rout of the enemy, and the end of their hope of finding the Prince, would free them of their old allegiances.

And so, every day, instead of hunting and making merry with the others, she went in search of the Moths' secret lair. A place of legend and mystery, it had stayed hidden for centuries among the slums of the city, guarded by glamours, impregnable except perhaps by treachery. But Skipper believed that Brimstone knew more than he had told them. And so she kept to the shadows, and watched as Brimstone walked the streets, and soon she found that he returned most often to an alleyway between two derelict buildings, where he would sometimes stop and wait for an hour or more at a time, or watch from a place on the rooftops, alone but for his thoughts...

2

Welkin Close was a cul-de-sac that ended in a blank brick wall. The wall was far too high to climb, and there were no entrances other than the tunnel by which they had entered. A couple of what looked like shops opened on to the cul-de-sac. Tom could see awnings, and lamps, and signs that read SILKWORM SUPPLIES, CHESTNUT CLEARWING'S PRINTWORKS AND PRESS, EMERALD'S TAP and HONEYDEW'S PANTRY. A crooked little half-timbered building, crammed into the space at the end of the row, revealed itself to be a public house, named the CLIFDEN NONPAREIL.

It was even darker here than in the little alleyway. Looking up, Tom noticed that the rooftops above him almost touched, their irregular shapes like the canopy of a forest. The only real light came from the lamps that hung from the awnings of the shops; their colours splashed the cobbles like watercolours in the rain.

'We're safe here,' said Charissa. 'No one comes here but our kind. The Folk can't see the entrance at all. To them, it looks like another wall. As for the Daylight Folk – as you can see, there is no daylight on Welkin Close. Daylight Folk don't like the dark. Lack of sunlight weakens them. I suppose that's how you were able to tap Pieris.'

Tom shivered at the thought. And yet—

It had felt good. Hadn't it?

'And the butterflies that came ... afterwards?'

'Remnants of quintessence. Nectar. His *spirit*, I suppose you'd say. It's what happens when damage, or anguish, or grief, is simply too great to withstand.'

Tom thought of Spider's story, and the lost prince who, in his sorrow, had broken apart into a cloud of moths and butterflies.

'So – he's really gone?' said Tom, who still couldn't quite believe it. 'He won't just – you know – fly back together again?'

Charissa shrugged. 'With that bastard, who knows? We'll see, if we ever make it home, which is unlikely if I don't get something sweet inside me soon.'

She turned to the little shopfront labelled *Honeydew's Pantry*. The door was painted a bright green, and as he looked in at the window, Tom could see shelves of glass jars, gleaming, stacked from floor to ceiling.

There was a bell chain by the door. Charissa stepped up and pulled it. From the back of the shop came a distant jangling sound. Then, the door opened to reveal a diminutive person of indeterminate gender, wearing a starched linen apron and a pair of rubber gloves.

The newcomer – Tom assumed this was Honeydew – viewed them with a slightly suspicious air. 'Let's see your daddles, folks,' they said, 'afore I let ye into my digs.'

Charissa pulled up the sleeves of her outsized overcoat, showing her hands. Tom did the same.

Honeydew scrutinised their palms for a moment, then stepped aside with a grin. 'No offence to you folks,' they said. 'But there's been some kind of benjo up town, and it pays to be careful, so it does.' Once more, the little person squinted up at Charissa and Tom. 'New to the city, are ye?'

Charissa gave Tom a warning look. 'That's right,' she said. 'I was told this was a safe house. And I could use a tap of something strong, if you have any to spare?'

Honeydew laughed. 'You've come to the right den. I've got a nectar as sweet as you'll find in any of the Nine Worlds. Come in, come in! You both look a trifle out of sorts, if you'll forgive me for saying so.'

'I've had a bit of a day,' she said. 'I'm Charissa. This is Tom.'

She and Tom followed Honeydew into the little shop, which revealed itself to be as diminutive as its owner. The ceiling was low, and a single lamp shone from a hook on the far wall. From floor to ceiling, shelves lined with jars glittered like sunken treasure.

The jars themselves were like sweetshop jars, but filled with a selection of mysterious substances, none of which Tom could identify. Some of the jars seemed to contain tiny fireflies that winked and glittered in the gloom; others, dried flower petals or brightly coloured pigments. And some held a liquid that to Tom looked like a kind of moonshine, sparkling like champagne and slightly phosphorescent.

Honeydew selected one of these jars, and poured three shots of the luminous liquid into three ceramic cups. It moved in a rather unusual way, as if it were slightly volatile; as Tom swirled it around his cup, he seemed to see it rise into the air like a cloud of tiny gnats—

Quintessence, he thought.

Charissa drank her share in a single draught, then deftly removed Tom's cup from his hand. 'You've had plenty,' she told him. 'Any more, you'll be climbing the walls.' She drank the second cup, and Tom immediately thought that she looked less pale, less tired. Her skin looked fresh and rosy again; even her hair seemed to shine.

'Was that – you know – *nectar?*' said Tom.

Honeydew gave him a curious look. 'New to the sweet stuff, eh? You'll learn.' The creature gave him a broad smile, displaying a row of pointed teeth. 'I'm guessing maybe the pair of you was part of that business across town after all.'

'No, not at all,' said Charissa.

'Not that you *look* like a skilmalink. But the mutton-shunters are out in force looking for a man they say robbed a flash mort near Fleet Street, then loped off like Springheeled Jack. I don't suppose you folks would have heard anything about such a thing?'

Charissa shrugged. 'Not a word,' she said.

'You?'

'Not a word,' repeated Tom.

'That's funny,' said Honeydew, 'because you look to me like a fellow that's on the lam. And you talk like a gentry-cove, for all you look like a wapstraw. What's your lay, eh?'

'Never mind his lay.' Charissa gave Tom a warning look. 'What do we owe you for the drink? And can we stay here for the night?'

'Nectar's on the house,' said Honeydew. 'And there are rooms at the Clifden Nonpareil for any of our kind who need 'em.' Again, that sideways look at Tom. 'Come over from the Colonies, eh? You've got that look.'

'That's right,' said Charissa. 'We'll just rest up for a couple of days, and then we'll be out of your hair again. I thank you for your kindness.'

Honeydew shrugged. 'My pleasure. Now, come with me, and I'll introduce ye to the gang.'

3

Charissa and Tom followed Honeydew out into the alleyway, and to the Clifden Nonpareil. At first glance, the building seemed very small – half-timbered, with a gable roof almost low enough for Tom to touch – but moving closer, Tom could see that its size was an illusion.

At Honeydew's knock, the door opened to reveal a very familiar face – it was Atlas, the giant he had encountered the first time he met Charissa. *Atlas Before,* Tom reminded himself, as the giant opened the door. Behind him, the tavern was crowded; in the light of a little fireplace and a handful of oil lamps, Tom caught sight of Cinnabar and, although he knew she was from *Before*, he flinched away instinctively.

'Welcome to the Nonpareil,' said a tall man Tom did not recognise. 'I am Commander Sable, and this is my second, Little Grey.' He indicated a figure with braided hair and a sleeve of tattoos.

'Don't speak unless you have to,' whispered Charissa as they went in. 'No one here knows you. You're perfectly safe, remember that.'

Tom nodded, feeling relieved. But just at that moment, the crowd parted and he saw a pale figure in front of him. It was Luna, the blind girl. In the gloom of the tavern, she looked like a ghost, her silvery hair giving her a corona of chilly fire.

'That's right, Luna,' said Honeydew in a suddenly harsher

voice. 'Tell us who he *really* is. Because if he's from the Colonies, I'm a bunce o' dog's meat.'

Tom glanced at Charissa. Her expression was unreadable. Luna took a step forward, just as she had in the tunnels, and came to stand in front of him. Her eyes were a striking violet, and Tom had time to realise that Luna *Before* was far from blind. She took his face between her hands and stared deeply into his eyes. For a moment, he felt the force of her gaze, her thumbs pressing into his temples. Then she released him and took a step back.

'This one doesn't belong here,' she said.

There was a murmur among the Moths. Sable looked at Atlas, who stepped aside to bar the door.

'He comes from somewhere far away,' Luna went on in her dreamy voice. 'Genus, Argent: common as dirt. But this one's different. Divided.'

'So where's his allegiance?' asked Cinnabar. 'What do you see in his colours?'

'It's confusing.' Luna frowned. 'It's like he's two different people. *Two* potentials, one of ours, and one in league with the enemy.'

'Is that so?' said Cinnabar sharply, and suddenly there was a knife in her hand. The blade was dark and unwavering, the edge as sharp as an eagle's eye. The point of it hovered six inches or so away from Tom's gut.

'I can explain,' said Charissa, addressing the group of Midnight Folk. 'He came to me as a chrysalis. We came together from London Beyond, with the help of the Spinnerman, by means of a stitch in Time. I had my orders. I was to keep him under my eye, to see which side would claim him. I thought to bring him to our way of things. To show him the truth of the Daylight Folk before it was too late to change. I thought he could be shaped to our ways. And he has potential. He took Pieris down before he'd even found his wings.'

'That was *him*?' said Honeydew. 'No wonder he was full of frisk.'

Charissa nodded. 'I had hope. I thought I could bring him to our cause. Make him forget Vanessa. But he's stubborn. Corrupted. Weak.'

Tom felt a numbness come over him. 'You brought me here to betray me,' he said.

Charissa's eyes stayed locked on his. 'No hard feelings, Tom Argent,' she said. 'But in the World of the Sightless Folk, the Midnight Folk have to fend for themselves.' She turned to Sable and Little Grey. 'You don't know me,' she told them. 'But I know you. Some are my comrades in London Beyond. Some of you are on Burnet's wall – our fallen heroes. This man was put into my charge by the Spinnerman himself, which means that he's important. And until we know exactly why, he needs to be kept under close watch.'

'Is that why you brought him here?' said Luna in a cold voice. 'Knowing his dual nature? Unsure of his allegiance?'

Charissa nodded. 'I didn't count on his taking down one of their Generals. Pieris is gone, and the Daylight Folk won't take his death lying down. Brimstone may not want outright war, but he'll want a full accounting, and when the sunshine hits the fan, it might be prudent to have someone ready to hand over.'

Sable turned to Cinnabar, who nodded briefly in return. Then he turned to Little Grey. 'Take him to the cellar,' he said. 'Let's see where his allegiance lies.'

Tom tried to protest, but found himself being dragged roughly towards the back of the room, where he saw a small, thick door, barred and heavily bolted.

'What do you mean, *allegiance*?' he said. 'I'm not part of your stupid war. What if I don't want to take sides? What if all I want is to get on with my life? To go back home?'

'Too late for that, Tom Argent, I fear. As for your act of allegiance—' Sable gave the grimmest of smiles. 'As you'll discover, we have a guest. If you dealt with Pieris as swiftly as your friend says you did, then you should be quite safe.' At this, Little Grey opened the door, and Tom fell down a short wooden ladder into a subterranean space. He fell onto his hands and knees onto a flagged surface, heard the ladder withdraw and the door slam shut above him, and found himself in darkness. Quickly, he checked his coat pocket. His camera was unbroken.

And then in the darkness came a voice, both languid and strangely familiar. 'Maybe this means you'll kill me now. God knows I'm bored to death waiting.'

Tom flinched. That voice. He knew it well. He'd heard it last in another world.

Once more, he felt for his camera. His fingers moved to the controls, finding the flash without thinking, and pointed it towards the voice. A brief and blinding flash ensued, but seared into his retina was the image it had revealed from the dark – the shape of a woman against the far wall, a woman he'd last seen with a shaven head...

Skipper.

4

A single flash of very bright light reveals more than you might imagine. The woman who had been Brimstone's second-in-command was visible for less than a second, and yet Tom was able to take in her appearance in surprisingly vivid detail.

When Tom had seen her in London Beyond, Skipper had shaved her head to the skull, but in this version of London, her hair was long and curly. Her features were recognisable, if a little more youthful, and she was wearing a light-coloured shift, startling against her dark skin. One arm was pinned against the wall by a metal cuff. The other lay listlessly in her lap.

Once more in darkness, with flowers of light blooming across his retinas, Tom heard her voice from across the space. 'Let me guess. You're not here to hurt me.'

'I'm not.'

The woman laughed, not pleasantly. 'That's what they all say at first,' she said. 'I thought they would have learnt by now. They can send me as many spies as they like. I won't give up my people.'

'I'm not a spy. I'm from London Beyond. I'm looking for Vanessa.'

Skipper laughed again. 'That and a penny will buy you a pint, assuming you live long enough to drink it.'

'You don't understand,' said Tom. 'We're in love. I came all this way to save her.'

'From what?' said Skipper. She sounded amused.

Tom explained about London Beyond, and his encounter with Brimstone, and how through his own ignorance he had missed his chance with Vanessa. 'But now I'm here in London *Before*, I know I can make her listen to me. Brimstone doesn't know me here. He can't keep us apart again. Vanessa and I were *meant* to be together, and he knows it. Well – maybe he *doesn't* know it,' said Tom, 'but that's because he doesn't know *me*, because none of this has happened yet.'

There was a pause, and then from the darkness came the sound of Skipper's rich laughter. 'Well, little man, no one can say you're not an entertainer. But you won't find the Daylight Folk through me, glamorie-glass or no.'

'You mean my camera,' said Tom.

'Chimera or glamorie-glass, it won't show you what you're looking for. And your friends can tap me all they like, I'll never betray my people.'

Tom sighed. 'Why would I betray you? I'm one of you. That's why they put me down here.'

'I don't know what you are, little man, but you're not one of us. You may be just hatched, but the Daylight Folk require an act of allegiance. Letting me out of here would help, if you're looking for suggestions.'

'It would?' Tom found himself thinking hard. 'And then you'd owe me a favour?'

'A favour. Of course,' said Skipper, sounding suddenly weary. 'And let me guess what that favour would be. A map to Brimstone's stronghold, perhaps? A hint at where they'll be sleeping tonight? Forget it, little man. Brimstone may be a traitor to his people and to his heart, but that doesn't mean I'll give him up, not if you were to keep me here for a hundred years.'

'I don't want Brimstone. I told you,' said Tom. 'Just give me some time with Vanessa. Get me ten minutes alone with her, and I'll get you out of here.'

There was a long and rigid pause.

'Skipper?' said Tom. 'Did you hear what I said?'

Now there was no amusement left in the woman's voice. 'You know my name,' she said. 'How?'

'I told you. I'm from London *Beyond*. I know you. Spider sent me.'

'You know the Spinner?'

'Of course. He's my friend. At least…' Tom trailed off awkwardly, thinking of their last meeting. 'At least, I *think* he is. He gave me this.' He felt in his pocket for Spider's token and drew it out, bringing it close to his face. He found that his dark-adapted eyes could just pick out the silvery thread, wrapped three times round the flap of card. 'He gave me a lifeline, Skipper,' he said. 'Give me what I want, and it's yours.'

In the darkness, he sensed her stiffen. The chain at her wrist made a ratcheting sound, and he knew she was straining forward.

'A lifeline? He gave you a *lifeline*?'

'I told you. It's yours, for some time with Vanessa.'

Skipper began to laugh again, a different laugh this time, high and reckless. 'Oh, you *are* a piece,' she said. 'So, it's Vanessa you want, then? All right. Give me the lifeline. That bitch can look after herself.'

Once more, Tom heard the sound of the chain. Moving slowly across the cellar floor, he edged his way towards Skipper. His outstretched hand touched her bare arm, then found her hand in the darkness. For a second, her cool fingers tightened over his—

'Now,' said Tom, 'you owe me. Remember—'

He heard her intake of breath, and then Spider's token was suddenly gone. Tom heard another clink of the chain, and then came a flash of silvery light, and then a silvery darkness.

'Skipper?' said Tom.

No answer. Not even the sound of her breathing.

Tentatively, he reached towards the place where she had been sitting. There was nothing. Empty silence, empty space; the empty cuff at the end of the chain still warm with the heat of her body.

Still, it counted, didn't it? Skipper had asked him for help, and now she owed Tom a favour.

But now, sitting alone in the darkness, Tom realised – a little too late – that, in fact, he had *offered* the lifeline. And if that was true, then maybe she had never asked for a favour at all...

5

Tom sat alone in the darkness for hours. Above him, the sounds from the Clifden Nonpareil taproom grew busier, then faded, then fell into a silence punctuated first by sleepy voices, and then by tiny creaks and squeaks that Tom guessed might be mice or rats. He supposed dawn must be close, and that his captors were sleeping. He wondered when someone would come for him, either (he hoped) to bring him food, or to check on his act of allegiance, which he guessed was to do to Skipper what he had already done to Pieris. *Your friends can tap me all they like*, she had told him, and now it occurred to Tom why both the Clifden Nonpareil and Honeydew's Pantry were so well supplied.

At some point, he must have dozed off, as he awoke at a sound to find the cellar door open above him, revealing Charissa framed against the pale rectangle of the doorway. A rattle announced the descent of the ladder down which he had fallen.

'Charissa? What are—'

'*Shh,*' she said. 'I've come to get you out of there.'

Tom looked up at her, puzzled. 'What?'

'Hurry *up*, Collector,' hissed Charissa impatiently. 'Do I have to explain everything, or will you – for once – just do as I say?'

Tom scrambled to his feet. 'But I thought you were on *their* side,' he said. 'You're the reason they put me down here.'

'I kept you safe,' Charissa said. 'I hadn't counted on Luna being here, and looking into your colours. I had to tell them *something*, or we'd both have been down here together.' She grabbed Tom fiercely by the hand and hauled him up the wooden steps. 'We have to get out quickly,' she said, 'while they're still sleeping. Something's about to happen here, something we can't be around for.'

Tom followed Charissa quietly through the empty taproom. It smelt of beer and honeycomb, and something even sweeter, a scent that simultaneously set him on edge and made his mouth water.

'Come on,' hissed Charissa again. 'You don't have time to snack right now.'

Tom looked at her, puzzled.

'Yes, I can tell you're hungry,' she said. 'I see it in your colours.'

Tom followed her obediently, trying not to step on any creaky floorboards. Charissa unbolted the taproom door, pushing up the overlong sleeves of her bulky overcoat, and then they were out in the courtyard, smelling the morning smoke in the air. From the light that filtered dimly into the alleyway, Tom guessed it was just before dawn. The awning to Honeydew's Pantry had been withdrawn. The shops were closed. From the thoroughfare that ran alongside Welkin Close, he could hear the distant sounds of carts, and carriages, and hacks, and people going about their business.

It sounded so familiar, and yet so very strange that he felt as if the whole thing might have been a very long and troubling dream. Only Charissa was real, he thought; Charissa, with her mousy hair and inelegant spray of freckles, and the way the fire had danced in her eyes that night at the Market on Old London Bridge—

For a moment, the memory pinned him helpless, like a moth under glass. The scent of the market; the fires, the smoke; and the woman who gave him the flower that somehow triggered his memories. And with that thought he realised that, once more, he'd forgotten Vanessa's face. He clenched his fists in frustration. Why didn't the flower work for *her*? Why was it that every time he tried to picture her beauty, all he remembered was her *shine*, like sunlight on the water? Was this what Charissa meant when she spoke of seeing *colours*?

'About those colours,' he said at last. 'What are they? What did Luna mean when she said I was two different people?'

'Later,' said Charissa. 'We have to get out of Welkin Close.'

She gestured at Tom to stay back, and cautiously approached the little arch through which they had entered earlier. It looked pretty ordinary to Tom: a sooty, narrow entranceway that led to a kind of tunnel. He was about to ask Charissa why she was being so cautious when he noticed a shimmer in the air across the tunnel's entrance: an almost invisible curtain of light, subtly veined, like a moth's wing.

He reached out a hand towards it.

Charissa slapped it away. 'Don't. They put a glamour on the gate. We can't get out without waking the house.'

'Oh,' said Tom. 'So, what do we do?'

'We'll have to get out a different way. I'm assuming you still have your lifeline?'

Tom swallowed. 'Yes, well, about that—'

'Because given what's going to happen here, we want to be a long way away when it starts. You, because of what you are. Me, because I helped you. This place won't be safe, not for any of our folk.'

'Why? What's going to happen? And how come you didn't know this before?'

Charissa shrugged. 'It was in the past. It was *history*. Who remembers every detail in case they're going to be history? But seeing those people – those *heroes*. Sable. Honeydew. Little Grey—' She spoke the names softly, reverently.

'Heroes?' said Tom.

She nodded. 'Everyone knows about Welkin Close. It's famous. It was the fortress of our folk, hidden by thousands of glamours. It was safe – it was hidden away. The Daylight Folk couldn't find it. The Clifden Nonpareil stood unseen for over a century. Until one day, someone escaped, revealing the location.'

'Er – someone escaped?' said Tom.

She gave him a look, and carried on. 'The Midnight Folk had a dungeon under the Clifden Nonpareil. They kept their prisoners in the dark, to tap them of their nectar. Some of them were there for years until the spirit left them at last, but this one somehow broke their chains and fled to warn the Daylight Folk. Brimstone was reluctant to act, but saw his leadership threatened. He had no choice but to lead, or be led. And so they ambushed Welkin Close by day, when our people were weakest. The Midnight Folk were slaughtered. Their names are all on Burnet's wall – Sable, Gypsy, Honeydew, Lappet, Magpie, Little Grey, Emerald, Chestnut, Yellow Belle, Pale Grass, Umber. So many. A hundred dead, or more. Luna managed to escape, but lost her sight in the battle.'

'Oh,' said Tom.

'Damn right. *Oh.*'

'This prisoner...' said Tom slowly. 'It wasn't... Skipper, by any chance?'

Charissa nodded grimly. 'That bitch was always the worst of them all. Vengeful. Hard. Relentless. She was in love with Brimstone, of course. That's why she needed to force his hand. She thought he'd become too comfortable, too happy with the status quo. Then, of course, there was Cinnabar—' She broke off. 'Like I said, history. But when I heard Skipper was down there, I knew I had to get us out. Lucky for us, we still have time. She's still a prisoner. *Isn't* she?'

6

'It would be really bad, right? If she got away,' said Tom.

'*Very* bad,' said Charissa. 'That's why we need your lifeline, Tom. We can't risk being here when it begins.'

'Maybe it won't happen at all,' Tom said in a weak voice. 'Maybe, if we warned the others, they could stop it, somehow.'

'The first thing they'd do is kill us both. They already think *you're* a spy.' She sighed. 'You're a liability. You're still in love with Vanessa. It's right there, in your colours. Spider knew as much when he sent you here.'

Tom was not entirely displeased that the subject had moved on from Skipper and the lifeline. 'So why do it, if not to keep me safe?'

She shrugged. 'Who knows what he's thinking? He's the Spinnerman, for gods' sakes. He's been spinning his lines since the day we first arrived here. He can't be trusted from one day to the next, which is why I had to make myself indispensable to him in the only way he understands.'

Tom looked at her blankly. 'How?'

'Tom Argent,' said Charissa in a very patient voice. 'What is it Spider treasures most? What has he been hunting since you rescued him from the Daylight Folk? What did he hope to exchange for you when you met with Cinnabar?'

Tom frowned. 'You mean, his overcoat? Cinnabar has it. She

said so. But she wouldn't exchange it for me. She said I was corrupted. *You* said so too—'

'Cinnabar lied. It wouldn't be the first time.'

'You mean I'm *not* corrupted?'

Charissa gave him one of her looks. In her outsized overcoat, she looked like a judgemental child. She stuck her hands into her pockets and opened the coat like a pair of wings. The lining, which was ragged and worn, seemed somehow, nevertheless, to *shine*, reflecting the light as if from a badly foxed mirror. Looking more closely, Tom thought he saw a kind of pattern in the silk; a kind of ephemeral pattern like the veins of luminescence he had seen across the gateway.

'*You* had it all this time?' he said.

'There's a saying among the Midnight Folk. *Trust the spider, but watch the thread.* I knew he wouldn't leave me here if I had his coat.' She closed the lapels of the evercoat, cutting off that ethereal shine. 'If only we knew how to use it, we wouldn't need him anymore. But it's filled with tricks and traps that only Spider understands. His threads, his glamours, his safeguards. His *maps*.'

'Maps to where?'

Charissa smiled. 'To *everywhere*.'

7

In the first years of his exile into the World of the Sightless Folk, the Spider Mage, tortured by guilt, fled the company of his people. He left the two warring tribes, taking with him his web, which was the map and microcosm of his presence across the worlds. This web was the source of all the Spider Mage's knowledge, containing within its woven strands all his dreams and devices.

But most of all, it contained his world, woven into the lining of what seemed like an overcoat, every detail painstakingly remembered and converted into an interwoven pattern of threads more complex than DNA, its infinite variety stretching out across every world, its powers only accessible to the Spider Mage himself. In vain his people tried to persuade him to unlock its secrets; to guide them back to their home world, long since made inaccessible. But the Spider Mage always refused. Only when the curse of the Butterfly Queen was broken – when a child of the Daylight Folk fell in love with a child of the Midnight Folk – could he return them to their home. Until that day, the two tribes would stay in exile for ever.

Years passed; and then centuries. The Spider Mage's promise was kept. The map in the lining of his evercoat slept, like some hidden chrysalis, containing worlds within it. And the Moth King and the Butterfly Queen awaited the return of the Prince, watching each other across the plain of their barren, broken marriage.

8

Tom stared, wide-eyed, at the evercoat. It looked like an ordinary coat again, thick and dark with broad lapels, and was rather shabbier than most. A button was missing; the rest were polished tortoiseshell, marked with a tiny star-like design. It had been mended in several places, using various differently coloured threads; it certainly didn't look as if it could contain the way to another world. It also smelt; and although Tom had learnt to believe many things over the past forty-eight hours, he still found it hard to accept a magic garment that smelt of goat.

Charissa was getting impatient. 'Look, maybe this could wait until we're somewhere a little safer?' she said. 'I mean, much as I'd love to give you an extended history of the Midnight Folk, maybe not while we're in imminent danger of getting caught up in the infamous Battle of Welkin Close. Now. That lifeline—'

'Ah. *That.*' Tom shifted awkwardly. 'I may ... not have it anymore.'

'You *lost* it?'

'Not exactly,' said Tom.

'Then *what?*'

'I'm sorry. I gave it away. I didn't know what else to do.'

Charissa took a moment. Then she said, in a very quiet voice, 'Please tell me you didn't give it to *her.*'

'I'm sorry,' said Tom again. 'I thought that if she owed me a favour, then maybe this time, Vanessa and I—' He paused, wondering – not for the first time – how it could be that someone so small and insignificant-looking could manage to look so dangerous. Once more, he thought of Old London Bridge, and the scent of smoke and fireworks. Once more, he wondered how it could be that the memory of a market was easier to summon than that of his beloved's face.

'You know what this means,' said Charissa. 'It means that Skipper knows where we are. She knows the location of Welkin Close. Which means that any minute now, we're going to be at the centre of the bloodiest battle our people have fought in centuries – *without a lifeline.*'

'You don't know that,' protested Tom.

'Don't I?' said Charissa.

Tom followed her gaze. Above them, the narrow ribbon of sky was starting to show the first signs of dawn. Out of the London smoke, it came – blush pink, absinthe green, ice blue, lemon yellow—

'That isn't the dawn,' said Tom.

And now through the colours, Tom thought he could see figures and patterns against the sky: patterns like magic lantern shapes against a screen of vibrant silk.

The Daylight Folk were coming.

9

They came with the dawn, and were terrible.

Thus began one of the darkest moments in the war between the tribes. Every detail was cherished and known; the names and photographs of the fallen displayed on the wall of Mr Burnet's camera shop. Of course, Tom was new to this, but Charissa knew it all too well. How Brimstone led the first assault, flanked by Pieris and Skipper; how Cinnabar had met him, stony-faced and silent. How bitterly the pair had fought, each seeking the other's weakness; how, finally, both had fallen, and were borne away by their people.

Of course, Pieris wouldn't be there this time, and that meant certain details might change, but what didn't change was the fact that Tom was about to see myth in the making.

'We have to leave, *now*,' Charissa said, looking into the brightening sky. 'We can't use the gate, or your lifeline. That leaves us with one remaining option. Remember how I promised to teach you how to use your wings?'

Tom's mouth fell open as she pushed back the skirts of Spider's evercoat to reveal the splendour of her wings. Dark they were, and golden, fanning into the gilded air.

'Now *you* do it,' she told him.

'I can't,' said Tom. 'I don't know how.'

'Well, you're going to have to learn on the fly. We don't have time to practise. Come on. You did it once before. Do it again.'

Tom closed his eyes and tried to summon the feeling he'd had in the alley behind Ye Olde Cheshire Cheese. The quality of light; the rush; the luminous feeling of power. He opened his eyes. Charissa was poised, her open wings throwing panels of golden light onto the sooty cobbles. His own were nowhere to be seen.

'Come on,' said Charissa. 'We have to go.'

Once more, Tom tried to summon his wings. The arch of multicoloured light; the feeling of invulnerability. He tried to imagine himself in the air, soaring over London—

Nothing. Not even a flicker.

'Oh, for gods' sakes,' said Charissa. 'This is no time for performance anxiety. You *know* how to do this. You always have. It's coded into who you are. All you have to do is let go of your inhibitions.'

Tom shook his head. 'I can't,' he said. 'It's like trying not to think of an elephant.'

'What?'

'It's an old psychological trick. The only really foolproof way to make someone think of an elephant is to tell them *not* to think of an—'

'For crying out loud,' she said. 'Think of Vanessa. Can you do that?'

'Oh, yes, I can do *that*,' said Tom, and tried to summon Vanessa's *shine*; the sound of her voice; his longing for her. He slipped a hand in his pocket, where the flower that blooms only once in a lifetime still released its scent to the air. Then he opened his wings without a thought, and rose into the turbulent sky in a blaze of nameless colours, just at the moment the Daylight Folk prepared to fall upon Welkin Close with all the rage of their bitter Queen's ancient, enduring sorrow.

Part 10

—

The Battle of Welkin Close

I

They came with the dawn, and were terrible. An army of five hundred strong, led by Brimstone, who had understood the cost of his earlier reluctance. Skipper, who knew his secret, and could easily have overturned his leadership, chose instead to stand by his side, and fighting together, they brought down dozens of the enemy.

The first strike was to let in the light. Welkin Close lived in darkness, hedged in by rooftops that almost met, and veiled from sight by glamours. The Daylight Folk attacked from above, setting guards on the alleyway to ensure that no one could escape. Then, from the rooftops, they smashed and burned their way through the ancient defences, letting in the sunlight and torching the half-timbered houses. The Clifden Nonpareil, built from oak that had been felled when the city was barely a township, went up in a bellow of flame, and the fire scampered from roof to roof, devouring timbers and shattering glass.

The light was even more damaging. It cut through the glamours of Welkin Close, and where it fell, the Midnight Folk dispersed into pure quintessence, becoming flocks of tiny moths that rose into the air like motes caught in the bars of sunlight. Those Midnight Folk who could fought fiercely, but they were trapped and outnumbered, their strength no match for the enemy.

As Welkin Close collapsed into a cauldron of smoke, Cinnabar, her eyes alight, stood to face Brimstone in combat. His cold eyes met the flame of hers, and whatever may have been in his heart, he fought her with all the strength of his will. Both took to the air with wings like scythes, the Sun and the Moon together in all their riotous colours. For a time, they were locked as close as lovers, and as fierce; no longer human in any way, but like colliding stars that fell together in smoke and flames. Finally, Brimstone claimed victory, and Cinnabar's proud heart was broken, and she knelt on the burning cobblestones and spilled her quintessence into the air.

But even as his people rejoiced, Brimstone too seemed to falter and fall, his wings dispersing into smoke, his spirit drained and exhausted. Skipper, who would have finished the enemy to the very last man, instead took charge of the Daylight Folk and withdrew in the hope of saving him, while the Midnight Folk crept away and found their refuge under the city. And there they endured and live to this day, in the dead space and abandoned stations of World Below. Somehow, Cinnabar survived, and continues to lead her people as Regent to the Butterfly Queen.

Even the Sightless Folk witnessed the rout of Welkin Close, but explained it away as a house fire, a gas explosion, an arson attack. The Great Extinction of insect life that ensued was barely noticed but by a few lepidopterists, who recorded the loss of species that once had been common in their land – creatures they named Stout Dart, or Lovegrass, or Chestnut Ermine, or Dusky Thorn – and wondered at their disappearance. But the war between the tribes remained, and the survivors grew more numerous, more tolerant to sunlight, and stronger, not least in their continued resolve to eradicate their enemy . . .

2

Flying is always so easy in dreams. Like so many Sightless Folk, Tom had often dreamed of flight – but now that he was in the air, he realised that there was a lot more to it than simply thinking rosy thoughts. The misty air of London Before was filled with all kinds of turbulence. There were bursts of electricity, like the onset of a lightning storm; there were currents of air that snatched at his wings, and threatened to drag him off balance. And his wings were not like the wings of a bird; his arms were not engaged at all. Instead, he felt the effort of flight as a kind of *tightening* throughout his core, a series of muscular contractions that felt both familiar and strange.

In spite of the danger, Tom felt a sense of blissful exhilaration. *This* was what he had longed for all his life, he told himself. *This* was what he'd been missing – these wings that held him up and completed him. He felt a sudden certainty that *this* was what would make him worthy in Vanessa's eyes – his wings must surely convince her that he and she were soulmates—

He followed Charissa from Welkin Close through the narrow space between the buildings. She was far more skilful in flight; Tom, still struggling with his technique, kept knocking his wings against gutters and walls and washing lines as he battered his way through the darkness towards the dawning light and the open sky. Every time he struck an obstacle, he felt those contractions intensify as the wings corrected his movements, and he spun dizzily, trying not to look down, or imagine his fall through the sooty air to the cobbled courtyard below.

He saw that Charissa had already reached the temporary safety of a nearby rooftop. Alighting on the ridge, wings spread, she looked almost part of the slates to Tom; her wings, so delicately patterned, were the same lichen-and-verdigris shade, and in the light of the early dawn, her pale and tattooed skin seemed to blend into the grey of the roofscape. Tom noticed that his own wings seemed more boldly patterned, with vivid markings of black and white; but as he landed on the roof, he found himself equally camouflaged.

'We've been doing this for a long time,' said Charissa with a smile. 'Our people prefer to go unseen, to blend into their surroundings. The Daylight Folk have a different style. They *want* to be seen. They crave the attention. It's how they find their prey. But it's also their downfall.'

'But back in the alley, my colours...' said Tom, remembering how bright they had been; how they had kicked into the sky like a spray of Northern Lights. 'And you told Sable my colours were fixed. That I was corrupted.'

'Oh, stop going on about that. I've explained already,' said Charissa impatiently. 'Some of us fix our allegiances straight away; some take a little more time to decide. Given how Vanessa got to you from the start, I would have thought you'd have joined them by the time you declared your colours. But spending time with Spider and me, I guess that must have changed things a bit. You're neither one nor the other yet. Don't worry. Sometimes it takes time.'

'Terrific,' said Tom, with feeling. 'That's why *both* sides want my blood.'

'Oh, don't be so dramatic,' said Charissa. 'Just keep your head down and let this pass. We're not meant to be part of it, anyway.'

This was the Battle of Welkin Close, which was already under way a hundred feet below them. As they were speaking, Charissa had managed to manoeuvre Tom onto the far side of the roof, which was still in shadow. From there, Tom could see that both of them could remain unnoticed, camouflaged against the dappled stone slates. The sounds of the battle – cries of alarm, the crashing of doors being kicked in, strange reverberations that sounded almost like music, a dangerous resonance that seemed to come from harp strings under stress – came to him from what seemed like an unimaginable distance.

And in among all of it was the light, reflecting against the sooty stone; a light that looked like sunlight shining through cathedral glass; a light that danced like marsh fire over the rooftops and houses. That was what Charissa called their *glamour*, Tom thought; the strange and marvellous energy that all the Daylight Folk possessed. Whatever glamours the Midnight Folk used were focused on hiding and camouflage; but the enemy's charm and flamboyance drew him like—

A moth to a flame.

'Stay down,' Charissa said. 'Don't change more than you already have.'

But Tom couldn't help staring at the dancing lights on the rooftops. The sun had just begun to rise, and the sky was a rich and glorious red. Winged figures occasionally dipped into the sunlight before diving down once more into the darkness of Welkin Close, and the sound of their beating wings filled the air with turbulence. Tom had no wish to intervene, nor to endanger himself or Charissa. But the beauty of that vision was such that he could not prevent himself from lifting his head a little more; and, staring into the sunrise, he saw a strangely familiar figure. She had alighted on the ridge of a nearby rooftop. Her face was half-turned away from him, and her figure was mostly obscured by her wings, but her glamour – her *shine* – was unmistakable.

'Vanessa!' he whispered.

Charissa looked up. 'Shh! So what?' she hissed at him. 'Where did you expect her to be? Waiting back at the homestead?'

'But I—'

'Yeah, yeah, *you love her*,' she said. 'So? You're not going to have a tête-à-tête in the middle of a battle, are you? Wait here for now, and if she survives, you can find her later. OK?'

'Wait, what do you mean, *if she survives?*'

'Tom, you've already changed what *was*. You killed Pieris, remember?'

Tom's eyes widened. 'And what does that mean?'

'It means all bets are off,' she said. 'Anything could happen now. That's why it's essential that you lie low, stay out of the way, and make sure— *Where the hell are you going?*'

Charissa's last words came out as a kind of muffled, anguished scream, as Tom stood up, wings spread, on the roof.

'Get down!' hissed Charissa. 'Tom, *get down!*'

But Tom simply looked down at her and put his hand in his pocket. Queen Orfeia's token was still where he had left it; the tiny silver bell that had fallen from the lining of her coat. *Remember, you have my favour*, she'd said. *Use it, if ever you want to lose your way back to my Kingdom—*

Impulsively, he held it out to Charissa. 'I'm sorry it isn't a life-line,' he said. 'And I suppose that, if I'm with them, I shouldn't be trying to help you. But—'

He was suddenly aware that, in the act of pulling out the silver bell from the pocket of his jeans, he had also pulled out what was left of the dried flower from the Moonlight Market. For a fleeting, final moment, he caught its scent, more tender and potent than ever before; and with it, the fugitive memory of a girl on Old London Bridge, a girl with a smile like the sunrise. But the petals – withered, translucent with age – disintegrated at his touch. The scent – and with it, the memory – dispersed like smoke into the air. For a second, Tom felt a terrible loss, and then, both feeling and flower were gone, leaving only the bell in the palm of his hand.

He looked into Charissa's pale face, trying to grasp the memory. Then it all came back to him. His love. His dream. His soulmate—

Vanessa.

Tom held out his hand and placed the silver bell in Charissa's palm. It gave a single, tiny chime, almost of protest: *True Thomas, be true!* – but Vanessa had all his attention, and the silvery sound was lost to him. 'I won this in London Beyond,' he said. 'I hope it can help you find your way home.' Then, raising his voice against the cries of dismay from the alley far below, he shouted: '*Vanessa! It's me! Tom Argent!*'

And all hell broke loose over Welkin Close.

3

Charissa's wings flashed open, her vivid face reflecting the dawn. She called Tom's name, but Tom's attention was wholly on Vanessa; Vanessa, all in scarlet and black, her beautiful wings a kaleidoscope, her skin burnished bronze in the sunlight.

The face that he had forgotten so many times before was now turned slightly away from him, and he could see her profile. In the light of battle, her beauty was almost unearthly; inhuman as that of a drawn sword, or a timber wolf, or a swarm of bees. He gasped; and the words he had *wanted* to speak vanished into the turbulent air, and all that was left was her glamour, her *shine*, and the terrible joy of sacrifice.

Charissa was shouting something at him, but her voice was almost inaudible. Instead, Tom Argent's head was filled with a marvellous silence. He felt as if he had been plunged into clear and sunlit water. He could feel its touch on his skin; the scent of salt in his nostrils. It made him feel refreshed, reborn; it went straight to his head like champagne. And in the stillness, he heard *her* voice, which was soft and yet commanding:

You again, she said, and Tom was not sure whether she had spoken aloud, or in some intimate part of his mind. *Who are you? Why do you follow me?*

Tom tried to answer, but found himself unable to speak. The unearthly undersea light seemed to be all around him; it filled him with joy and energy. He felt utterly fearless; invulnerable in the light of her gaze.

Come closer, said Vanessa, and Tom obeyed instantly. He vaguely remembered someone saying that she could be dangerous. The memory made him laugh aloud.

Vanessa seemed to be laughing too, as if he had spoken his thoughts after all.

Everything is dangerous, whispered the silken voice in his head. *Everything is dangerous, and beauty—*

Beauty is everything.

Tom found that he was moving lightly over the roof slates. He no longer had any fear that he would fall. He did not consider the drop to the ground, or the sounds of battle beneath him. Welkin Close was forgotten. Charissa was forgotten. Even the fact that he'd started a war almost single-handed seemed as distant as a tale in some childhood picture book. His half-formed plan was wholly eclipsed by her terrible glamour.

You knew me, she said. *Who are you?*

'Tom Argent, from London Beyond,' he said, hearing his voice from far away. 'I came all this way to find you. To *save* you...' He was close to her now, close enough to smell her scent, which was like bluebells in the rain, and the aroma of a forest in spring, and the peppery sweetness of petrichor.

How sweet of you, Tom Argent, she said, looking straight into his eyes. Tom started to feel faint, and knew that it came from being near her. The first time she had kissed him, back in the alley at King's Cross, he had put it down to drunkenness. But his near miss with the Daylight Folk and his recent encounter with Pieris had shown him his mistake. He knew that if he let her touch him, she would drain him of his life as surely as he had drained Pieris'. He was not afraid of this. To be consumed by his beloved seemed at that moment as glorious and as inevitable as the movements of the stars.

But first he wanted to explain: to tell her why he was different. He wanted to confess his love in words that would win her dangerous heart. He wanted to tell her that he was the one she'd been waiting for all this time, a man with no allegiance, balanced between midday and midnight, born to save her and her kind from their bitter, endless war.

Vanessa laughed. 'But it's *my* war,' she said. 'It's *my* war, and I like it.' Reaching out her strong brown arms, she drew him gently into her embrace. 'It's *my* war, and *I* started it, and only I can end it.'

Then, looking deep into his eyes, she kissed him, and began to feed.

4

Tom had always imagined his death as a descent into darkness. But Vanessa's embrace was the opposite: it was like dipping into an ocean of light. *She loves me,* he thought, and the words seemed to shine around his head like a circlet of stars. *It may be for just this moment, but this moment is eternity—*

The world outside might be at war, but Tom Argent didn't hear any of that. The Battle of Welkin Close – the battle *he* had started – was reduced to nothing but a whispering, like the distant sound from a shell, and Vanessa was the ocean drawing him into her loving embrace, consuming him with sweetness. For less than a moment, he recalled the flower seller on Old London Bridge, the wistful scent of smoke, and her words: *You'd dare put a price on true love?*

Then, just as he was about to sink into bright oblivion, something struck him sharply and painfully on the back of the head, and a voice he almost recognised shouted, very close to his ear: 'Oh, for the sake of the Nine Worlds, why do you have to be so *dense?*'

The shock was like plunging his head into a bucket of icy water. Momentarily half stunned, Tom gasped and flailed as he found himself yanked backwards out of Vanessa's embrace and dragged across the roof slates. Gone was the sweetness; the ocean of light; the certainty that she loved him. Instead, he saw the sunrise, and heard the cries of dismay from below, and smelt

225

his own sweat, and the reek of smoke, and something that he *thought* might be goat—

Charissa was standing over him, holding the piece of broken brick that she had used to strike him. Her dappled skin was coloured scarlet with the sunrise. Around her, the lining of Spider's evercoat gleamed like shaken tinfoil.

Tom put a hand to the back of his head and gaped at her. 'You *hit* me with a brick!'

She shrugged. 'Well, *someone* had to. Vanessa would have tapped you witless otherwise. That is, if she'd found any wits to tap.'

Tom looked over the rooftop and saw Vanessa watching him. 'I thought you loved me, Tom,' she called. 'I thought you wanted to save me?'

'Oh, do shut up,' said Charissa. 'Your girl, Skipper, owes him a life. That means *you* owe him a favour.'

'Is that so?' Vanessa smiled.

'They're *your* rules,' said Charissa. 'Besides, you got a bargain. Ten minutes, alone and unharmed, with you. That's all he wanted. That's the price you have to pay for wiping out my people.'

For a moment, the two of them faced each other silently over the rooftops; one tall and burning bright as the sun, the other pale and small and drab, and shaking with ill-concealed fury.

'All right,' said Vanessa at last. 'But we won't have much chance to be private here.' She glanced at Charissa. 'I'm assuming we don't need your little friend for the conversation you had in mind?'

Charissa gave her a sullen look. 'If you think *I* care what he says to you—'

'Very well.' Vanessa laughed. 'Then come with me, Tom Argent,' she said. 'Ten minutes' grace for my favour. I confess

I'm a little curious. I know a place – a *safe* place – where we can be undisturbed.'

'Pff,' said Charissa, and pulled a face.

'It's OK,' said Tom, 'I'll be all right. I know what I'm doing.'

And then he spread his wings and prepared to follow Vanessa wherever she led, while, below them, the Battle of Welkin Close unfolded like a bloodstained sheet flung over the alleys of London Before, and as the enemy descended en masse, it just as rapidly started to burn.

5

The battle was as localised as it was ferocious. As he left the epicentre, Tom saw the column of greasy smoke rising into the rosy sky, and overflew a fire engine, drawn by two heavy horses, heading towards the conflagration. But once they were clear of Welkin Close, there was no sign of glamours, or of carnage.

Tom had always felt that most Londoners lacked curiosity. To live in the city meant to refuse engagement with the unusual. In this regard, this version of London was not dissimilar to his own. People dressed predominantly in brown, blue and grey, and refrained from meeting each other's eyes, or acknowledging what did not concern them directly, lest they become entangled in something dangerous or profane.

Tom Argent had always been more curious and perceptive than most, but flying over the London streets, he realised how little even he had seen of the city that was his home. From this new angle, he was repeatedly struck by the beauty of grime: the detail and the intricacy of ridge tile and chimney pot, the gilding of the sun's rays on the grisaille of the smog. The whole of London seemed to reflect the dazzling shine of the Daylight Folk; and he longed to capture it on film, and share its secrets with the world. So too he longed to capture Vanessa, ahead of him, in flight; and fumbling his camera out of his overcoat pocket, he took several shots of her as they flew, hoping for one of those splendid juxtapositions of subject and light, those accidents of movement and form that only ever happen on film.

He had barely taken a dozen shots when Vanessa slowed her flight, looped down and alighted on a path by the north side of the river.

Tom took a moment to find his bearings. There was Vauxhall Bridge, he saw, but the rest of the terrain was unknown to him. There was no main road, no buildings; just the dirt path leading up to the bridge, and a number of miserable wooden shacks too small to be thought of as homes, but which nevertheless, he realised, housed some of the poorest of Londoners. A pair of wide-eyed children sat on the bank, watching them pass; a woman washed a handful of rags, her skirts hitched up, her feet in the mud. As Vanessa passed her, the woman flinched and looked away, as if to avoid meeting her gaze. Tom wondered whether she knew that she was in the presence of a superior being, a predator.

Out of her winged aspect, Vanessa was once more discreetly clad in a bronze-coloured gown and dainty half-boots, her thick dark hair gathered beneath a broad-brimmed bonnet of the same shade as her gown. Tom thought she looked stunning; reaching again for his camera, but keeping it hidden by his side, he took another couple of shots of Vanessa in profile. He sensed that she might not approve of his taking her image without consent. But Tom was used to collecting images in secret, and if he had photographs, then he would never again forget her face, not if she displayed herself in a hundred different forms.

Vanessa had not noticed the small sound of the shutter. Nor had she seen Tom furtively hide the camera under his coat. She made her way delicately over the dirt path towards the bridge, where a community of boat builders had left a giant stack of logs and unfinished craft by the water's edge. Tom wondered why Vanessa had not chosen the nearby pleasure gardens for their meeting, and thought, in a rare moment of clarity, that the river would be an easier place to dispose of a body. Chilling as that was, and in spite of everything he had been told, he still did not quite believe that Vanessa – lovely Vanessa *Before* – would be willing to harm him. And so he followed her to the shelter of the bridge's steel pillars, where she finally turned to him and gave a smile of such luminous sweetness that Tom almost forgot his plan, and the camera hidden inside his coat.

'Well, Tom Argent, tell your tale. After all, you've paid the price.'

Tom nodded, almost too awed to speak. Beneath the borrowed overcoat, the camera collected her image again. He hated to deceive her, but he remembered Spider's warning: *they say it steals their soul away, although, of course, they never had any in the first place.* Of course, Spider had been referring to Charissa, as yet so unremarkable that he had not even seen her. But when Tom had seen the negatives, he'd found that not only could he *see* her, he could also *remember* her. More than that, in his negatives she'd been anything but unremarkable. The Charissa he'd collected on film had been—

'*Beautiful*,' Tom said aloud, still caught up in the memory.

Vanessa gave an impatient shrug. 'Please don't tell me you have done all this to spout *platitudes*.'

'No. I ... I was just thinking,' said Tom. 'Bear with me. I have a story to tell.'

And so Tom Argent began his tale in as much detail as he could. He told her about the camera shop, and the photographs, and the evercoat, and the champagne bar at St Pancras, and of Brimstone's debt to him. He told her of his choice, his mistake, and how, if he had known then what he knew now, he would never have let her go.

'But now we have another chance. Together, we can end this war. Now that I finally know who I am – a Moth, in love with a Butterfly—'

'What?' Vanessa frowned at him. Her beautiful face was no less beautiful for it, but for the first time, Tom saw petulance there, and cruelty. 'What are you talking about? Did you not hear what I told you, over Welkin Close?'

Tom began to stutter. 'B-but... you loved me. I know you did. That's why Spider sent me here. To give me a second chance with you. Just like in the story. To break the curse. To end the war. A Moth and a Butterfly, in love, bringing their people home.'

Vanessa laughed. 'Oh, please,' she said. 'Is *that* what you took from all this? I told you before, Tom. This is *my* war. Only I can end it, and I have no inclination to do so.'

'Then why am I here?'

Once more, she laughed. 'I imagine Spider sent you here because he thought you'd be safer in London Before. And because he had no choice. Both sides were the enemy. Only the contents of his coat gave him any power. Without it, he's no one. If the Midnight Folk hadn't somehow managed to steal it away, my people would have destroyed it, and with it, any further chance of returning to the Kingdom.'

'But why?' said Tom. 'I don't understand.'

Her voice grew sharp with impatience. 'Tom, do you even know who I am? Can you not see, with your glamorie-glass?'

Tom moved his hand protectively over the camera in his coat.

'You think I didn't see you?' she said. 'Collecting your little memories?' Her laughter was hard and cruel now, and nothing like the tinkling of bells. 'Ask Imago Burnet who I am. Tell him to show you *his* photographs. I'm sure he still has them, though I can see why he might not want to display them. Tell him his plan has failed, Tom: his ridiculous plan to melt my heart.

Imago Burnet knows I *have* no heart. Tell him that he and the Spinnerman have lost their chance of ending this war. And tell him' – she gave Tom a smile, devastating and inhuman – 'tell him Queen Vanessa says his son is *not* the lost Prince, for *my* son would have known me, even through my glamours.' She looked at Tom again, and her eyes were hard and as dead as fallen stars. 'Thus ends our pact, Tom Argent,' she said in a voice from which all kindness had gone. 'Now fly, little Moth, and spare your wings. Next time, my flame will burn them.'

Part II

—

Imago

I

Love never ends — but it changes. In some cases, it grows like a tree, stronger and more fruitful. In others, it changes its nature, like chrysalis to butterfly. The Moth girl had loved her young man for so long that she never saw it coming: that sense that the hunger she'd felt all her life was about to be satisfied.

She'd kept him safe for so many years, had followed him through perils, protecting him at the cost of her own safety and that of her people. And all the time, she'd hoped that he would finally see her, love her in his own world, and not simply in dreams. But now, she understood. The Butterfly Queen, in her glamours, would always eclipse reality. Her young man had been lost to her from the moment he saw her.

She clenched his parting gift to her tight between her fingers. It was a tiny silver bell, the shape and size of a cherry stone. She doubted he knew what it was. But she understood its chime. It was the call of another world, the sound of another seduction. Love was a cheat, an illusion, it said. To pursue its little light would always lead to heartbreak. What mattered — what really mattered — was something else entirely. Something that commanded love without ever being at its command. Something that shone as bright as the sun, and collected its light like a glamorie-glass. Something that was cold at heart, so the heart could never be broken. This was what the bell promised her.

Power.

2

Tom walked back to the shop in King's Cross. The thought of using his new wings did not even occur to him; in fact, he could hardly believe they had ever existed. The thought that he could summon them into being at will, as Vanessa had, seemed like some kind of fairy tale, the kind his father had taken away as soon as he had realised how much Tom wanted to believe.

There was no sign of Charissa. This did not surprise him. Charissa and her people had always had the skill of going unseen when they needed to. Nor was there sign of the Daylight Folk, nor sound of the sacking of Welkin Close, nor the rout of its people. But Charissa was strong and resourceful. She was more than capable of looking after herself. And maybe, with the help of Queen Orfeia's token, she'd managed to find a way out of this world and back to her own London. It should have been a comforting thought. But the thought of a world with no Charissa in it made Tom feel unexpectedly bleak. Somehow, he'd got used to her being around. Her sarcasm. Her matter-of-factness. The unexpectedness of her smile. Even the dreadful overcoat. That feeling of having *known* her, been friends with her, for years and years.

The sun had already risen above the narrow, smoky streets. Now Tom was surrounded by the sounds of human activity. There were drovers, workmen, traders, piemen, road sweepers and hackneys, and though he attracted the odd sideways glance, he mostly managed to pass unseen, in spite of the slight out-landishness that his borrowed clothes had not quite managed to conceal.

But his mind was not on his surroundings. Thoughts of Charissa continued to intrude upon his consciousness. With an effort, he forced himself to focus on Vanessa, the shock of her rejection and on the words she had spoken by the river.

Tell him Queen Vanessa says his son is not *the lost Prince.*

Was Vanessa the Butterfly Queen? Was Burnet the Moth King? And why had she called Tom Burnet's son? It sounded like one of the fairy tales his parents had so discouraged, and yet it was no more bizarre than anything else he had experienced. He had followed a stitch in Time. He'd followed the road to Faërie. He had taken quintessence from Pieris, and flown over London Before on wings that he could summon at will. Charissa had called him Prince Argent. Vanessa herself had called him Moth. And if he *wasn't* the lost Prince, then just where did that leave him?

His head was aching as he reached the little shop by King's Cross. The door was locked, and the CLOSED sign hung against the dusty glass. Tom tapped on the glass panel, half expecting no one to answer, but the door opened almost at once with a rustle of silken skirts and a woman's voice saying: 'Thank God, you're safe. We've been so worried about you.'

'Charissa?' said Tom. The shop was dark, and he had only the vaguest impression of who had opened the door to him. But already he was sure that the woman was not Charissa. This woman was too tall, too slim, in her brown silk dress and her long, curly hair. Her voice was not Charissa's, though it did seem oddly familiar.

It was the Temperance woman he had saved from Pieris. Of

course, he'd sent her to find Burnet. It felt like a hundred years ago.

'Quick, come in before someone sees you.' The woman took his hand in hers, drawing him in and closing the door. 'I'm so glad you're safe, Mr Argent. I believe I owe you my life.'

He followed her through the darkened shop, which smelt of dust and chemicals. A single gas lamp burned at the back. Now Tom found he could dimly make out the photographs on Burnet's wall, like insects in a collector's case. He shivered. What *had* seemed like a whimsical thought now proved to be only too close to the truth. And Burnet himself had told him that he, too, was a collector.

'Is Mr Burnet here, Miss, er . . . ?' said Tom, feeling a little awkward.

She smiled. 'You can call me Temperance. Mr Burnet is waiting for you. He's told me so much about you.'

'And Charissa? Is she here?'

Temperance shook her head. 'Not yet. I heard there was trouble on Welkin Close. Mr Burnet was very concerned. Here, come and sit in the parlour, and you can tell him what happened.'

Tom followed her into the anteroom, where the gas lamp was burning. Imago Burnet was sitting in a vast old leather armchair, surrounded by over-stacked bookcases and pictures and curiosities. On a small table, there was a tray, a decanter and three tiny glasses filled with some kind of yellow liqueur. Burnet handed Tom a glass, though Temperance, who was drinking tea, looked somewhat disapproving. 'I'm very glad you're here, my boy. I heard what happened on Welkin Close. How much did you see? How did you escape?'

Tom found the liqueur deceptively strong. It seemed slightly luminous in the glass, and he guessed it must contain nectar. Feeling revived, he told the tale of his escape from the Clifden

Nonpareil, his bargain with Skipper, Charissa, and the evercoat. Burnet showed no surprise until Tom mentioned the evercoat, at which he leaned forward, eyes suddenly keen.

'She has it?' he said. 'Where is it now?'

But Tom was frowning. 'I don't understand. *I* was the one who let Skipper escape. *I* started the Battle of Welkin Close. I'm the one to blame for all that. But all *you* seem to care about are stupid things like Spider's coat, or a—'

'Tom,' said Burnet patiently. 'The Battle of Welkin Close was already history when you were born. How could you be respons-ible for it?' He poured himself another glass of the strange yellow liqueur. 'Time is a mysterious thing. It changes according to where we stand. Objectively, you might even say that it doesn't exist at all. What do we have to show, after all, for the moments of our lives? Memory. That's all we have. Whatever happened at Welkin Close would have come to pass anyway. The fact that *you* triggered it this time round doesn't alter anything.'

Tom felt at the same time relieved and faintly offended. 'Is that why I never had a second chance with Vanessa?' And he repeated what she had said to him by Vauxhall Bridge. Burnet listened in silence, sipping from time to time from his glass.

'Dear boy,' he said at last. 'I'm sure you are aware that Vanessa is not like the rest of her folk.' He reached for a box on one of his shelves, and opened it with a small silver key. Inside was a stack of artwork: drawings, sketches, photographs. The box itself was old and ornate, made of some dense dark wood, and chased with intricate silver designs that had faded and blackened with age.

'What's this?' Tom asked.

'Memories,' said Mr Burnet, and lifted out the contents. He carefully placed the artwork onto the side table, then reached into his breast pocket and drew out an ornate fob under glass, in which a tiny portrait gleamed like a fly in amber.

'It looks like Vanessa,' Tom said. 'But this is *old*—'

Burnet gave a sad and bitter smile. 'Time is a complicated thing,' he said. 'Especially for the likes of us. We have passed across the worlds, across the web of Time itself, in service of our quest to bring the lost Prince back to our people. Over the centuries, I have collected many Aspects of the Prince – fragments of his scattered self – in the hope that the Queen might one day relent, and permit love back into her life. But Vanessa has long since abandoned hope of ever finding happiness. All she cares for now is revenge. And however hard I try to prepare any potential chrysalis, she always somehow manages to charm and corrupt them to her purposes. But the price has been high for both of us. Look at her. See for yourself.'

Tom looked again at the miniature. It was unmistakably Vanessa, but as he'd never seen her before: Vanessa in the court clothes of another century, her hair dressed in elaborate curls, her wings unfurled in a fan of inhuman colours. But the most startling thing about it was the expression on her face – that look of openness, of *love*, that seemed to shine from her features.

'This was Vanessa when we first met.' Burnet's voice was wistful; his face in the lamplight was lily pale. 'She was loving, in those days – bright and full of mischief. But with the loss of our son, she changed. She forswore love on behalf of her kind, and grew ever colder and more cruel. It was my fault, I admit it, and if I could change the past, I would. But that past cannot be changed. Our son was the stitch that bound us together. Without him, we flew further apart. And over the years, under her rule, the Daylight Folk became increasingly cruel and predatory, feeding on what nectar they found and hunting my Folk whenever they could, for *her* people have long given up hope of ever finding our son, or going home to the Kingdom, and instead have built a court of dreams in the land of the Sightless Folk.'

Burnet took a last long look at the portrait in the fob, then returned it to his breast pocket. 'The Vanessa I knew died a long time ago. Our quarrel is too old for mending. And when the last Moth has been hunted down, the last part of myself removed from the fragments of our son, then will her vengeance be complete, and she will have become, at last, the monster she once swore she would be.'

Tom said: 'She isn't a monster.'

'Look at the pictures,' said Burnet. 'See her without her glamours.'

Tom looked through the pieces of artwork spread out on the table. All of them were portraits, arranged, he saw, by age. Now Tom could see the change that time had wrought in his beloved. She was no less beautiful, but he could see how, over the years and the centuries, her features had changed, growing harder and more angular.

Mr Burnet opened a box to reveal a display of glass negatives. 'These are the most recent and faithful of my portraits,' he said. 'Here we see her true face, stripped of all its glamours.'

Tom studied the negatives. Here, the change was more pronounced. Like those flower images that had once excited him, these negatives seemed to reveal so much more than the eye could see. In the portraits, Vanessa had looked human. But in the negatives, Tom saw a woman of inhuman age and otherworldly beauty, her hair pulled back from a face that seemed hacked out of volcanic glass. The lips were full, but scornful; the brows arched in perpetual query. And the eyes – those *eyes!* – were enormous, pupil-less and devouring. They were the eyes of something that was eternally, morbidly hungry. To look into those eyes would be to fall into a pitcher plant; to drown in the pit of her appetite.

'How did you get these?' Tom asked, his professional instinct momentarily overriding his horror.

Imago Burnet gave a bitter smile. 'She comes to me once a year,' he said. 'She knows how much it pains me. She knows she is perfectly safe in my house. My people will not harm her. She sits for me in my studio, and shows me the face of her grief and despair. She knows that this will hurt me more than anything else her people might do, and besides, she is vain and vengeful, and she wants to be sure that I still love her.'

'How would she know that?' said Tom.

'Only the eye of true love can pierce the glamours of our Folk. That's why it's so clear that the love you felt for her is an illusion. You don't see Vanessa. You see only what she wants you to see. Compare that with Charissa.'

Tom frowned. 'Charissa's different.'

'Of course she's different,' said Burnet. 'You could see her from the start. Her glamours never worked on you, not even as a chrysalis. And didn't Spider send her here to try to break Vanessa's spell? If you and she had had the time – or if you had remembered some part of her love for you—'

'Remembered her *what*?' said Tom, perplexed. 'Charissa doesn't love me. She hit me with a *brick*!'

He stopped. The idea was absurd. Charissa didn't love him. True, she had saved his life at least twice, but she had also called him a bread roll, sneered at his photography and told him he was thick as mince. He found himself smiling at the thought, and at the sudden memory of the farmyard smell of her stolen overcoat, and the scatter of freckles across her face, and the unexpected touch of her hair against his mouth in the alleyway.

He shook his head to clear it. *No!* He was in love with *Vanessa*. Vanessa was the woman of his dreams. Vanessa, his goddess.

Vanessa, his queen. Vanessa, whose face he had once again forgotten the moment he had left her.

'Without memory, there can be no love,' said Burnet. 'It changes everything. That's why you never remembered her, even though you wanted her. That's why the Moonlight Market conducts most of its trade in memories.' He indicated the books on his shelves, where among the leather-bound novels, and books of poetry bound in suede, and pamphlets and sermons, and Bibles, and scientific journals, there were more colourful, cloth-bound books, with gilded spines and titles such as: *Holly Blue, 3 Months*, and *Hairstreak, 19 Weeks*, and *Meadow Brown, 8 Months*, and *Vanessa, 13 Days*.

'The Market!' said Tom, remembering WILLOWHERB'S BARTERED BOOKS. 'Spider was buying those books for *you!*'

'So, you do remember *something*.' Burnet nodded. 'Yes, Spider was buying books for me. Vanessa was trading her memories for baubles at the Market. I sent him to retrieve them. I told you, she was never wise.'

But Tom had noticed another book, shelved between a dictionary and four volumes of Spenser's *The Faerie Queene*. Its dark-coloured spine was almost concealed behind an ornate carriage clock, but it had drawn him nevertheless.

'I don't think you should read that, Tom,' said Mr Burnet in a warning tone.

But Tom had already pulled out the book from the dusty, crowded shelf. It looked at the same time old and unread; familiar and strange. Holding it between his hands, Tom was surprised by the weight of it; the detailing on the frontispiece; the thickness of the paper; the richness of the marbled edges.

The silken cover was midnight blue, and embossed with the shape of a moth on a flower, in outline against a full moon. And the title, in intricate lettering, read: *Tom Argent: 101 Moonlit Nights*.

3

Tom scanned the pages of the book in growing fascination. It felt both real and impossible, like one of those half-remembered fairy tales, lavishly illustrated and read under the covers by torchlight, before his parents quietly deleted them from his childhood.

It was his story. A hundred and one forgotten nights, spanning fourteen years of his life, which was exactly the number of times the full moon had risen during that time, unclouded, on Old London Bridge. A hundred and one Moonlight Markets. It seemed impossible. And yet, somehow, all the details were there. His fanciful childhood; his camera; his lonely adolescence. His sense that there existed things outside of his line of vision, things that his parents had warned him against; a magic not born from chemicals, or celluloid, or lenses. And running through his story, from adolescence to adulthood, always by moonlight, but bright as the sun, there was Charissa. But this was a different Charissa to the one he thought he knew; that fierce and cynical Moth girl, loyal only to herself.

Here was Charissa as a girl, hopeful and filled with laughter. Here, as an adolescent, wise one moment, childish the next. Here, she glanced out from the pages as an adult, a lover, a friend; dancing in the firelight, poised against the starry sky. Here, she was trusting, loving, unmasked, gentle and filled with confidences. Here, by the light of the full moon, she was not only beautiful, she was by far the most beautiful woman Tom had ever seen.

And now Tom Argent realised what he should have guessed before, what he should have seen in her eyes while he had been dazzled by someone else. *She* was the girl on the bridge, the one who had kissed him so tenderly. *Hers* was the shine he had recognised, reflected in Vanessa. *She* had been the memory contained in the flower seller's gift, the flower that only blossoms once, like innocence—

Like true love.

The knowledge was wormwood, ashes, dust. Now he saw with terrible clarity how, through his selfishness and greed, he had forsaken his true love, time and time again, across a hundred and one incarnations of the Moonlight Market. He'd fallen in love with her every time he'd seen her during those a hundred and one nights. And yet, every time, he'd forgotten her, disappointed her, cheated her – and for what? For the sake of a fantasy. For a collection of photographs. Now he understood her scorn as he had pursued Vanessa, not knowing that *she* was the one, that she had *always* been the one. He understood her mockery, her insults. He understood her tone of voice when she had called him *Collector*. He winced at the contempt he had shown for her love, her trust, her loyalty.

Except that wasn't what it was. What had the flower seller said? *Never mind. It remembers you.* Love, the flower that blooms only once, had kept those buried memories; had stored them in a place where even magic could not follow. Love cannot be snatched away as readily as memory; and even as he returned to his world like a man awakening from a dream, a part of him had remembered, not only that she was his love, but that her image had to be *kept*, that only film could be trusted.

'*That* was why I couldn't stop taking photographs,' said Tom. 'I wanted to prove she wasn't a dream. I wasn't stealing memories. I needed to be sure it was *real*. Oh, God. If only I'd *trusted* her!'

Mr Burnet watched him patiently. 'I told you,' he said. 'Hindsight is a window that shows nothing but disappointment. Spider wove his plans, in the hope that the two of you would fall in love, but once Vanessa came along I knew that it was useless. Vanessa always wins that game. Even if you'd remembered—'

'But I *do* remember!' said Tom. In a trembling voice, he explained about the flower seller's gift, and the memories it had brought back. 'I remember everything. I love her, and I always will.'

'So, where is she?' said Mr Burnet. 'Because if you really love her, then she is in terrible danger.'

'She's safe,' said Tom. 'I sent her home.' He explained about the silver bell, and how he had given it to her in exchange for Spider's lifeline.

'That's *not* a way home,' said Mr Burnet.

'But the Queen said it led to her Kingdom,' said Tom.

'And where do you *think* Queen Orfeia rules? *Death has no power in my realm, and neither has Grief, nor Memory.* Isn't that what she said to you? There's no coming back from her Kingdom, any more than from Death itself.'

Tom felt his blood run cold. 'I have to find her! Stop her!' he said.

Burnet looked at him pityingly. 'It's too late, Tom. Charissa's gone. If she used the token, it means she no longer cares for you. And if she stayed, why isn't she here? I can only think of one reason. The Daylight Folk would do anything to stop my people from ending this war. Including hunting down anyone who might be dangerous to their plans. If Charissa loves you ...'

'But how could they possibly know?' said Tom. 'Nobody suspects she's here. No one even saw her, except—' He swallowed, then said in a small voice, 'No one except Vanessa.'

4

For a moment, Tom sat in silence. He felt at the same time numb, stricken, anxious, ashamed, and now, strangely, *wide awake*. Burnet's collection of images had opened his eyes in a startling way, showing him Vanessa as she *was*, instead of how he had dreamed her. He had come to London Before convinced that she was his destiny. He had risked his life for her, willingly and without hesitation. He had started a war for her sake without the slightest pang of remorse.

But now he could see clearly again. He understood how his desire to be a hero had blinded him. He saw how his need to be special, to capture true love like a butterfly, had made him see only the glamours of love, and none of its reality.

But Charissa – he'd always seen her exactly as she really was. He'd taken it for granted that everything about her was true. Her small, freckled face. Her fierce scornful voice. The delicate spiral tattoos on her arms. Her eyes, like blades. Her golden wings under Spider's old coat.

Tom was aware of a sudden feeling in the pit of his stomach. It was a feeling he'd had once before, as a boy, when he'd tripped over the rug at the top of the stairs, while carrying a breakfast tray from his mother's bedroom. That eerie sensation of freefall; of knowing that something irreparable had happened, but not yet having experienced the terrible moment of impact—

It can't be too late, he told himself. *There has to be something I can do*. But what could be done, when the outcome was known? When every possibility had been played out again and again?

Turning quickly to Burnet, he said: 'Vanessa called me Moth. But Charissa told me I hadn't declared my true colours yet. What did she mean?'

'She meant that your allegiance remains undetermined,' said Burnet. '*Argent* is a name that can refer both to a Moth *and* a Butterfly. It means that you choose your colours, instead of having them imposed by birth.' He sighed. 'But all this comes too late. Just like me, you have lost your chance to change the course of our destiny.'

'Not if I go after her!'

'You've already lost her,' said Burnet. 'If they have Charissa, Tom, the Daylight Folk will consume her. They will end her life, or worse: they will make her one of their own, a soulless thing, with no memory of love, or comfort, or kindness.'

'There has to be something I can do,' said Tom. 'What about Spider's evercoat?'

Burnet shrugged. 'Without him, the evercoat is useless. A relic from a vanished world. Even Spider has forgotten half of what's inside it. Midnight Folk, Daylight Folk – we've all tried to unravel its truths at one time or another. But only Spider can do that – and he refuses to do so until the curse of our people is ended.'

'But this is *true love*!' said Tom in despair. 'I can't give up on true love!'

Burnet shook his head sadly. 'The Daylight Folk feed on love,' he said. 'In the absence of yours, they will consume hers, and make of her a thing like them, to taunt you with their victory. And then, like me, you will spend your life in misery and bitterness, collecting fragments of what might have been – without her, for ever.' He looked at Tom with a kind of sad and terrible affection. 'You asked me once how I knew you, Tom. I know you just as you know yourself. I know you because we are the same – creatures caught in amber. I am *you*, Tom. You are me, seen from different points in Time. Today, you are Tom Argent. Tomorrow, you will be Imago Burnet. Both of us tangled in her hateful web. Thus it has always been, since the start. Thus is her vengeance satisfied.'

5

'But I don't *want* to be you,' said Tom. He hadn't understood all of what Burnet had said, but this much at least was clear to him. Both of them were part of some kind of repeating pattern, reflected across the centuries like figures in a mirror maze. And Vanessa linked them – though Tom had never loved her; what he had *believed* he had felt was no more than an illusion. *Charissa* was real. Charissa, who had risked her life to help him—

'You have no choice,' said Mr Burnet.

'There's always a choice,' said Tom fiercely. '*True love and certain death, or eternity without her.* That's what Queen Orfeia said.'

'True love, *and certain death*,' repeated Burnet with emphasis. 'This isn't one of your fairy tales, Tom. There's no *happily ever after*. There's only certain death, or the rest of your life without her. And even if you knew she was there, and even if you could find them, the Daylight Folk would never let you live long enough to see her.'

'What do you mean, *if* I could find them?' said Tom.

'The greatest strength of the Daylight Folk is their adaptability. They move to a different place every night, they adapt to suit their surroundings. If you'd kept your lifeline, you might have followed them to their lair. But you gave away your chance, Tom, like every other fool in love.'

'I'm not giving up, Mr Burnet.'

'Brave words. But how will you find them?'

'I could follow Vanessa's signature,' said Tom, remembering the light trails that he and Charissa had followed through the tunnels under London Before. He'd seen the signatures left by the Midnight Folk with his camera – why couldn't he use it again to find the lair of the Daylight Folk?

'Signatures decay too fast in daylight for that to be possible.'

'I took some shots of Vanessa. Perhaps, if we could look at them, we might see where she was heading.'

For the first time, a flicker of hope passed over Burnet's tired features. 'Pictures of Vanessa?' he said. 'Taken without her knowledge?'

'I know, it's kind of creepy,' said Tom. 'But—'

Burnet had put down his liqueur glass. His look of resignation was gone. 'We need to develop these pictures at once. Come with me to the darkroom.' In two strides, he was out of the room, with Tom following eagerly at his heels, leaving Temperance holding her cup of cold tea, a study of perfect confusion.

Part *12*

———

Quintessence

I

Memory or power, she said. It's a simple choice to make. One is a constant turbulence of grief and disappointment. The other is a cloudless sky filled with new possibilities. Imagine being able to cast aside the things that keep you earthbound – the pain, the guilt, the rejection – and replace them instead with joy and delight, and music, and dancing, and pleasure. And love! Why tend to such a dull garden when you could have your pick of blooms: adoration, and worship, and applause, without any of the suffering? So the Moth girl told herself as she went over her memories, and let them fly into the air like ashes from a bonfire. Let my garden burn, *she thought.* Let my memories go free. Let me die as a Moth and be reborn as a glorious Butterfly, to live in the sunlight and feed upon your blind infatuation. I should have known from the first, *she thought,* what to expect from the Sightless Ones. Why did I cling to him for so long? What did I hope to find in him that I could not find in myself?

Thus did the girl of the Moth Folk consider the choice that was offered her. True love, and certain death, or to be reborn into sunlight? To be a Moth, in darkness, or a Butterfly, sipping nectar? And yet, for a second, she seemed to recall a moonlit bridge, and the touch of a hand against hers, and the scent of a flower that blooms only once – before the Moth she had once been was consumed by the flame of the Butterfly.

2

'I don't have quite the same chemicals as you have in London Beyond,' said Mr Burnet to Tom. 'I'll have to improvise, I'm afraid. I hope the result will be good enough.'

Tom waited restlessly for Burnet to develop the film. The chemicals were toxic, he said: best not to be exposed to them unless absolutely necessary. Then the two of them waited for the roll of film to dry – Tom with an impatience that twisted inside him like hot wire – before finally going to look.

The darkroom was small, with a bench, a stool, an oil lamp, and a stretched line on which the film hung like a piece of curling flypaper. '*There*. There, in the final frames,' Tom said, squinting at the negatives in the light of the oily-smelling lamp. 'I see her. That's Vanessa.'

Burnet cut the negatives and slid them between two pieces of glass. Then, holding the lamp in place, he peered over them for a moment. 'Yes. There she is. How she has changed.' He passed the slide once more to Tom, his face a mixture of sadness and longing. 'Here she is in true Aspect,' he said, 'without any of her glamours and veils. Here is the creature she has become – a creature of sorrow and hunger, seeking what she can never find, forever exiled from herself.' He sighed and turned away. 'Go on. Look for yourself. See if you can find a clue to the whereabouts of the Daylight Folk.'

Tom squinted over the slides. There were half a dozen of

them in all, taken at various stages of his flight with Vanessa and their walk towards Vauxhall Bridge. Most showed her profile, but one, taken just as she turned her head, had caught her face almost perfectly. That face! For a moment, Tom was transfixed. Of course, he already knew Vanessa was a monster. But the images in Burnet's collection had at least had some human features. These had none. In negative, Vanessa looked nothing like a woman at all; what lurked beneath her image was a being all horror and pity. Its hair was white, its skin whiter still; its eyes like those of a creature that has never seen the sun. And in its unguarded expression he saw both inexpressible sorrow and an insatiable appetite that at the same time made his skin crawl and filled his eyes with sudden tears.

'I had no idea,' he said, remembering the woman who had come into his shop, the woman who had seemed to shine with all the brightness of summer.

Burnet sighed. 'You did well,' he said. 'I know of no one else who could have captured her soul so faithfully.'

'But what about her signature?' Once more, Tom scrutinised the image. Hard to tell from a negative whether there was anything more for him to find. It was so hard to look at her; the woman – the *thing* – that he had so blindly yearned for—

He tore his eyes from Vanessa's face. Charissa still needed his help. And while he felt a kind of grief at the loss of his illusion, the thought of harm to Charissa was an almost physical pain. Again he scanned the negatives for a sign – the faintest scrawl of a signature – that might lead to the Court of the Butterfly Queen.

And then he saw, at the edge of the frame, a kind of scribble of darkness across a sky that would have been bright with colours, had it not been a negative. A scribble; maybe a signature – but what did it mean? Where did it lead? Tom looked closer, hoping to see an image in the negative, but there was nothing more than a blur that might have been a watermark. He realised how much he had longed to find something more tangible – a map, or even a poster, like the ones for the Moonlight Market.

He looked again. That blurry stain might almost be a Rorschach test. For a moment, he thought it looked like a bird; then a badger; then some kind of reptile. He narrowed his eyes, desperate now to evoke some kind of image, but still the meaning eluded him. The signature – if that's what it was – remained indecipherable.

Tom groaned and put his head in his hands. Failing simply flying about all over London in search of a trail, there was nothing he could do. *True love, and certain death.* No words had ever carried such a dreadful resonance.

There came a tiny knock on the door.

Tom looked up and saw Temperance, holding a flyer in her hand, looking shy but determined.

'Oh, please,' said Tom. 'No tracts, OK? I'm really not in the market for tracts.'

'It isn't a tract,' Temperance said. 'That man in the alleyway dropped it, just before he spoke to me. I thought maybe it might be a clue.'

'Pieris had this?' Tom said, taking the printed flyer.

Temperance nodded.

Tom read the flyer, which was printed on cheap yellow paper. Images of animals – badgers, birds and reptiles – under the heading: MR SLOANE'S COLLECTION.

He felt a tiny glimmer of hope.

'Do you think it might be a clue?' Temperance was still watching him with the air of a bird who had been saved from the claws of a vicious tomcat. Her moth-coloured eyes shone now with a mixture of caution and gratitude.

Tom looked up at smiled. 'You know, I think maybe it is,' he said.

Then, ignoring Burnet's questioning, he headed out of the camera shop and back into the streets of King's Cross, where, heedless of traffic or passers-by, and without any hesitation, he summoned his wings and took to the skies of London, in pursuit of true love and certain death, like a prince in a fairy tale.

3

Not since Mr Coxwell's famous balloon race had London seen such activity in its skies. The Battle of Welkin Close had been mostly conducted by stealth, the worst of its ravages hidden from sight by the glamours of the Silken Folk, but now that it was over, the sky seemed filled with vapour trails and strange lights. Even the Sightless Folk could see that something unusual was afoot; and there were several reports of a man – or maybe more than one man – flying over the London fog on wings just like a butterfly's.

Thanks to Temperance, Tom had a destination. MR SLOANE'S COLLECTION had been a haven of his childhood; and now at last he recognised the terracotta images of row upon row of creatures, standing guard at every turn, on every tile and surface.

When Tom Argent was a boy, he had loved the Natural History Museum. Alfred Waterhouse's design – the ceilings, the doorways, the gargoyles – had fascinated him at least as much as the museum's contents. There was magic here, of a kind; a magic born from wonder at the endless diversity of Nature. In London Before, it was still very new – and it was filled with visitors. What better place for the Daylight Folk to parade their charms and glamours? And what better place for them to collect than the roof of that fabulous building?

It was harder to find than he'd thought. He wasn't used to a bird's-eye view, and London Before was an alien place, very different to the London he knew. He tried to keep to familiar streets, to pass familiar landmarks; but even so, it took some time to reach his destination. His new wings felt at the same time marvellously a *part of* him and strangely out of his control, pulling him this way and that until he was quite exhausted.

It was almost noon by the time he arrived. He selected a piece of parapet, shielded from view by a section of the building's elaborate fronting, where wolves and ermines and weasels and wildcats preened and stretched themselves against the sunny red stone. There were insects up there, too: mantises and crickets and beetles and moths. And, of course, there were butterflies. Cast into the ridge tiles, carved into the intricate facades. And lounging there in human form, looking suspiciously unsurprised, Tom saw the Daylight Folk, and knew that they were expecting him.

He landed rather clumsily, having not yet mastered landings. Thus, instead of arriving neatly on his feet with a majestic swoop of his new wings, he misjudged his step and went sprawling onto the terracotta tiles, landing almost at the feet of the Butterfly Queen and her retinue.

Looking around him at the ring of half-familiar faces, he saw Brimstone, and Argus, and Swallowtail, and Skipper, and at least a dozen more, all of them in silks, and lace, top hats, and velvets, and crinolines. All of them warm-skinned, bright-eyed and beautiful beyond belief, basking in the sunshine above the streets of London Before.

For a moment, Tom blinked, bewildered by so many colours. It was like stepping into a circus ring; all spotlights and sequins and costumes. And there was Vanessa, brightest of all, in a dress of pale leaf green, with her long hair coiled like a crown and pinned with gleaming gemstones. She was so radiant, so beautiful, that Tom could barely look at her, and yet, with his

JOANNE HARRIS

new knowledge, he found that he could see *behind* her charm, her glamours, to the thing that he had seen in his negatives; the soulless creature behind the fantasy. He picked himself up, still blinking away her glamours, and made a little gesture that might have been a bow.

'Vanessa.'

She smiled. 'I hoped you'd come.' Her eyes were warm and luminous. But behind the shine Tom saw something else; something hungry and playful and cold. She held out a hand that was at the same time long-fingered and graceful but also a hideous, clutching claw, tipped with narrow fingernails. 'I knew you were a fighter,' she said. 'I knew you wouldn't just give up.'

She smiled, and behind her smile, Tom saw a deep and insatiable maw, with teeth that went halfway down its throat. He saw a monster, but there was more: behind the monster, he saw a woman, old as the city itself, her long hair white as spider silk, her face a net of wrinkles and lines – a creature of sorrow and hunger.

'At last, you came,' she repeated, and Tom realised that she was not speaking to him at all, but to someone standing behind him. He turned and, to his surprise, saw Imago Burnet on the parapet, his colours flaring into the sky; his face as pale and calm as despair.

262

4

For a moment, the Moth King and the Butterfly Queen looked at each other across the roof of the Natural History Museum; Burnet with a look of deep sadness, Vanessa with a brilliant smile. Glamours played all around her, glancing from the statuary and off the banks of London fog, so that she looked like a firefly in a silken cage, sending out stuttering signals of light and colour in every direction.

She took a step forward. 'You came,' she said.

'But not for you. For the children.'

Vanessa laughed, and her voice was a wild music that tore at Tom's heart. '*These* children?' she said, indicating the Daylight Folk. 'These are no children of yours, Burnet. My children live in the light. Yours can only dream of it, be drawn to it, be consumed by it.'

Burnet shrugged. 'I don't care what you think. I came for Tom and Charissa, and I will not leave without them.'

Vanessa gave that smile again. With his new vision, Tom could see both her beauty and her damage, snarled together like silk and barbed wire rolled into a golden ball. But his attention was not on her. Since his arrival, he had been scanning the group for Charissa. Her drab brown wings should have marked her out among their brilliant colours, but Tom could see no sign of her, although Burnet seemed to think she was there. Now he scanned the faces again, and this time he saw her in the crowd, right between Brimstone and Skipper, but she looked so different now that he almost missed her. The Charissa who met his eye was not the fierce and defiant creature he'd last seen on the rooftops above Welkin Close, in Spider's shabby, oversized coat. *This* version of Charissa was cool, and poised, and elegant, in a gown of rose-pink silk, her hair entwined with flowers. Her sleeves were embroidered with butterflies; around her neck gleamed a collar of gems. There was no sign of the evercoat.

'Charissa!' he said. 'Thank God you're all right.'

She gave him a tiny, mocking smile. 'Nice of you to drop by, Tom. But, as you can see, I'm doing fine. In fact, I'm in my element. I wonder why I resisted so long, when freedom tastes so sweet.'

Tom thought back to what Burnet had said and, instead of relief, felt a sinking despair. 'They changed you,' he said in a low voice. 'They made you one of their kind.'

Behind him came the sound of Vanessa's delightful laughter. 'Such a low opinion you have of us, Tom Argent,' she said. 'You think *we* changed Charissa? How? By tapping her nectar? No, Tom. She made a choice. She *chose* to live in the light with us, and to give up her life in the shadows. And, in exchange, we gave her a new name – *Annulet* – to celebrate her acceptance into our circle, and to reward her for bringing this ridiculous and costly war to an end.'

'An end?' said Tom. 'But I thought you didn't *want* the war to end.'

Vanessa laughed again. 'Not quite. I didn't want the war to end in anything but my complete, unequivocal victory. But now, thanks to Annulet – and to *you* – I have what I wanted. The Battle of Welkin Close was only one part of my strategy. I have you to thank for that, Tom. You gave Skipper your lifeline in exchange for a meeting with me. But you were much too weak for my cause. Luckily, Charissa was not. She gave us the one thing we needed, Tom – the one thing that would win me this war, not just here, but *everywhere*, in every time and place in the worlds.' She turned to Burnet and smiled. 'I'm glad you're here to see this, Burnet. I've been waiting for it for a long, long time.'

With a gesture, she stood aside, revealing a drab individual on his knees at Charissa's feet; an individual whom Tom recognised only too well.

It was Spider.

5

Burnet stepped down from the parapet. His wings – a flamboyant red and black – withdrew into his shabby aged coat, and he was the Burnet Tom had always known, old and drab and mournful.

'Listen to me, Vanessa,' he said. 'I've seen what this has done to you. I've seen how, year after year, your grief and rage have hollowed you out. Let us end it now, my love, and go our separate ways in peace. Just give me Tom and Charissa, and I promise—'

'Really? You *promise*?' Her voice was cold. 'I've had enough of promises. You promised we would find our son. You promised me the Kingdom. And a thousand years later, here we are, still searching. Still living on scraps in a world where we are nothing but *insects*—' She stopped for a moment, regaining her poise.

To Tom, her beauty was almost unbearable. Motes of soft light surrounded her, gilding her with mellow gold. Her hair was a braided coronet, intricate and regal. And yet, though her beauty was peerless, Tom found that he felt nothing for her but an aching kind of pity.

'But we are insects no longer,' she went on. 'Today, we reclaim the Kingdom. Thanks to my girl Annulet, and, of course, to our friend Spinner here' – she gestured to Spider, still on his knees – 'I shall rule again, this time alone, and for ever.'

She made an imperious gesture towards Charissa – no, *Annulet*, Tom told himself – who handed her what seemed to be some kind of rolled-up garment. Vanessa shook out its folds to reveal Spider's evercoat.

'This coat is everything I need,' said Vanessa to Burnet. 'Woven into its lining is the world we left behind, and more: the key to *every* world, every world in the Honeycomb. With Spider's help, I can rule them all, and we will return victorious.'

Burnet's eyes did not leave her face. 'Spinner is loyal to me,' he said. 'He won't give up our secrets. Your shadows have tried so many times, in London Beyond and elsewhere. But he has always stayed loyal to me – to me, and to the lost Prince. The way back to the Kingdom is woven into his evercoat, and he will never give it up, not until our son is found, and love returns to your withered heart—'

'Oh, such a pretty story,' said Vanessa in a mocking voice. 'But it is only a story, Burnet. Our son was lost the moment he set foot in this world of shadows. Not once in a thousand years has a Moth loved a Butterfly, and been loved by them in return.'

'That isn't true,' said Tom, looking at Charissa. 'I did – I *do*. And she loved me.' He took a step towards her, addressing her directly. 'I loved you from the start,' he said. 'But I was stupid, and greedy. I thought I could cheat the Market. I thought a photograph of you would help me remember, and every time, I paid for it with my memories. But some part of me never forgot. I *saw* you, in spite of your glamours. I saw you as you really were, not some perfect illusion—' He broke off, seeing the look in her eyes – her beautiful, *expressionless* eyes – his resolution faltering.

'Oh, don't stop now,' said Charissa. 'You're just getting to the good part. I really want to hear the bit about my personality, and how you loved me for myself.'

'I did,' said Tom. 'I do.'

Vanessa smiled. 'Oh, Tom,' she said. 'You think *that's* love? And if it is, do you think it lasts?' She laughed. 'You people are so naïve. So blinded by the illusion of love that you'll fly right into the candle. Today, you love Charissa, you say. Yesterday, you worshipped me. Love doesn't last, Tom Argent. Love is a moth at a candle flame, consuming itself in its eagerness. But *power* – there's something to hope for. And power feeds on weakness.' She turned to face Charissa, and smiled. 'So *feed*. Feed, my pretty Annulet, and show these Moths what true power is.'

At that, Charissa – no, *Annulet* – took Tom Argent by the hand, and he felt a strange kind of dizziness. The world about him tilted and turned. The air around him seemed to fill with a kind of luminous energy – *his* energy, he realised. His life force. His nectar.

6

When Tom had kissed Vanessa in the alley behind King's Cross, he thought he had experienced the same kind of troubled dizziness. At the time, he'd attributed this to being in love, and being overwhelmed, and to the bright thrill of her proximity. But now, as Charissa – no, *Annulet* – gently touched his face with her hand, he realised that what he had felt with Vanessa was nothing but the fleeting glimpse of a candle flame through a window. He had never been in love – not before this moment. And love was not a flame at all. Love was a shadow, he realised, and the shadow was always *hungry*.

Annulet's hand on the nape of his neck was as light as a butterfly. She smiled as she drew him closer, and he felt the warmth of her breath against his face. She smelt of honey and woodsmoke, and cinnamon and iris, and her lips were all he'd longed for: soft and warm and loving. He felt his resistance slipping away; his consciousness hung by a golden thread. Would he be consumed, he thought, just as he had consumed Pieris, or would he, drained of love, become another of the Daylight Folk?

'It's all right,' whispered Annulet. 'Don't think about anything else. Just come to me, and I promise, Tom, no harm will ever come to you.'

Now, Tom Argent was starting to drift right out of his body and into the air, blossoming into euphoria; dissolving into fragments of light. A cloud of golden butterflies, small as motes in a sunbeam, seemed to diffuse from his fingertips, filling the air between them with a luminous energy. It was a strange sensation; he felt as if every cell in his body was made from floating particles.

'*I love you, Charissa,*' he whispered, and his words became yet more of the golden butterflies, escaping from his altered lips, gilding the air with sweetness.

Annulet – who was no longer Charissa, but something far more dangerous – gave a bright and unearthly smile. 'I know you do,' she told him. 'Now come to me, and make me whole.'

Tom nodded. *Goodbye, Charissa*, he thought, and closed his eyes, awaiting the inevitable.

For some time, nothing happened. Instead of receding into the dark, Tom felt a bright surge of energy. He found himself thinking vaguely, *When people die and go towards the light, could it be that they've been reborn as a Moth?*

He opened his eyes.

The scene was unchanged. Well – almost unchanged. The Daylight Folk were still there, watching him with their luminous eyes. Spider was watching from Vanessa's side, looking pale and rather grim. Burnet stood on the parapet. Tom looked down at his body, his hands, half expecting a transformation. Both were unchanged. His hands, he thought, looked a little grimy.

A cloud of tiny butterflies, golden like pollen, hung in the air. 'Where's Annulet?' asked Tom.

For a moment, no one said anything. Vanessa shot Spider a scornful look. The cloud of tiny butterflies – fragments of quintessence – gently continued to disperse into the grey-gold London air. Looking down, Tom saw a very familiar silver bell at his feet, no larger than a cherry stone.

'*Where's Annulet?*' he repeated.

'Gone, I'm afraid,' said Vanessa. 'But look on the bright side – you turned out to be one of my people, after all.'

Tom remembered how Pieris had dispersed into a cloud of butterflies. How *powerful* it had made him feel. He looked around wildly, as if he might see Charissa hiding among the crowd. 'No,' he said. 'She can't be gone. *I'm* the one who was meant to be gone.'

Vanessa shrugged. 'What can I say? Power wins over weakness, Tom. She was weaker than you, that's all. You should be glad. Your instincts won. Now, you're truly one of us.'

'I'll *never* be one of you,' said Tom. 'I'd rather die than be one of you.'

'That's what *she* said at first. She thought her love could save her. Instead, it consumed her. It always does.' She laughed. 'Poor Tom. Don't you understand? Love is not a partnership. It is a perpetual hunting ground, where only the strongest can survive. Our meat is their hunger, our drink, their thirst. And we feed. We feed on their dreams of love, Tom, we thrive on their little tales of romance. This world of yours is filled with them, and they have made my children strong.'

'Your children?' said Tom.

Her smile was both poignant and terrible. 'My son was lost an age ago. The pain of simply being in this world broke him into pieces. Since then, I have sought out those fragments of him, separating the weak from the strong, the daylight from the darkness.'

'The Moth from the Butterfly?' said Burnet.

She shrugged. 'That, too. Our son is gone. We will never see him again. But *my* son – yes, *my* son can live. My son, as he *should* have been without your pernicious influence. My son, as he always was: bright, and strong, and powerful.' Once more, she smiled at Tom, and said: 'You started as a common Moth, weak and sentimental. But you have proved yourself. You have learnt to conquer Love. You have rejected sentiment and shown your true colours, in spite of Burnet's interference, and earned your rightful place at my side.' She held out her hand to Tom, and said: 'Time to claim your throne, my son. Come to me, Prince Argent.'

7

For a moment, Tom could hardly believe Vanessa's words were addressed to him. All his life he'd longed to be special; to be chosen. All his life he'd dreamed of being something more than what he was – that one day, he would be revealed as someone extraordinary. And now, this glorious, magical being was telling him his dream had come true; was giving him the chance to be the hero of a fairy tale—

He shook his head. 'I don't want it.'

'You don't know what you're saying,' Vanessa remarked. 'I'm offering you a place at my side. The crown of my people. *The Kingdom itself.*'

'I thought the Kingdom was lost,' said Tom.

Vanessa lifted her hands. Between her fingers was an intricate cat's cradle of light. 'It was never lost,' she said. 'The Spinner kept it safe in his web, woven into his evercoat. The old fool never stopped hoping that one day a Moth and a Butterfly would fall in love and end the war. He hoped it of you and Charissa. It's why he sent you both here from London Beyond, to keep you safe – to give you time. He was so sure of your love for her that he wagered his evercoat that Love would win.'

Tom looked at Spider. 'You did that?'

Spider shrugged. 'Call me romantic.'

Vanessa looked at him indulgently. 'You don't think he *knew* my Annulet had the evercoat? Of course he did,' said Vanessa.

'He sent it with her on purpose. The fool imagined that somehow it would be safer with her, in London Before, than with him in London Beyond. Fortunately, she brought it to me, with all the memories it contains. After that, it didn't take much to find Spider and make him co-operate.'

'But what about Charissa?' said Tom. 'She *can't* be gone. She can't be.'

Vanessa shook her head. 'But she is. Only one of you could win.'

'And if she'd consumed me, instead?' said Tom.

'Then I would have welcomed my daughter. What matters, Tom, is the Kingdom,' she said. 'Take your rightful place at my side, and we will take our people home.'

'What about *my* people?' said Burnet in his quiet voice.

'Your people?' said Vanessa. 'It was *your* people that lost us our son. You've relinquished all rights to the Kingdom. You've found your place in the darkness here, in the backstreets and sewers of this stinking world. I return now to my own, its Queen. I wish you joy of your shadows.'

Tom had barely heard all this. Charissa was all he could think of. There seemed to be no room in his head for anything more than her absence. His lips felt numb, as if her mouth had left a lasting impression there. His fingers, too, felt strangely numb; he looked down, and saw what he took at first to be smoke rising from his fingertips.

He brought a hand closer to his face, and saw now that the smoke was in fact a swarm of tiny, pale-winged moths, rising like thistledown into the air. They hovered around him at head height, and he realised that they were coming from his mouth, his eyes, his nostrils. He took a single, trembling breath.

Charissa, he began to say...

And then, in that instant, he broke into a million tiny fragments, pale and winged and luminous, that rose like a column of turbulent air above the rooftops of London.

8

Vanessa dropped the evercoat, the gleaming threads of the cat's cradle falling from her fingers. '*No!*' she cried, and around her, the air seethed with luminescence. 'Come back! My son, my Prince, come *back*!'

Spider picked up the discarded threads and tucked them into the sleeve of his shirt, where he had already concealed the silver bell dropped by Charissa. Addressing the Queen, he said: 'You may have celebrated your victory prematurely. Love has a way of persisting, you know, far beyond what is reasonable.'

Vanessa gave a wounded laugh. 'Oh, don't I just know it,' she said. 'It's like a troublesome insect that will not die, however much you swat it.' She turned the full force of her wrathful gaze upon the figure of Burnet. 'You never give up, do you?' she asked. 'You keep on finding them, *sending* them – these broken fragments of our son – to prove what, exactly? That Love can save us after all? That even you and I – after all the pain and suffering we have inflicted upon each other over the centuries, after all the blood our people have spilled – could one day be reunited?'

Burnet took a step towards her. 'I never once stopped loving you,' he said. 'You know I never will.'

She laughed again, more harshly now, and it seemed to those who were watching that behind her flawless features, *another* face was now visible – a creature of hunger and sorrow, marked by a grief as deep as Death's domain.

Burnet went on: 'My faults – and yours – will never change what I feel for you. My love can see beyond them. And I am not fooled by glamours. I see the shadows in your light. I see you as you really are, and I accept you completely.' From the pocket of his coat, Burnet pulled out a negative. It was one of the photographs that Tom had taken by Vauxhall Bridge, and Vanessa glanced down instinctively as Burnet held it out to her.

For a time, she was frozen, looking down at the negative. One hand – one graceful, tentative claw – moved up to touch her luminous face. Her glamours swam around her, making her beauty flicker like images in a lantern show, shifting from maiden, to mother, to crone in a flash of fretful turbulence. Spider watched her silently from behind the round lenses of his spectacles.

Burnet took a step closer to her and put a hand on one of hers.

'Don't *touch* me! Don't you dare touch me!' she cried.

But he held more tightly to her hand, and now the glamours enfolded them both, flinging their hectic colours against the glowering clouds over London. Whatever was happening to Vanessa was having its effect on him, too; the air between them shimmered, as if from some violent, powerful charge.

'Cry peace, Vanessa,' said Burnet. 'There is no peace in victory. There is only emptiness, and a hunger that cannot be satisfied. I ask your forgiveness, and offer you peace, for the sake of our vanished son, and the love that brought him into the world.'

'*Peace!*' she cried. 'Another lie. Another word for *weakness*.'

'No, Vanessa.' Burnet shook his head. 'Love is stronger than hatred. Peace is stronger by far than war. Look at yourself as you really are, and see what your hatred has made of you.'

Her luminous eyes flicked back towards the photograph in Burnet's hand, and the fitful glamours swirled around her like angels in a snowstorm.

'What does that matter to me,' she said, 'when I have glamours aplenty?'

'Your glamours may fool the Sightless Folk,' said Burnet. 'But they never once fooled me.'

Once more, Vanessa shook her head. The volatile air between them both was fizzing and popping like champagne. 'This comes too late, as always,' she said. 'You were *always* the King of Much Too Late.'

'And you were always Queen of my heart,' said Burnet, and held out his arms to her.

For a second, Vanessa said nothing. Her angry profile was turned away; her dark hair shimmered silver. Burnet put his arms around her, and for a moment, she turned her face into the curve of his shoulder…

Then the air gave a giant sob, as if rushing in to fill a space, and the interlaced pair dispersed into dazzling fragments. Millions of butterflies and moths exploded into the turbulence, fluttering madly to escape; bright wings torching the London smoke into a cacophony of colours.

Golden-winged and orange-tipped; peacock-eyed and painted; speckled, stippled, spotted; striped; fretting the kaleidoscope air. And then, they slowly began to dissolve like smoke into the atmosphere.

The Daylight Folk observed the scene, open-mouthed and trembling. Now they looked less like predators and more like frightened children, dressed up in their parents' clothes. Some of them began to weep. Spider, who in the confusion had somehow reclaimed his evercoat, sat down on the parapet and pushed his hair out of his eyes.

'Not all love stories end happily,' he said, picking at a loose thread in his lapel. 'But that doesn't mean Love isn't real, or that it isn't worth pursuing.'

Skipper looked at him bleakly. 'What happens to us now?' she said. 'Where do our people go from here?'

Spider shrugged. 'Wherever you like. But if I were you, I'd hang around. This story isn't over.' He pulled again at the loose thread, winding it around his thumb. The thread was long and silvery, like a thread of moonlight. Spider's skilful fingers teased and pulled on the delicate thread. And as they did so, the Daylight Folk gradually became aware of the cloud of butterflies and moths returning. Softly, they settled onto the stones and terracotta tiles of the roof. Softly, they settled onto the stones of the parapet where Spider sat. Softly, they clustered and blossomed and bloomed, hanging like grapes in the luminous air – and soon the onlookers started to see a figure – no, *two* figures – taking shape among them. For a moment, it was impossible to see more than an outline. But as the shapes became clearer, the Daylight Folk were able to see a man and a woman, hand in hand. Their faces were almost familiar, and yet not *quite* the same as before: the woman small-featured and freckle-faced; the man dark-haired and soulful. Each of them was staring at the other in amazement.

'Tom?' said Charissa.

'Charissa?' said Tom.

He put out a hand to touch her face, as if he couldn't believe she was real. 'It really *is* you, isn't it? I mean, you're *Charissa*, not Annulet?'

Charissa gave him a look. 'Oh, please. Do I *look* like an Annulet?'

Tom gave a trembling sigh of relief. He touched her hands, and then looked at his own. Both pairs seemed substantial. 'I thought I'd lost you. I thought you were gone.' Then, turning to Spider; 'What happened? Where are Burnet and Vanessa?'

Spider tucked the silver thread into his inside coat pocket. 'They were reunited,' he said. 'As were you.'

'But *how?*' said Tom.

'Love tears us apart, and rebuilds us,' said Spider, 'every day of our lives. The love of the King and Queen for their son tore them apart for a thousand years, but their love for each other never died. All it did was make them angry. They could not be together, but they could not exist apart, and so they waged war against their love, until at last it consumed them. But you' – he smiled at Charissa and Tom – 'you were both a part of their love. Fragments of the lost Prince, broken into pieces. And against all her efforts to claim you or consume you, you came together. You fell in love. A Moth, in love with a Butterfly.'

Tom looked at Charissa in wonder. She seemed to him to have acquired a certain luminous quality; a *shine* by far exceeding that which he had ever seen in Vanessa. Her eyes were like the moonlit sky. Her hair was filled with silver stars. Motes of light, like fireflies, danced in the air around her. He looked at his hand. He, too, seemed to *shine* with an iridescence that gilded the air.

'We've changed,' he said. 'What happened here?'

Spider was pulling another thread from the lining of his coat. It gleamed like a strand of starlight. 'Long ago and far away,' he said, 'when the worlds were honeycomb, there was a King too proud to relent, and a Queen too angry to forgive. Between them, they caused the loss of their son, and a war that lost them their Kingdom. Every time the King tried to mend the rift between them, the Queen pulled away, and every time she sought love, his frozen heart rejected it. And so they destroyed one another at last, and scattered their children to the winds.

But from them came a *new* King and Queen, brought together in a love too powerful to be broken.'

There was a silence as Tom tried to make sense of the words he was hearing.

'So... I'm... the King,' he said at last.

'Burnet told you,' Spider said. 'He said that one day you would find yourself taking his place in the Kingdom.'

'I thought he meant the camera shop...'

Spider shrugged. 'It's a learning curve,' he said. 'Don't worry. You'll get there.'

'So what happens now?' asked Tom. 'I mean – where do we go from here?' He had become aware of the eyes of the Daylight Folk on him. Hopeful, expectant, suspicious or dazed, they watched him from the parapet and from the crenellations of the Natural History Museum, their wings spread like banners against the sky. And now he could see the Midnight Folk, too, drawn by whatever mystery had been at work on these rooftops: Atlas, and Luna, and Diamondback, and Cinnabar. For a moment, Cinnabar stood aloof on the parapet. Then Brimstone held out his hand to her, and she went to join him.

My people, Tom thought to himself, and put up his hand to cover a smile. It was ridiculous, of course, and yet it felt so natural. As natural as being in love. As natural as flying.

Spider pulled at the silver thread again. Between his fingers, Tom now saw an intricate cat's cradle of light that seemed to extend in multiple directions. 'With this, you can go anywhere,' said Spider, lifting the cradle of light. 'You could stay here, in London Before. You could go back to the London you know. Or you could reclaim your Kingdom, and lead your people home. Your choice.' He passed the cat's cradle over Tom's head. As it touched him, the net of light settled over Tom's shoulders, becoming a kind of mantle: golden, soft as spider silk, light as woven thistledown. He made the same gesture over Charissa, and she too was draped in gossamer. And with the mantle came a scent of green woods and of summertime; of distant spices, unnamed blooms, and blackberries, and honeycomb.

'So what is it to be?' said Spider. 'The Kingdom awaits your answer.'

Tom put his hand to his mouth again, as if to check the smile was still there. He thought about the camera shop, and the changing skyline of King's Cross, and all the people in black and grey, and the smell of the canal at dawn. He thought of the noise and the traffic, and the litter that always lined the streets, and the neon sky that drowned out the stars, and the sounds of buses and taxis and trains, and he tried to imagine not going back; never again being a part of that world.

Then he tried to imagine a life with Charissa in another place, a place he already knew from his dreams.

He put his hand to his mouth again, and was not surprised to find that his smile had grown even broader. 'But – I don't know how to rule,' he said. 'Me, a king? Where would I start?'

Charissa smiled. 'Don't worry,' she said. 'The Queen has all the power. The King has more of a secondary role. You just sit next to me, looking pretty, feeding me honey cakes and wine and making sure I don't get bored.'

'Really?' said Tom.

'Really,' she replied. 'Oh – and, of course, being Queen, I have the right to call for your execution the morning after the wedding night if I feel even the *slightest* bit unsatisfied.'

Tom gave her a startled look.

For a moment, she held his gaze, regal and implacable. Then she gave a wicked grin, and said: 'Typical chrysalis. Thick as mince.'

Epilogue

*Long ago, and far away, the Butterfly King met the Moth Queen.
They were very different. She was nocturnal and he loved the sun;
she was fierce and warlike, and he was a gentle dreamer. And they
were both from different worlds. He was from a land of towers, and
trains, and roads, and aeroplanes; she was from a land of dreams,
and silent wings, and falling leaves.*

*But Love has always found a way of defying boundaries. And
after warring for a time, and making their share of mistakes, and
overcoming many dangers and obstacles, they were at last united in
love, and thus united their people. And with the help of the Spider
Mage and his web, they passed through the Honeycomb, and led the
way back to the Kingdom all who chose to follow them there.*

*There, they were crowned, and made their pledge – she in a garland
of autumn leaves, he in a circlet of spider silk – to rule the Kingdom
wisely; to fight against injustice and fear; to honour their love, and
to guard it well, and to tend it, and give it time to grow.*

*And if she was not always moderate in the way she expressed
herself, and if he was sometimes a little naïve, this surprised no one,
and was only to be expected. But between them, they ruled both wisely
and well; with passion and moderation. And when their children
were born, she taught them how to stand their ground and how to
fight for what they loved; and he taught them how to see their world
and appreciate its beauty.*

And so their children grew fearless and true, and loyal and adventurous; and they were loved by the King and Queen as fiercely as the lost Prince had ever been loved by his own kin. And the couple reigned over the Kingdom for a thousand years or more, and had many joyous adventures. And the Spider Mage folded his evercoat and sealed it away in an iron chest, for he had walked through the Web of the Worlds to reunite his people at last, and his wandering spirit was satisfied.

The End

Acknowledgements

A story is like a butterfly. It starts as an unformed larva, then hardens, gestates, and finally emerges into the sunlight as a fully-formed imago. But the chrysalis stage is what matters most. That's where the real transformation starts. And although it's tempting to attribute the magic to just one individual, this kind of metamorphosis is often the work of many.

So thanks to those who helped this book achieve its potential. To my agent, Jon Wood; to my editors, Gillian Redfearn and Claire Ormsby-Potter; to Rachael Lancaster for her elegant cover design, to Ruth Sharvell in Production, Yadira de Trindade in Comms and Jenna Petts in Publicity. Thank you also to my son Fred, who helped me come up with the germ of the tale one day on the Tube to Saint Pancras. That was many years ago; since then, we have both experienced our own kind of meta-morphosis. Thanks to our fellow-travellers, for their kindness and their loyalty. Thanks too to the booksellers, the bloggers, the tweeters, the skeeters, the tooters, Tubers, Tik-Tokkers and reps. And thank you, as always, to you, who have stayed constant throughout everything; the readers, without whom no book is ever more than just words on a page. I hope you enjoy this story, which comes from love and transformation; and remember that those who live in fear of change – or its turbulent counterpart, love – are often those who need it most.